CONQUERED
PAULA QUINENE

A WWII EROTIC HISTORICAL
ROMANCE SET IN GUAM

INFINITY PUBLISHING
1094 New DeHaven Street, Suite 100
West Conshohocken, PA 19428-2713
Toll-free (877) BUY BOOK
Local Phone (610) 941-9999
Fax (610) 941-9959
Info@buybooksontheweb.com
www.buybooksontheweb.com

Conquered is a passionate love story, as much about its main characters, Guam native Jesi Taimanglo and American GI Johan Landers, as it is about author Paula Quinene's passion for Guam itself. As her characters try to find a place for themselves amid the war, Jesi's relatives, and the Chamorro traditions, Quinene charts a path through a seldom told story: Guam's place in WWII. An original idea written with an original voice that invites readers in to the exotic world of the Pacific, complete with coconut trees, banana doughnuts, dolphins swimming in the ocean, and moonlight on Pago Bay, *Conquered* also recounts the brutal horrors of the Japanese occupation on Guam, a US territory largely forgotten back in the States. In addition to learning about a singular and little-known culture that has played a part in the world wars of the Pacific, readers will undoubtedly crave the recipe for banana doughnuts.

—Stacey Donovan, Writer, Editor, and Author of ***Dive***

DEDICATION

To the survivors of WWII on Guam

To the families of those who died on Guam during WWII

To the military families who lost loved ones
fighting for Guam during WWII

To the veterans and their families who have served
Guam and the United States of America

To the men, women, and their families who still serve, protecting
and defending Guam
and
the United States of America

I thank you. We thank you.

Special Thanks To

My detailed, generous, and invaluable editor
Stacey Donovan of Donovanedits.com

My creative and friendly book cover artist
Fiona Jayde of Fionajaydemedia.com

My meticulous and jovial cover models
Jimmy Thomas and Heang Lay of Romancenovelcovers.com

My informative and enthusiastic Guam reading group
Sandra Gray Santos, Vanessa P. Toves
Silas Kadiasang

My encouraging and cheerful supporters
Family, Friends, Fans

My very own comical and loving US Army soldier
Edward J. Quinene

AUTHOR'S NOTE

*C*onquered is a project that is very near and dear to me. But it's not my story. It's the story of Guam and her people, woven within the romance of an American soldier and a native girl during WWII. It is my way of sharing and preserving Guam's history.

When I was a teenager in the early 1990s, I felt I had some connection with Guam – not just having been born and lived there, but that I was destined to do something for my island. I spent a few months trying to figure out what I was supposed to do then life led me far away. It was in the midst of working on *A Taste of Guam, Remember Guam,* and this novel, that I realized that what I was meant to do in this world was to write my cookbooks, and most especially, to write *Conquered.*

I started working on this book in the summer of 2006. I gave myself ten years to finish, never dreaming it would actually take me ten years. It's been an emotional, educational, and rewarding journey. I'm thrilled to share this work with you.

The original design of the Guam flag did not include a red border until 1948. I approved the use of the new version because of the beautiful contrast on the cover as a whole.

If you have any questions, feel free to write to me at pquinene@paulaq.com.

Always,

Paula Quinene

1

July 20, 1944 — Central Guam, Eastern Coast

"FIFTY-SIX, FIFTY-SEVEN." JESI'S ARMS trembled, her body weak. "Fifty-eiiight. I can't do this, I can't."

"Don't give up. Never give up," *Mames* whispered.

"Fifty-niiine. One more push-up," Jesi said, talking herself to the finish. "Help me, *Ma-miss*."

"You can do it," Mames whispered again.

"Siiixty." Jesi face planted on the ground. *I did it, I did it!* She took two deep breaths then turned sideways to rest her right cheek against the cool *guåfak,* a mat of woven pandanus leaves. Both arms stretched above her head. *Mames is always there when I need her.*

Chirping geckos ran across the dirt and made her smile. The little buggers kept her company in the cave. A small bulb attached to the D battery furnished enough light at night, to exercise, and to read the notes she took for grandma's medicine. *Thank you, Peter.*

Jesi rolled to her back. Peter, one of her older brothers, had worked odd jobs for the cable company and the Pan Am Hotel. He collected discarded equipment, including broken lamps and flashlights. Some bulbs worked, even three years later.

She remembered the push-up challenges against Peter and her oldest brother, Tommy. They always beat her. Then when they were done, Tommy would tickle her to no end. Tommy enlisted as a mess attendant in the US Navy so he could see the world. That was before the war. He was only permitted to work the lowest job. "You're not an American citizen," he was told. Tommy didn't care; he said he'd be the "best food server the navy had." Jesi blinked away a tear. *I hope you're safe.* Tommy's last letter came home in October 1941, two months before the Japanese soldiers invaded the island.

Jesi was almost nineteen now, and had a good chance at beating her brothers in push-ups. Exercise was invigorating. There wasn't much else to do hiding out. Jesi hopped up, rolled the guåfak, and put it back in its place then walked deeper into the cave. She wet a washcloth and wiped her hands then picked up her toothbrush. Jesi moved a few feet to her right toward the table where she stored her food. She trod along the wall of the cave to the opening, a cave hidden within the cliffs on the eastern coast of Guam.

Jesi stopped once she reached the door of vines and trees. She listened for unusual noises from outside. The sounds of bombs and airplane engines continued their unforgiving raid. The entrance to the cave was close to the edge of the rock face, looming over the Pacific Ocean.

No one other than her dad and Peter had been here since that awful day. Jesi never strayed from the vicinity of her hiding place. She never saw a Japanese soldier, but figured they looked like the Japanese lady who owned Dejima store. *And the man that helped her was Japanese.*

Jesi used to tag along with her mom and Peter when it was time to stock up on household items and foodstuffs. They bought imported goods from Mrs. Dejima such as coffee, corned beef, and razor blades.

She pushed the vines aside, stepped between trees, and sat with her legs crossed. The coolness of the ground against her thighs comforted her. Ten feet of grass covered the ledge until the land gave way to a wall of limestone. If the Japanese ever found her, she couldn't even escape by jumping. The sharp rocks at the base of the cliff would cut her to pieces.

A sliver of moon reflected off Pago Bay. The stars sparkled in the night. She ate her nuts and dried meat, and took a gulp of water from her canteen. Jesi pulled off the elastic band then wriggled her fingers through her hair. With her head tilted back and her eyes closed, she inhaled, filling her lungs. The ocean breeze brushed against her face and skin, giving her goose bumps. It was cooler in the evenings, and it was windy. The aroma of salty water and the fragrance of the jungle filled her nostrils. The waves crashed against the rocks. She yearned to swim. Lucky if she got a rinse in the freshwater stream. It was nothing compared to swimming across Pago Bay.

Grandma. She cocked her head upright then pressed four fingers against her nose and lips, imitating the way her Grandma had kissed her hand a thousand times. Jesi's heart grew heavy. Grandma was an esteemed Chamorro medicine woman on the island, and Jesi was being trained to follow in her footsteps.

She straightened her legs and leaned backwards, bracing herself with her hands. *I'm so alive in the ocean. Free. I can never tell them I'd rather teach kids how to swim.*

"They'll understand," Mames whispered.

Jesi stood up and walked to the side of the cave to brush her teeth then walked back in to put everything in place. She retied her hair and undressed. Her nipples hardened from the damp washcloth as she wiped her tummy, arms, and legs. *When did I get muscles?* Jesi slipped into a clean panty and pajamas, removed her slippers then crouched with her butt on the makeshift *kåtre.*

The "bed" was constructed on the ground using a much larger guáfak, extra clothing, and pillows, which were all covered with a blanket. It was late now, perhaps past midnight.

Jesi hadn't seen Peter or Chief, her dad, for a week. Peter stayed in the cave with her except the few times he left to rendezvous with Chief. Their last meeting was six days ago. Peter had yet to return.

"In the name of the Father, and the Son, and the Holy Spirit. Lord, please keep my brother and dad safe, and protect my mom and grandma from harm." She recited the Our Father and Hail Mary before closing her prayer.

The Taimanglos had left their home in Mangilao as soon as they learned the Japanese bombed Guam. Chief dropped Peter and Jesi off a mile from the trail to the Pago Bay cave then took Jesi's mom and grandma to the Ylig cave which was south of Pago Bay. The women had not seen one another since.

The horrible thoughts of what could have happened to Peter and Chief popped into her head again. The tears came. Her chest tightened. *If I could just fall asleep.* The ground still vibrated from the bombings.

"You are strong," Mames whispered.

Jesi lay down and hugged her pillow. Years of worry, fear, and little to eat took their toll. *When will this end? Mom, when will I get to see . . .*

"No, no, no!" Jesi screamed against the Japanese man in military clothes. He let her go and she ran to her friend. "Carmen, Carmen," she cried as she dropped to the ground to hug the ravaged and nearly beheaded body below her. Then she heard his footsteps, and his laugh. She looked up. He was coming for her.

July 21, 1944 — USS *Starlight*

Soldiers on the USS *Starlight* were alerted as Mount Sasalaguan came into view. The *Starlight* carried American army men from the 305th Regimental Combat Team. They prepared to fight on Guam alongside the marines.

The Statue of Liberty Boys, as the army soldiers were called, were attached to the marine brigade and made up of guys in their late twenties and early thirties. These men were much older than the typical GI. Their mission was to liberate the Chamorro people and recapture Guam from the Japanese. The island's airstrips were crucial for refueling and resupplying and to stop the enemy from staging their own aircraft.

Staff Sergeant Johan Landers left his tent and walked toward the railing on the port side of the ship. With his back against the rail, he looked left. The bow was blocked by a chimney and the quarterdeck. He looked right. The gun turrets didn't completely obstruct his view of the stern. It never failed to amaze Johan that these ships were much longer than a football field. Some ships were built twice as long. Soldiers and equipment were packed so close together on the deck Johan felt as if he were training in the deserts of Arizona. He turned to look out at the ocean.

Johan pressed his hips into the metal. *Mount Sasalaguan is at the center of southern Guam.* Johan checked the time; it was 0140. The glass and frame of the Bunn Special sparkled when it caught one of the lights on the ship. The silver-cased watch was the only keepsake he had from his old life. It was a gift from his grandfather who had worked the railroads that ran through the Catskill Mountains. *It was a pocket watch,* Pops had said. Johan cleaned the glass with his thumb, and a smile touched one corner of his mouth.

Pops and Granny spent more time with him than his own folks. As a kid, he looked forward to being sent to live with them every summer. Johan loved being away from the controlling life of rich-kid private schools, mean nannies, and parents too busy for a young child. He was ten and twelve years younger than his older brothers. By the time he came along, mom and dad were wrapped up in growing their fortune in banking and investing. *Like we needed more money.* Johan shook his head. A low grunt escaped his throat.

He crossed his arms on his chest and filled his lungs with air. Soon, even sleep would be tinged with thoughts of battle, a welcomed retreat from the nightmares he'd had since losing Lily. Johan shouldn't have bothered with his mother and father that day. *If I had left on time.* The ache in his heart threatened to consume him. *They should've just let me die.*

The wind brushed across his tanned, naked torso, giving him relief from the sweltering conditions on the ship. The smell of saltwater was exhilarating compared to the odor of sweaty men. His chest muscles twitched. Johan gazed into the dark sky. Minutes passed.

"Boom, boom. Boom, boom, boom." Distant naval gunfire and the light from star shells near Guam snapped him out of the empty hole he'd learned to retreat to.

He turned around from the railing and made his way through the rows of tents and trucks on deck to the designated pickup area for ammunition. A long line of soldiers had already formed. Horrendous lines were the norm in the army.

"Godspeed, Sarge," the ordinance corporal handed him two belts of ammo.

God? "You too, man." Johan slung the belt across his chest. "Just keep the ammo coming." He grinned at the corporal as he accepted a bag of rifle grenades, and a pouch of hand grenades.

"Sure thing, Sarge."

Johan walked back to his spot on the deck where he'd already packed his duffel bag of government-issued clothing, a copy of *Time Magazine*, and playing cards. He set all his ammo down then rolled up his half of the tent and stuffed it into his combat field pack. The field pack also contained his food. The long-sleeved uniform shirt he put on was overkill in the heat of the tropics, but after training in the jungles of Hawaii, it was a plus. The sharp-bladed grass and ever-present mosquitoes may just not eat him alive. Johan tightened his boot laces so they were snugger. He stood up, donned his field pack and helmet then grabbed his pouch of grenades and strapped it to his right thigh. It took less than a minute to secure his cartridge belt around his waist. After he picked up his rifle, he stood still. Eighty pounds of equipment was a piece of cake. Johan looked around to ensure his men were ready to head below deck. It was too hot during the ocean crossing for the troops to stay under. But now that they were getting ready to head into shore, all men would soon be ordered to their compartments. Johan saw an open spot along the port side and made his way back again. It was his one last chance to get his head right.

Jesi sat up breathing heavy and fast. Beads of sweat formed along her forehead. She pushed her hands into the bed beneath her, willing the man away. Nothing happened. *It was a nightmare, only a nightmare.* She stared into the dark cave, eyes creased, nose flared, and lips pursed.

Her subconscious reminded her of the terrible news in the early months of the Japanese occupation. Carmen was Jesi's classmate and Carmen's family was thought to have been hiding an American GI radioman named George Tweed. In an effort to scare Carmen's family into giving them information, the Japanese soldiers took Carmen, raped her, and killed her.

Jesi slid into her slippers and grasped the walls of the cave as she walked to the door. She felt dizzy and her lips trembled. Her heartbeats seemed as loud as the bombs that exploded. Jesi braced her back against the cave, closed her eyes, and took three deep breaths to calm down. Once the dizziness subsided, she pulled the vines aside and stepped between the trees. The sun would rise soon. Jesi eased herself to the ground, lay back on the grass, and closed her eyes. She bent both knees so her feet were flat. *They are fine. Chief told you to stay put. He will be madder than mad if you go out. You can't go out there.*

The *Starlight* neared the transport area. Forgiveness didn't come. Not for himself, or his parents. Johan looked at his watch. It was 0530. He heard the ship's engine turn off. The roar of 16-inch battleship guns blitzed the air. *"Baboom, baboom, baboom."* It was dark and distant, but the navy's artillery power lit up the beach and the mountains behind it. Fighter planes buzzed. The crackle of the loudspeakers on the quarterdeck pierced the air.

Johan turned left to the direction of the noise. You'd hear a fly if it flitted from the stern. Men stared at the loudspeakers. Many crossed their arms. Some wiped sweat off their forehead. All were quiet.

"This is Marine Major General Roy Geiger."

Of course.

"The eyes of a nation watch you as you go into battle to liberate this former American bastion from the enemy."

Hooah!

"The honor which has been bestowed on you is a signal one."

Signal, or single?

"Make no mistake; it will be a tough, bitter fight against a wily, stubborn foe who will doggedly defend Guam against this invasion. May the glorious traditions of the Marines' esprit de corps spur you to victory. You have been honored."

"Hooah!" the men busted out.

Fighting words, General.

Men returned to packing up.

Johan looked across the sky. It was light now, but black and gray smoke covered the sun.

"All troops report below deck."

"Baboom, baboom, boom, boom, boom."

Jesi awoke and bolted to her feet. Her body flinched at another bang. It took a moment to realize she dozed off outside and the bombs weren't falling on her. It was daylight. The explosions were faster and louder. And she heard more planes. Jesi ran back in. She took her slippers off and sat curled up on her bed, clutching her chest, and rocking forward and back. Her heart pounded fast and her stomach churned. She stared in front of her. And rocked. And rocked. But the sounds of the bombs continued their torture.

"You'll be all right. Be strong," Mames whispered.

What did dad say? Think, think! Chief said that after plenty of bombings, the Americans would land and kill the Japanese. It's what they did on Saipan. OK, it's OK then. The Americans are here.

9

Jesi's spirits surged, and she knew she'd reunite with her family and go home today. She stripped off her pajamas, donned a T-shirt and jeans cut at the knees, and washed up. Jesi picked up her calendar and pencil and bit her lip, making a big circle around July 21. A smile crossed her face and her tummy grumbled.

I forgot to eat breakfast. The stash of coconuts in the corner beckoned her. There were four *mánhas*, the young coconuts with green husk. There were also two star apples, nuts, and dried meat on the table. *Mánhas will do.* Jesi went outside.

"Whack, whack, whack."

Ai adai.

Frustrated with the blade, she drank from the jagged hole of the first coconut.

So worth it.

"Whack."

Don't cut your hand.

"Whack, whack."

Jesi finished the juice of the second coconut.

"Hugh! Hugh!"

The extra oomph in heaving the machete was enough for the dull blade to cut both mánhas in half.

"That's how you do it," she mimicked Peter.

Peter enjoyed messing with her. It was because she expected as much from Peter after his accident, as before.

Delicious.

She rinsed her hands and chin then walked back into the cave to tidy up. Jesi and Peter stashed necessities in the Pago and

Ylig caves before the Japanese invaded. Chief said they had to be prepared if the Japs were serious.

"This can wait."

"Boat team No. 5 proceed to your landing station. On the double, boat team No. 6," the voice on the loudspeaker continued.

"We're next boys," Johan called.

It was almost 1030 hours. Johan and his men started their way up to the deck from the compartments.

"See you on the other side," Johan said as he gave a half hug to a fellow soldier.

"Hooah," another hollered.

Johan felt a pang of sadness knowing that he might never see these men again. He shook the thought out of his head. Johan's platoon and the rest of the Second Battalion reached their assigned stations on the starboard side of the ship. The coast guard boats were waiting.

"I'm first, you be last," Johan said to Sergeant David Lucas.

"Yes, Sir."

Sergeant Lucas was the noncommissioned officer who would be next in line should Johan get killed, wounded, or go missing. He was several inches shorter than Johan, but equally muscular and fit. They were in the same platoon, in charge of separate squads. Together, they commanded a fine group of soldiers.

Johan clenched the cargo net as he and another soldier made their descent. The small boat bobbed and heaved in the ocean. The rough waters from all the moving ships made for a treacherous drop. There was a man down in the boat pulling the net taut on either side.

"Hot damn," Johan cursed as he lost his footing and held his weight up with one hand.

"Sarge, you good?"

"You best hold the hell tight!" he yelled up to his guys. Johan made it into the boat and helped the others jump in.

The boat pulled away from the transport ship.

"Sarge, it's for you."

Johan rose to his feet from his seat up front and took the radio from the driver. "Sir, yes, Sir." He gave the radio back to the guardsman. "Word just came down that General Shepherd doesn't need us yet," Johan hollered over the artillery noise. Much of the heavy bombing from the battleships had slowed down. The sound of rifles, grenades, and smaller canons took over.

"Hurry up and wait," Miller said.

Johan gave the private first class a "shut-your-big-mouth" look. Miller outshone most soldiers during the 305th's training in the States, but he had problems with how slow the army seemed to move and make decisions.

"Get your head down, man."

The rocky ride made a good number of soldiers ill.

"Right, Sarge."

All the boats carrying the Second Battalion made circles in a holding pattern on the ocean. They waited for the go-ahead to the line of departure. These men were combat-ready even if this was their first turn at war. They wanted to fight.

Landing amid battle on W-Day, Johan felt he could conquer the world and the enemy. He'd lived for this moment since Lily was killed in June 1941. *If I were there just a minute earlier, she would never have crossed the street and gotten hit by a drunkard.* Leaving New York City to restore his grandfather's homestead in the Catskills didn't erase his nightmares. The horses distracted him for a while, but Lily's scream and the image of her body on the road haunted him. He tried to work himself to death, collapsing in the sun. Anything to erase the pain from his heart. Combat training was intense, and took him all over the country. Still, the nightmares persisted. Even the arduous abandon-ship drills around Eniwetok didn't cure him. *I'll meet my so-called maker on this rock. And what god would take her and my baby anyway? There was no God. But in war, there was death. Perfect.* The boat driver handed him the radio again, startling him out of his hole.

Finally, having circled for almost three hours, Johan was given the order to come to shore at 1400.

"All right, men, it's a go!" He yelled above the noise of the engine.

The boat neared the line of departure at the reef where they would load into landing craft to take them ashore. Johan swept his eyes along the beach. American Ducks, or six-wheeled trucks that could float, were strewn across and partially submerged in the water.

What's all that floating?

Several types of amphibious trucks and landing craft lined the sand delivering supplies.

"What the hell!" Johan furrowed his brows and coughed, and coughed, and coughed.

Most of the men on his boat nearly choked from the ash.

"There are no landing vehicles to take you guys in," the officer in charge said.

"Hot damn, figure." *Christ!* "Listen up boys, attach your radio up top and get across in one piece." Johan removed his radio from his belt and secured it. "Lucas, you head 'em up and I'll pull the rear."

"Got it, Sarge. Jump boys, we're going in." Sergeant Lucas was the first to get wet and he raised his rifle above his head. The water was covered half his buttocks. The other men followed, lifting their rifles, too.

Johan stepped in and was drenched up to his groin. The pouch of grenades around his leg was waterproof. He saw the men to the left of his platoon struggle to maintain their balance. One soldier walked in water that was up to his waist then in the next second the water was over his head. Johan trod a different path, hoping to avoid the same fate. It was a quarter mile to the shore. His neck muscles twitched and he glowered. His nose flared. "Goddamn it." The floating debris was the bodies of soldiers and marines. The corpses were strewn along the sand. Men worked feverishly to collect their fallen friends. Johan picked up on a stench. It was the burning of human flesh.

Much of the Second Battalion veered far off to the right of their assembly area near Gaan Point, separating and faltering as they tried to find a safe path to shore.

"The Japs aren't firing at us, easy targets that we are," Johan said to the soldier beside him. The marines had already secured the beach, and many were pushing inland. A bullet whizzed past his helmet. "Son of a bitch." Johan stood still for a moment then fired his rifle in the direction of the bullet. He ran until he caught up with the last of his platoon. "Hurry up, boys."

"Race you, Sarge."

On shore, bomb holes still threatened to trip them. Spent artillery shells littered the coral ground. Coconut trees were half bald if not decapitated. Johan and his men reached their designated spot on White Beach One, four hundred yards inland of Gaan Point in the village of Agat. Small mountains just beyond the beach loomed over their command post.

All the 305th were sandwiched between the Twenty-Second Marines on the left and the Fourth Marines on the right. Johan's platoon settled in for the night. He hastened to dig his foxhole. The skirmishes along the front lines were discernable as the Japs tried to break through the hold the marines had. Johan was satisfied his pit was as deep as it could get. *Not enough has to be enough.* He walked around to check on his guys. They finished with their own holes and started to hunker down.

It's as good a time as any to eat. Each of them carried enough D-rations for a few days. Johan sank into his trench then reached into his field pack. He pulled out a small rectangular package a bit shorter than his hand, and not much thicker. The "candy" bar.

It was dark and her stomach grumbled. Jesi had been pacing outside the cave for a while and forgot about lunch. The beginnings of a worn-out track between the cave's entrance and the edge of the cliff started to form. Still, there was no sign of Chief or Peter. *Where are they?* Jesi's eyes narrowed and she rubbed the back of her neck. *Why was it taking them so long to get here? The bombings were not as bad as earlier today.*

Jesi walked into the cave and stuffed a handful of peanuts in her mouth. She lay down on her tummy and hugged a pillow against her cheek. *I'm leaving tomorrow.*

2

July 24, 1944 — Early Morning —Maanot Ridge,
Southwest Guam

"RISE AND SHINE, SLEEPING BEAUTIES," Johan made sure all his men could hear him.

"Getting up, Sarge," Calhoun said in the adjacent hole.

"Breakfast awaits you."

"Out—damn—standing," Miller chimed from the other side.

Johan tossed each of his guys a C-ration. They were now able to eat boxed food, an improvement from their so-called candy-bar meals the first few days. However lousy the bars of chocolate powder tasted, they provided much needed calories.

Johan and all the Second Battalion of the 305th previously moved out from the Agat beachhead and had already relieved the Fourth Marines along the front lines near Maanot Ridge.

"Listen up," Johan called to order his platoon of thirty men when they finished cleaning their weapons. He smoothed an area of dirt and drew a map. The crude depiction showed their westerly location in reference to their objective along the southeastern region of the island. "Today, three squads will head out and recon toward Talo fo fo and Yo na. Did I say that right?"

"Don't remember," Smithy said.

Johan gave two squads their specific instructions.

"Where we going?" Smithy asked.

"Smithy, you, Calhoun, Miller, and I, will go east, first toward the Tokcha Bay, sweep north toward Ylig Bay, then finish up and head west back to camp." Johan looked around to ensure the men understood their tasks. "And for you other boys," Johan faced his fourth squad, "make a doggone latrine." He was both serious, and not. The recon squads loaded up with their packs, helmets, and weapons.

"See you all tonight," Johan said as he turned to leave.

"Yes, Sir," someone replied.

Johan's squad finished the first leg of their route by midday and headed north.

"It's hot as an oven," Calhoun said. *"Yoooooo . . ."*

Johan turned his head to see Calhoun sliding down a hill.

"Jeez, Calhoun," Smithy called down, "You sure are clumsy as heck, man."

"Close your mouth and help me outta here."

"I think you need to cool off more in that there pond."

"Smithy boy, you best lend a hand if you know what's good for you!"

Smithy, or Specialist Smith, was a courageous pint-sized man. But his whims sometimes got him in a load of crap.

"Aw shit, Smithy, get him out," Johan ordered.

It rained. Then shone. And rained again. Then shone. Wet leaves from bombed branches littered the ground. Where once grew coconut and bamboo trees now stood tree trunks that looked like a few lone toothpicks in a dispenser. They saw two houses thus far. Two shacks was a better description.

Specialist Calhoun got on his feet alongside the others and they continued on.

Johan's arm muscles tensed. He bit down hard on his jaw. His eyes narrowed to the hill just ahead of them. He raised his hand to bring his squad to a halt.

The men quieted. Something flashed in the hill. The hairs at the back of his neck frizzed at attention. They were in lush, shrubby and flat terrain now.

"There it is again," Johan whispered. He and his men had decorated their helmets with jungle leaves to blend in with the surroundings. Johan hoped it was enough to fool the Japs as they had the advantage right now.

"Let's head over to those trees there, to the left of the hill. Calhoun and I will come up behind them. Smithy and Miller, you take the front."

Smithy nodded confirmation.

Johan and Calhoun reached the trees then crept their way to ten yards from the base of the hill. They heard the Japs talking. One tank and one platoon. Miller and Smithy were in position.

"It's a go, it's a go," Johan said into the radio. He and Calhoun stood up to launch grenades and as soon as the grenade left Johan's hand, an American plane came out of nowhere and began strafing the hill. He froze for a second then realized Calhoun had about-faced and run. Something exploded behind Johan that sent him flying through the air. Johan landed with a big thud on the ground. He heard them calling out to him, but he couldn't speak. *Here, over here.* The words didn't come out. Nobody came. He could see his own body sprawled on the ground. *I'm dying; I'm finally going to see her again.*

Contentment and relief covered his face.

-----

*July 24, 1944 — Late Morning — Ylig Bay Cave,
Central Guam, Eastern Coast*

Jesi woke up to her second day in the Ylig cave. Her trek down from Pago cave was uneventful and she didn't see any Japanese, or Chamorros, or even Americans. She was grateful that this side of Guam appeared to be untouched by any of the bombs, but her mom and grandma should have been here.

Where are they? She couldn't stand being alone much longer. *Perhaps they're at Uncle Kin's house.* Uncle Kin was her grandma's brother, and before the war, there was always a barbecue or fiesta there. His house was not far from the Tokcha River, along the northern edge of Talofofo village.

I am going to find them. Jesi opened a can of corned beef and ate it with a papaya she had picked on her way down. She got ready for yet another hike by herself.

Jesi reached the edge of her uncle's property. She waited awhile behind *tångantångan* trees and looked around. No one was there. *I don't hear any chickens.* Uncle Kin sold eggs at the Agana market. Some of his chicken coops backed up to a shelter that had a lone tin wall and a tin roof. It was just ahead of her. Jesi walked closer to the coops. She covered her mouth and nose with her T-shirt and rounded the corner of the shelter. Jesi's eyes widened. "Oh god, oh my god! *Ai Yu'us, Ai Yu'us!*" Bloated bodies lay on top of each other. Flies swarmed. Head were decapitated. She heaved, and heaved again.

Jesi tore off down the dirt road. "Help, oh my god help!" Her aunt's small house was just ahead and it looked like there were people there. "Help, help me!" Tears blurred her vision.

"Don't go there. Turn around," Mames whispered.

Jesi slowed to a jog and wiped the tears from her eyes. The figures got closer to her. First it was one, then another. Jesi stopped. They started to run toward her.

She bolted in the opposite direction. This time she didn't scream. *Focus.* Her heart pounded. *They're talking in Japanese.* Jesi looked behind her and saw that they were still running toward her. She looked forward again and tripped over something. "Oh god!"

Jesi jumped back up. Out of nowhere one of them stepped in front of her and grabbed the back of her shirt as she turned around. He pinned her against his chest. She tried to break her hands free, but his arms were locked around her abdomen. Jesi swung her head back against his face. The soldier cried out and released his hold. She turned around and kicked him in his groin.

The Japanese crouched down protecting his organs and blood dripped from his face. She ran, but crashed right into the other two. "Heeelp!" The bigger Japanese held her with her back against his chest and covered her mouth with his free hand.

Johan was startled awake by a high-pitched shriek. *What was that?* It was bright all around him. *I see the light.* The throbbing in his right leg was intense. He looked down and pulled his uniform up. The gash from yesterday bled through the bandage. *Damn, I'm still alive.*

"No! Get away from me. Heeelp!" The cry filled the air.

That was a girl in trouble. The shrubs were just low enough for him to peer over without having to stand.

"Stop, don't touch me!"

The scream came from the direction of the shack. Johan looked to make sure it was safe to leave his spot then hobbled closer to the dilapidated structure. The entrance to the dwelling appeared to be a porch-like area with nothing for a floor except the ground. Johan rubbed his leg. *Son of a bitch.* There was a junked pickup nearby.

As he hid behind the truck, he saw there were three Japs and a local girl. Her arms were pinned behind her with her neck locked in place inside a Jap's arm. And they had a gag on her now. The other two tried to get at her clothing. The girl kicked them when they got close. A foot landed right on one man's chin. He fell back then stood up and slapped her cheek. Johan gasped. The girl appeared to lose consciousness. The Jap with dried blood all over him held her legs while the other bent down to lay her on the ground. She became conscious again and continued fighting them off. They held her so stiff Johan feared she would dislocate her shoulder as much as she was struggling.

This was the best chance he had to take them out as all three Japs were on their knees. Like a caged wild animal let loose on his prey, Johan lunged forward, kicked one across the face, and shot another between the eyes. "Ah shit." He felt a sting through his left arm. "Just for you, you son of a bitch." Johan shot the third man through the heart. That left him with the semiconscious Jap on the dirt. Ignoring the enemy's plea, Johan dropped his gun so it hung across his chest. With a trench knife in hand, he grabbed the Jap by the neck and pulled him to his feet then plunged the knife deep inside the Jap's gut, driving it all the way up until he felt a gush of blood. Adrenaline surged through his body. There were no other Japs running toward the shack. Johan could hear his own breathing and his heart pounded. Sweat ran down his cheek.

The squirming reminded him of the girl lying on the ground. He cased his knife and wiped his hands along the back of his legs. He looked at her. Johan raised a blood-stained index finger to his lips to keep her quiet then removed the gag. Tears streamed down her temple, but her eyes were wide open. *Green eyes?* The girl was panting.

"I'm not going to hurt you. You need to calm down."

The girl shook her head sideways.

"Do you speak English?"

She nodded up and down.

"Breathe slowly. Take a deep breath in like me." *Good girl.* "Breathe out now." Johan continued to inhale and exhale with her until she calmed down.

"I'm going to slide your pants back up and untie your hands, all right?"

She nodded.

As soon as her hands were free, she sat upright and scooted away from him.

"It's OK; I'm not going to hurt you."

She looked at her ankles.

"I'll untie your feet."

Once freed, the girl sprang up and stood back. Johan closed his eyes, sickened at what could have happened had he not heard her. *Thank God, if there was a god.*

His left arm hurt. Blood oozed from a bullet hole. The girl bolted past him. Johan turned and looked after her. *Ah hell.* "Stop, I won't hurt you." He ran after her, pushing past the pain in his limbs. *There are still Jap stragglers out there. They would not get their hands on her if it killed him.*

"Go away!" She was still on the dirt trail that ran along the outskirts of the hidden path to Ylig cave. Dead tired, she ducked into the brush, ignoring the branches that scraped her. She reached the secret path and looked over her shoulder. *Oh, thank you, Jesus.* Her breathing calmed now that he wasn't there. *Get to the cave, get to the cave,* was all she could think about. And how he killed those men. It was horrific. His eyes reminded Jesi of a trapped wild pig. That frightened her.

Jesi hiked down a steep slope, but she had done it many times. The entrance was easy to miss because it was covered by jungle. She found the big *ifet* tree with its recognizable trunk. "One, two, three . . . twelve." She turned to the left then took three steps between the trees and was at the front of the cave. This cave had lots of light shining through compared to the Pago cave. *My machete.* She patted her back. *Oh god, it fell off.* She rummaged through the stockpile of necessities to find another machete, just in case.

3

July 24, 1944 — Late afternoon — Heading to Ylig Bay Cave,
Central Guam, Eastern Coast

JOHAN FOLLOWED THE GIRL FROM FAR enough behind so she would feel less threatened. His arm and leg were killing him. *She turned here.* Johan took a few steps to the left and walked into the cave until he saw her. The girl stopped whatever she was doing and turned to him holding the longest machete he'd ever seen.

"I'm not here to hurt you. Just wanna make sure the Japs don't get you."

She stood looking at him.

Johan braced himself against the wall of the cave, took his pack off, and slumped to the ground. *It's so damned hot! Where's my radio?* "Shit!" Johan released the ammo belt around his waist. The radio was gone. Pain tore through his arm as he writhed out of his top. He grabbed his canteen of water with his uninjured hand and took a swig. The water felt good as he poured it down his face.

Johan heard the girl rummaging around. She walked toward him carrying a container. The girl didn't have the knife anymore. She motioned to his bloody arm and showed him the contents of the tin. Johan nodded his approval, and looked at her eyes again. *You're not seeing straight, Landers.* Her hair was tied but disheveled, and her cheeks were dirty.

There was blood on her shirt. The girl reached for his canteen then for a wet cloth. After cleaning around the wound, she grabbed a bottle from the tin. Johan clenched his teeth. It hurt like hell.

"Your eyes," he blabbed, "I thought they were green."

No response.

He was light-headed so he stretched his arm out for more water. The girl got up then came back with a green coconut and a cup.

Johan watched her through half-opened eyelids. She flattened a box and held the coconut on top of it. With her other hand, she took a small swing of the machete to the coconut and cut off a piece of the skin. The girl placed the piece between her teeth and made another cut. She inserted the tip of the machete into the exposed area, set the machete down, and turned the coconut over so the liquid drained into a cup.

"Drink," she said.

Johan closed his eyes and took a sip. Then a gulp. Coolness spread through his body. *She's nice.* It was the most delicious thing he'd put on his tongue. Refreshing. The girl held the cup for him until he finished.

"Thank you."

The girl nodded.

She set the cup aside and stepped away to pick up the coconut and machete again. Keeping her left hand out of the way, the girl held the machete in her right hand, centered it on the coconut, and hit the coconut in the middle. It split in half. She brought the coconut to him. Using the skin that was between her teeth, she scooped the coconut flesh and fed him.

Johan savored the soft meat. It wasn't as sweet as the stuff his granny used to sprinkle on cake. But it was really good.

The girl was about five feet and a couple inches, and it looked as if she could use something to eat, though she wasn't as thin as the other refugees he'd seen. She wasn't trembling anymore. When she finished, she set aside the spent coconut and cardboard.

"Thank you, Miss. My name is Johan. What's your name?"

She narrowed her eyes at him for a moment.

"Jesi, my name is Jesi."

Her voice was pleasant. He was exhausted. *What is it about her eyes?* She stood up, startling him, and walked deeper into the cave.

Johan winced as he reached for his knife. It was covered in dried blood. The way he had killed that last Jap was gruesome. *Perhaps it was a bit much.* He wondered if that scared her. *Can it be any more hot and humid!* The knife was still so sharp that it cut through the right side of his uniform pants all the way down to his boot without a snag. "For Christ's sake." Johan stabbed the knife into the ground and let out a heavy sigh. A lot of blood seeped through the bandage and the area below his knee appeared swollen.

The big army soldier lay in front of her. She barely got him on the guåfak before he became unconscious. He needed medicine right away. *But what if they catch me again. I can't go, I can't.* Jesi took a deep breath and closed her eyes. *You have to go. You must go.*

"I will protect you. Go now," Mames whispered.

27

Jesi snapped out of it. She looked for coconut oil and found a bottle near her grandma's *lusong* and *lommuk*. The mortar and pestle of a *suruhåna* was akin to the rolling pin of a baker.

Jesi knew where to pick the leaves of the *sinamomu* plant. It was not far from the cave. Once she reached the patch, Jesi asked permission of her Chamorro ancestors, the *taotaomo'na*, *"Guella yan Guello, kao siña mañuli' yo' tinanom-mu? Ya yanggen måtto hao gi tano'-hu, chule' ha' håfa malago'-mu."*

"Si Yu'us ma'åse'." Jesi said thank you when she finished then walked back to the cave.

Once the leaves were washed, she put them in the lusong with coconut oil and pounded the mixture to a paste.

"Fanohge Chamorro . . ." Jesi hummed the Guam hymn. The song came to her head from out of nowhere. Perhaps it was because there was hope for her people, that the Americans were here and would chase the Japanese away. With a lightness on her shoulders, she unwrapped the bandage from Johan's leg. Jesi cleaned the wound, applied the thick paste, and covered the injury with a new bandage.

It started to get dark. There were two lamps filled with coconut oil. Jesi lit both. She found another guåfak and laid it along the right side of him. After cutting away the remainder of his clothing, she did a thorough check of his body. There didn't appear to be other major wounds.

She picked up the cloth she used earlier and wiped along the side of his chest closest to her. He had sparse body hair. Jesi wiped his abdomen. *So much muscle.* She grew hot. It was warm in the cave. And she was still in her long-sleeved shirt.

Jesi stood up, grabbed one lamp, and walked to the stack of containers. She opened one, but it had dishes. She opened the next container. It had clothes. Jesi sifted through what was there and found one of her mom's blouses and shorts. *Oh mom.*

Jesi remembered how Chief would fuss with her mom when it came to wearing dresses. *Thank God mom didn't force me to wear a dress all the time. Those poor girls.* Cave hiking with her brothers in a dress didn't seem right anyway. Most Chamorro women and girls had to wear a dress every single day. Jesi took her shirt off to change, and sensed that her bra was loose.

Her skin felt as if it were crawling over itself. Nausea washed over. Ignoring the sick feeling, Jesi took the bra off and threw it down, followed by her cutoff jeans, panty, and hair tie. *I need water.* She filled two pitchers with water from a big bucket, and grabbed a washcloth. The washing area of the cave was farther back. There was a piece of soap in a cup, enough to make a lather. After pouring water over her head and body, she scrubbed her skin so hard that it hurt, never mind that the scratches burned, too. Tears streamed down her cheeks. Jesi stood still.

She touched her mouth. It felt as if the gag were still there. Her left hip throbbed from where they yanked her jeans off. *They could have killed me. Oh god, they could have killed me like Carmen!* The tears came faster and her sobs were louder. Jesi dropped the soapy cloth then crouched on the ground. *Mom, where are you? I need you.* The ache in her heart was heavy. She hugged her chest and couldn't stop crying. *How could this happen to us? Please, God, help us. Save us from these terrible people. Please keep my family safe.* Jesi cried for a while.

Enough. Stop this crying. Get up! She remembered what her mom always said to her when she had heard too much of her daughter's silliness. *You were always so strong, Mom.* Jesi willed herself to stop crying and blocked the horrible men out of her mind. She stood up and took a deep breath. And another. More coherent, she finished washing up.

"Lily, Lily! No, Lily!"

That was him. Jesi wiped down as fast as she could and jumped into the blouse and shorts, forgetting to put a bra and panty on.

"You're safe, Mister, um, Johan. You're all right." He was sweating so she wiped his forehead. *Un ramas lodigao, tres hagon mumutong sapble, tres hagon betbena.* She needed too many different plants to make the medicine drink for his fever. And it was dark. *What am I going to do?* Jesi grabbed the bottle of coconut oil and smeared some between her palms. She massaged his uninjured body parts to help bring his fever down; it was all she could do since she could not make the concoction.

"Check his bag," Mames whispered.

That's it. Jesi got up to grab his bag and brought it close to the light. There were brown boxes labeled as rations. *He's got to have some kind of medicine.* Looking at his belt, she noticed there was a couple of pouches and another canteen hanging on it. Jesi got back up and brought the belt to the lamp. She opened the first pouch. *These look dangerous.* After closing it and leaving the grenades alone, she opened a second pouch. "Foot powder, Frazer's Solution, battle dressing, aspirin," Jesi read. *Aspirin.* She opened the jar and spilled four tablets on her palm then grabbed Johan's canteen and sat beside his head.

"Johan, Johan." She nudged his right shoulder "You must get up and take these pills." He stirred. Jesi could see he was trying to open his eyes. "Just tilt your head up a little bit so I can help you." Jesi held out her hand with the aspirin in front of him, but he couldn't sit up. She moved above his head and eased her knees under the pillow. "Take these." Johan reached for the pills and put them in his mouth. She held the canteen up to his lips. Johan pushed on her hand to tilt the canteen upward and sipped the water.

"Thank you."

He went unconscious again. Jesi slipped out from under his head. *I hope this American medicine helps.*

She put his things back in the bag then prepared another makeshift bed next to him. Exhausted, Jesi sat along Johan's right side with her legs crossed under her thighs. She was about to lie down when she noticed he was still sweating. Jesi got back up to get a piece of cardboard then used it as an improvised fan to cool Johan's body.

Jesi jerked her head back up. She had dozed off. *Just a little longer.* It felt as if she were holding a gallon of water out in front of her. *Who was Lily?* After a while, Johan's breathing was steady and he stopped sweating. His forehead was warm against the back of her hand, not hot like before. *The Chamorro medicine and the American medicine worked.* Jesi blew out the lamps then lay down on her left side. With her head propped up on her hand, she stared at him. *He hadn't shaved in a while.* His hair was dark, and his chest moved up and down with each breath.

Johan blinked and focused on the ceiling above him. It was bright inside and earthy, like dirt. He looked down at his body. *I'm almost naked.* His right leg was bandaged. He raised his left hand to scratch his nose. "Damn it." It was bandaged as well. Johan laid his head back on the pillow. *What had happened? The girl.* He turned to his right. She lay asleep beside him. After adjusting his body and turning over onto his side, he rested his left arm across his abdomen. Jesi was on her tummy and her hair covered the pillow. Her right arm was bent with her hand tucked under her cheek. *A nice small nose.* Johan reached across to push away the black wisp that lay over her mouth. *Full lips.*

A strange noise came from her throat and she had a grin on her lips. Her legs shifted under the blanket. It looked as if it were the blanket that was supposed to cover her cushions. She hugged her pillow closer to her head. Jesi opened her eyes, blinking.

"Good morning," Johan said, "or is it afternoon?" He nodded toward the front of the cave. "What were you smiling about?"

She stared at him. Her brows crinkled. Jesi sat up and looked around.

"It wasn't a dream. You really are here?"

"I am. How are you doing?" Johan asked.

"Good." She reached across and felt Johan's forehead with the back of her left hand. "You look better, too."

"My leg isn't as swollen. Thank you."

"What about your arm?"

"It's not as bad either, thanks to you."

"I, I was a little scared. You were burning up and I couldn't make the medicine."

"The one you put on my leg?"

"No, I wanted to boil twigs and leaves to make a medicine drink, but it would have taken too long."

"I see."

"I looked in one of your pouches and found aspirin."

"Your eyes are gray."

"And?"

"It's different. I can't put my finger on it."

"They turn green when I'm angry."

"That's it. I thought they were green, but then today they are gray."

"How old are you?" He didn't mean to ask. It just came out.

"Nineteen."

"How old are you?"

"Thirty." He decided that he would not mention he'd be thirty-one in December. Johan's stomach grumbled.

"Was that you?" Jesi asked.

"Yup, sorry. I'm starving."

"Let me see if I can—"

"Bring my pack over here. When was the last time you ate?"

"I don't know. Breakfast yesterday?"

"You haven't eaten for a day? Reach into the bag and get one of the brown boxes."

Jesi folded her bedding to one side of the guåfak then grabbed the bag. She pulled out a box that said C-rations and emptied the contents.

"Inside you'll find a P-38, it's a small metal can opener."

"This is neat," Jesi said, admiring the strange packages of food in front of her.

"It doesn't taste all that great."

"But you can eat it, right? And at least you get food." She shrugged her shoulders. Her stomach growled. "Sorry. I guess I'm hungry, too."

"Don't be sorry. Open the big can. It's meat or chicken, and something or other. There are crackers in one of them. And a spoon should be there."

"They sell food in cans here, but I've never seen them like this. Is it just army food?"

"It's for all US military, and sometimes a little different depending on where you're at."

"How do I put this on the can?"

"Hook that little piece under the rim then push that top part down into the can."

"Like this? And push here?"

"Yup, just like that."

"We take the tip of a knife and poke it into the top of the can then push the knife down." Jesi worked her way around the can with the opener.

Johan studied this girl in front of him. Her hair was wavy and all over the place. Her fingers were long and slender, and her nails were clean and cut. His manly part hardened at the sight of her nipples poking through the fabric.

"All done," she said, interrupting him from his carnal thoughts.

"Now you eat," Johan said.

"Um, no I can't. It's your food and you need it more."

"You've been taking care of me. How about we share?" Johan reached over with his left hand to lift her chin. "We both need to eat. Where's that smile?"

"That's fair. Thank you."

His finger traced her smile. *I'd kiss those lips if I could move.* Johan pulled his hand back. He couldn't decide if it was the pain in his arm, or his conscience. Having not been with a woman in over a year, his need for sex was taking over.

"You first," Jesi brought a spoon up to his lips. It was chicken and vegetables. "Is it OK that we use the same spoon?"

Johan nodded.

Jesi tried the stew. "Not bad. And it's nice to have something other than nuts and *tinalan kåtne*."

"What's *ti-na-lan-kawt-knee*?"

"It's dried meat."

"How do you make dried meat here?"

"The men catch and clean the deer, and the women boil ocean water for salt. I don't know what they do after that."

"Your English sounds very good. Who taught you?"

"We could only speak English in school, not Chamorro. My mom makes me speak English to her, too, and I had an American friend. Suzie and I went to the same school and we talked all the time in English. Suzie had to leave with all the other Americans."

"What do you mean?"

"Peter said that he saw the American families leave on a ship. It was just a couple of months before the Japanese came."

"Just Americans?"

Jesi nodded.

"I see. Your skin is not as dark as I expected."

"You're making fun of me?"

"Not at all. I just thought the locals would be darker."

"I know. Most Chamorros are pretty dark. But not me. A lot of kids made fun of my eyes and my skin."

"I'm sorry they picked on you."

"It's fine. My mom says that one of our ancestors from a long, long time ago must have been light-skinned. And someone was a tiny bit Asian."

"Probably." *That's why your eyes are different.*

"Where do you live, Johan?"

"May I have some water please?" he asked.

"Of course." Jesi reached for the canteen and helped him drink.

Johan lay back on his pillow.

"Could you get me more aspirin?"

"OK." Jesi knelt over to the pouch and retrieved the bottle. "Four?"

"Yup. I lived in the Catskill Mountains in New York."

"Where the Statue of Liberty is?"

"Close. You know where that is?"

"Uh-huh."

Johan leaned up again and Jesi helped him with the medicine and water. "How about we talk later, OK? Finish the rest of the food. There's another box in my bag and a chocolate bar. The chocolate is terrible."

Johan lay down and closed his eyes.

Jesi finished what was left of the crackers, but was still hungry. Chocolate sounded good. She hadn't eaten candy since the Japanese came. Jesi unwrapped the bar and took a bite. Or tried to. She took a smaller bite and was able to get a piece off. A frown spread across her face. It wasn't like the candy bars she remembered. She ate it anyway, drank water, and cleared up the trash.

She sat beside Johan and checked his forehead. The fever was gone. Jesi used her blanket to cover him. And thought about the way Johan held her chin. *Did he want to kiss me?*

Jesi at one time built up the courage to ask her father if she could go to the community center dance with a boy. He kissed her once and wanted to go out. She just started high school. Chief was almost out of his skin. "If I catch you wif a boy Jessica Marie Taimanglo, I'll whip you hard you cannat sit down. An den I'll get my speargun out and shoot him der." Jesi laughed at her imitation of her father.

Chief used her full name when he was mad. She gave up on having a boyfriend. It wasn't worth the wrath of her father.

"What's so funny?" Johan asked.

"Sorry. I didn't mean to wake you."

"I'm glad you did. What were you thinking about?"

"I was copying my dad. He can get so mad. His eyes grow all wide and his neck muscles, you can see his veins." Jesi contorted herself to copy her father. "Why are you smiling at me that way?"

"Because you're funny. Help me sit up?"

Jesi placed a couple of pillows behind his back.

"I don't laugh when I make my mom mad though. She actually whipped me."

"And it really hurt?"

"It did."

"More than your dad's whipping?"

"My dad didn't spank me, not that I can remember anyway."

"When was the last time your mom took the belt to you?"

"Belt? It was a branch from the tångantångan tree, ah, one of the trees in the jungle." Jesi massaged her bottom.

"It was that painful?"

"I was ten years old. It was the first and the last time."

"What did you do?"

"I sprinkled flour all over the living room floor so my brothers and I could slide around." Jesi grinned and let out a small chuckle.

"We all got spanked. She had us lie right there on the floor and whipped us one by one. We cried, even before we got it. She was more than mad . . ."

"What's the sad face for?"

"I used the flour she was saving to make my dad's birthday cake. After she whipped us and told us to clean up, she went to her room. I could hear her crying and I felt terrible. I apologized. She said she would make something else, but that I should not play with food."

Johan reached over to wipe the tear at the corner of her eye.

Jesi blinked and swallowed. "I miss her so much. I haven't seen my mom and my grandma since the Japanese came. They were supposed to be staying in this cave, but nobody was here when I arrived." Jesi tried to control her emotions. "I don't even know if they are alive." She put her face in her hands and sobbed, noticing that he pulled her against his chest.

"There now, sweet girl."

His lips rested on the top of her head as he stroked her back.

I'm going to be OK.

Jesi wrapped her arms around his torso. His chest nestled her cheek. The beating of his heart was that of a soft drum, *da dum, da dum, da dum.*

"Jesi, Jesi," he whispered. She had dozed off. "Good girl." Johan closed his eyes. Jesi was creeping in doors he had vowed to keep closed forever. Forever as in dead. *Maybe there's a reason I'm still alive.*

Johan felt her move and looked down, "Hi there."

"Hi." She leaned back and glanced up at him.

Johan shifted his gaze. *Don't do it, Landers.* Her mouth was somewhat parted. He enveloped her upper lip with his. She stiffened for a second. As he pulled her tight against his chest, she opened her lips enough for him to tease his tongue into her. Johan wanted to be inside her, and he knew he could take her now, injuries and all. He peeled his lips from hers then wrapped her snug in his arms. *Christ, what are you doing?*

"I'm sorry." Johan pulled away.

"Don't be. I've never been kissed like that before."

"I shouldn't have done it."

"I'll be right back."

He watched her as she got up and walked away. Johan couldn't hide the grin that emerged while admiring her butt. Jesi walked back toward him with matches and a lamp, smiling. She set the lamp next to the other one, lit the wicks then held one lamp and knelt by Johan's right leg.

"Let me look at your leg."

"All right."

"The swelling has gone down. Can you bend your knee?"

"Yup, it doesn't hurt much."

Jesi stood up and walked to his left side.

"What are you looking at?" Jesi asked.

"You."

She smiled.

"Does your arm hurt?"

He raised his arm to shoulder level then lowered it to his side. "Not bad."

Jesi unwound the cloth around his bicep. "It's healing well. I'm going to make more paste to be safe then we'll have dinner."

Johan sat back and relaxed.

"Who taught you how to make that?"

"My grandma. She's a medicine woman, a suruhåna is what we call her in Chamorro."

"Cha-mo-row." He had heard the word before in conferences, but it didn't mean anything to him at the time. "What's Cha-mo-row?"

"It's the name of our people, the people of the Mariana Islands, and it's our language."

Jesi finished making the paste and applied it to his left arm. "Are you a *sue-rue-haw-na*, too?"

"I'm still learning."

"You get an A plus, suruhåna-in-training." Johan grinned at her.

She wrapped his arm then worked on his leg.

"How do you say 'you are a very beautiful girl'?" It slipped. There was a bashful look on her face.

"*Gof bunita na palao'an.*"

"*Gough boo-knee-ta na pa-louw-an.* You are gof bonita na palao'an."

"And you're funny," she chuckled.

"You are a very pretty girl, Jesi." *Enough, Landers.*

"If you say so."

"I want to kiss you again." Johan stretched his arm out and pulled her right beside him. He cupped her chin in both of his hands so her face was close to his. Johan pressed his lips on hers. She kissed him back, but this time he sensed with more conviction, more desire. He tugged on her hair, tilting her head back. Jesi went rigid.

"I'm sorry, I got carried away."

"I just remembered those men."

Johan leaned her against his chest so her head rested on his shoulders. "They're dead now. I'm sorry that I scared you."

"I'm OK."

Jesi arched backwards then surprised him with a quick peck on the lips before she stood.

"I need to find something for dinner."

"Do you think you could help me up and walk a little?"

"Are you sure? I think you should still rest."

"I've been lying around for a day. I'd really like to stand up, and I'm not in much pain."

"OK, if you're up for it."

Johan looked under his blanket and smirked. "Do you have an extra pair of jeans or pants, and a shirt?"

"I'm sure there is." Jesi smiled back as she got up and walked toward the containers.

"You're in luck. I think these will fit." She held up an old pair of jeans and a T-shirt. "They're my dad's, and are stiff from drying in the sun."

"Come around to my right side." Johan bent his left leg so his foot was flat on the floor. He extended his right arm for Jesi to grab, and pulled to stand on his good leg. "Now that was easy."

"Show-off."

"We'll see." Johan put weight on his injured leg. "Not bad."

She helped him put on the jeans.

"Do you have something I could use as a crutch?"

"Me," Jesi smirked.

"You're right. You're short enough to be my crutch." Johan looked down and returned her grin.

Jesi gathered what she could find for dinner. They ate a can of corned beef, one young coconut, a box of rations, and the last chocolate bar. The two of them were so hungry that they even finished the "candy." Jesi cleared the dinner mess, fixed her bed then stood up and looked around. She needed to wipe down and couldn't find anything to hide behind.

"I need you to turn around while I wash up for the night."

"What do you mean?" Johan asked.

"I mean I need to undress so you'll have to turn around."

"I see." Johan started to turn around.

"Not yet. When I tell you."

"OK."

Jesi picked up one of the lamps and went to look for something to wear. She found a white T-shirt, a pair of smaller jeans, and a belt. Jesi took the scissors from the first-aid container and cut the jeans. "There."

She turned to Johan. "You're watching me."

"It's calming. You know what you're doing."

Smiling, she grabbed a pick and combed the tangled mess on her head. There was a hair tie on the handle so she put her hair in a bun to keep it from getting wet. *He's still watching me.* After retrieving a towel, washcloth, and some water, she headed to the washing area.

"Now you need to turn around please."

"Are you sure?"

"Of course I'm sure." *I think he's flirting with me.*

Jesi undressed then squatted to wash her private parts. As she dried herself, she felt that tingly sensation between her legs. She hung the towel around her neck, moistened the washcloth, and wiped the rest of her body. The scratches had already crusted over.

"Are you done?" Johan called.

"Almost."

"I need a wipe down, too."

Is he serious? "You got one last night and all you've done pretty much since is lie around."

"A man can try."

He is flirting with me!

Jesi finished putting on the shirt and shorts then stacked the dirty clothes and towels along a dry side near the wall of the cave.

"You can turn around now," she said, as she walked toward him. Jesi sat down on the guáfak as he lay on his side looking at her. "You have a nice smile, too."

"I don't think I've smiled so much since . . ."

"Since what? Who's Lily?"

Johan looked at her, surprised.

"You had a nightmare last night and screamed for Lily."

"I see." His face went blank.

"We don't have to talk about it, I was, it's just that, you were trembling and—"

"It's OK. I've been running from that night for a long time."

Johan rolled on his back and took a deep breath. His big, beautiful grin was gone. "She was my wife. We were married for two years and lived in Manhattan." There was a long pause, and he crossed his arms over his chest. "One day, she called the bank and said she had a surprise for me so I left work early. We were going to move to Texas where Lily was from. My parents didn't like her much because she wasn't as proper or high class."

"I'm sorry." *What else should I say?*

"It was a rainy day in the summer. My folks just got back from a trip so I stopped by their place to tell them we were moving. They tried to convince me otherwise, and of course we got into a fight as always. I ran late getting home. She was killed by a drunkard driving a car as she crossed the street to meet me for dinner. If I just went straight home she would still be alive."

Jesi didn't know what to do. A teardrop shimmered down his cheek. "I'm so sorry." She swallowed the lump in her throat then wiped his face.

"The doc said she was two months pregnant. That was her surprise." His voice cracked.

He had picked up Jesi's hand in his, and was squeezing her fingers so tight she was sure they melded together. Jesi was determined not to pull away.

"I left the city to work on my grandfather's homestead in the mountains. I was full of rage and hatred; I didn't even visit my parents for over a year. I blamed them, I blamed myself. Then war broke out and I thought . . ."

"Thought what?"

"It would help me forget. I'd go to bed spent then get up and train again, day in and day out. But sometimes, I still have nightmares."

She felt his grip soften. *Thank God.*

"When I buried Lily, I vowed not to endure that kind of pain, ever." He closed his eyes.

"I'm sorry you had to go through that."

Johan turned his head toward her.

"Will you lie next to me tonight?"

4

July 26, 1944 — Early morning — Still in Ylig Bay Cave,
Central Guam, Eastern Coast

"JESSICA MARIE TAIMANGLO!" JESI AWOKE startled. *Oh no, Dad.* His booming voice knocked the wind out of her, which was fitting because their last name meant "without wind."

Jesi saw that Johan was reaching for his rifle.

"No, Johan!" She grabbed his arm.

"Dad." Jesi got up to hug her father. He didn't budge.

"What's wrong?" Chief looked at Jesi then Johan. "It's not what you think."

"*Háfa nai,* Jessica?" Chief asked in Chamorro.

"Nothing. Johan's an American soldier and he saved me. The Japanese men—"

"Tell me." Chief switched to English.

"They would've killed me, but Johan heard me screaming."

"Sir, I mean no disrespect to you or your daughter." Johan got up and held out his hand to the man in front of him.

"I'm Staff Sergeant Johan Landers of the United States Army. I was injured and your daughter was kind enough to treat my wounds with her medicine."

Jesi could see her father's scowl ease up.

"Dad, please, he hasn't hurt me."

Chief shook Johan's hand and nodded his head. "My name is Chief."

"Where've you been? You didn't come back for so long that I had to come down here and look for you."

"I tole you nefer to leaf da cave wifout me or your brother!" Chief was mad again.

"I was worried."

"Ai, Jesi."

She could see that her father was tired. Chief sat on one of the containers and slumped his shoulders. He never backed off scolding her until he knew that Jesi understood his meaning. There was something wrong.

"What is it?"

"Dey were marching people. We followed dem. Da old people, some cannat walk anymore an jus drop to da ground. We wait nai for da Japanese to leaf den we pick dem up. We try to hide dem, but dey could hardly walk nai . . ."

It was morning, and bright inside the cave. She could see tears in her father's eyes. The last time she saw him cry was when they buried the little coffin of her baby sister Teresa. Teresa died at birth. Jesi was worried.

"What happened?"

"Dey kill so many people in da caves. I saw deir bodies burned and da heads cut off." Chief broke down in front of her. Jesi knelt next to her father and held him. His body trembled, and it killed Jesi that he was in such pain. *Be strong, Jesi. Be strong for him. It's what mom would have done. Don't you dare cry.* She took a deep breath and swallowed, blinking back her tears. Jesi held her father, the man that had been her rock for her entire life. She would be strong for him.

Jesi looked at Johan with a fake smile. He returned one in kind, comforting her.

"Ai, I'm sorry, Jesi."

"It's my turn. You've always held me."

"Ai, my girl." Chief wiped his tears then hugged Jesi. He stood and he looked at Johan. "How long youf been here?"

"Two days."

"Where's mom and grandma?" Jesi asked as she stood.

"I saw soldiers out der. Dey help me take mom and grandma to da American shelter." Chief shook his head. "Dey are still fighting out der. Dey pushed da Japanese towart Yigo, but der are still some Japanese in da jungles."

"My unit is supposed to go through the eastern half of Guam, all the way up to Mount Santa Rosa. I need to get back to them."

"But you're not well yet." Jesi's chest tightened.

"It's my duty. My men are out there."

Johan seemed taller to her.

"Your leg is not healed, and your arm."

"They are better."

"Jesi," Chief said in a warning voice.

"Peter!" Jesi saw her brother walk into the cave.

"Oh, Peter, I've missed you so much." Jesi held her brother tight.

"I know, Jes. Who's that?" Peter said in a harsh tone as he looked over Jesi's shoulder.

Of her two brothers, Peter was the most protective of Jesi. They were the closest in age, and he was the one on Guam.

"He's an American and he saved my life." Jesi stepped back from her brother. She was not usually short with Peter, but she did not like his tone.

"Peter," Chief called. "Stay here wif Jesi. I'm going to help dis man get back to da army."

"He hasn't eaten yet." Jesi thought she was being reasonable.

Johan took a step in her direction.

"By now, they've got hot food for us. Thank you so much for your kindness and for getting me back to good health, Miss," Johan said, as if nothing had happened between them.

Why is he being like this?

"I'm in your and your family's debt," Johan looked at Jesi, Chief, and Peter. "Once this is over, should you need anything, just go to the army post and ask for Sergeant Landers of the 305th."

"Thank you." It was the only reply she could muster.

"Sir," Johan addressed Chief. "If you would give me a minute, I'll be ready."

Jesi's heart sank. She didn't want him to go. He was hurt and going back out there. It wasn't right. Johan should be healed first, and not even be allowed to fight until he was well. Jesi forced the tears away, not wanting to get emotional with everyone around. She turned and began looking for something, anything.

"You can rub this on your skin to keep the mosquitoes away." She held out her hand to Johan, "It's coconut oil."

"Thank you, Miss."

Jesi watched as Johan placed the jar in his pack. He looked like the soldier that rescued her, except for the jeans he was wearing. He put his pack on and took a few steps toward the entrance then turned around. Johan stared right into her eyes. "Thank you, Jesi. I look forward to seeing you again."

5

JOHAN AND HIS PLATOON REACHED THEIR objective for the night. The thick, almost impenetrable jungle was tough to get through, but he and his guys pushed hard. The men of the 305th army combat team lived up to their "305th Marines" nickname, bestowed on them by the Marine Raiders. The Raiders were an elite group of marines who were so impressed by the performance of the army soldiers on Guam that they referred to their combat buddies as the 305th Marines.

"Forget about slit trenching," Johan ordered his guys. "This ground is too damn hard. Calhoun, Miller, and I will pull first guard. The rest of you settle in and try to get some sleep."

Johan found a spot in one of the trees to keep a lookout. His leg and arm were in good working order less his scars. The tree trunk was comfortable enough to sit on. And he could almost reach the big green fruit that was growing on the branches. It wasn't a coconut, but instead had a lumpy exterior. It was as big as a soccer ball, somewhat oblong. Johan scanned his eyes over the area. He was grateful he didn't lose any of his men in the battle for Barrigada a few days ago. They were able to push the Japs out of their positions thanks to the overhead fire cover of the 706th Tank Battalion.

He thought about Jesi every night. Her smell, that's what it was. The coconut oil she gave him smelled like her, and indeed kept the mosquitoes from eating him alive. It felt so good to sleep beside her that last night. Chief was upset. Livid. Johan sat up straighter, shook his head, and took a deep breath. *Forget about her, Landers.* The reality was he would be leaving soon anyway.

"Sarge, you ready to switch?" Specialist Smithy whispered up to him.

"Yup." Johan climbed down from the tree.

The night was quiet other than the occasional gunfire in the distance. Johan picked up a green coconut from the pile the men had collected. He had taught the guys how to open the young coconuts just as Jesi had done. Johan cleaned the inside of his steel helmet then set it aside. Once he poked a hole through the shell, he emptied the månha juice, as she had called it, into his helmet. Johan cut the månha in half then took the "spoon" between his teeth and scooped out the soft, wholesome flesh. He did the same for another one.

Johan threw the empty husks, not skins, into another pile then sat down in Smithy's spot, next to Calhoun. He savored the sweetness of the fruit in his helmet. Johan smiled. It dawned on him that he missed Jesi. No matter what he told himself, he couldn't stop thinking of her.

"Maybe it was meant to be, Sarge," Calhoun said. Calhoun was a few years older than Johan and left behind a wife and two sons. He joined the army because it was the right thing to do and to be a good example for his boys.

"What do you mean?"

"I mean you were there and she was there. You could've been killed, but you weren't. She could've been killed, but she wasn't.

"Uh-huh."

"Do you believe in fate, Sarge?"

"Hell no!"

"Sarge, I know you're not a Godly man, but I am. And I believe that God's plan was for you to meet this girl."

"Was it God's plan for my wife to be killed?" That came out of nowhere.

"What?"

"Forget about it."

"Sarge, I'm sorry. You, ah, have never said anything."

"Forget about it."

"It was meant to be," Calhoun said.

There was a long pause. Johan hadn't thought about Lily since he woke up with Jesi. He hadn't had any nightmares since, either.

"Perhaps you feel guilty." Calhoun broke the silence.

"Guilty?"

"It's no dishonor to love again."

"Love? I don't love her, Calhoun. And shut up already."

"OK then. It's no dishonor to want to sleep with the girl."

"You're right, Calhoun. I'd love to get me a piece of that ass!" As soon as those words crossed his lips, Johan felt an acrid taste in his mouth. He stood up and went to take a piss.

"Sorry, Sarge. I, um, didn't mean it like that."

Johan returned to his spot. He dozed in and out of sleep. He dreamed of Jesi again, but this time she was riding a horse across the meadows.

The chirping of wild birds and chickens woke him. It was the morning of August 7. The Seventy-Seventh Infantry, including Johan's unit, would soon be closing in on their final objective. The army's mission for the war on Guam would be over in a few days.

The men who pulled guard duty through the night came back to their buddies, just as the sleeping soldiers were waking. They swallowed their rations then were on their way toward the base of Mount Santa Rosa.

"Quiet," Johan said. "Ah shit, take cover, take cover," Johan yelled as bullets flew over them. He and Calhoun retreated behind a tree.

"Damn, Sarge, that's two tanks up ahead."

"Yup, but they've been hit."

Calhoun peeked out from behind the tree. "You're right."

"Listen up," Johan said into the radio. He gave his orders to Calhoun and the rest of his men.

Johan and Calhoun made their way closer to the tanks. They had to take out the Japs that manned the guns. "I got one," Johan said, looking through his scope.

"Got mine," Calhoun replied.

"Three, two, fire." Johan hit his target, straight through the heart. He saw that Calhoun ripped one Jap's head to pieces, splattering his brains everywhere. "Jeez, Calhoun, thought you were a godly man."

"That was an act of God."

6

"**P**ETER, THERE IT IS," JESI WHISPERED TO her brother.

"Don't move. I got him."

Jesi watched as her brother cornered and captured the loose chicken. Since Peter was with her, she had a little more freedom, and could even boil a pot of soup.

"Yes!" Jesi said. "We're eating good tonight."

"Get three coconuts, Jes." Peter was the only one that called her Jes. Peter attended a year at George Washington High School with Jesi, long enough to lose his thick accent.

Jesi walked to where the *heggao* was dug into the ground. It was a pointed piece of metal rod for husking coconut. She looked up, to the left, and to the right. It was a beautiful day with the jungle so green and the sun poking through the patches of clouds. Jesi loved the way it smelled the day after it rained.

Jesi held an unhusked coconut in both of her hands with the pointed end of the fruit toward her tummy. She pushed the middle of the coconut in to the heggao until it hit the hard shell inside. Jesi slid the coconut off to the side of the heggao, tearing a piece of fibrous husk off. She continued to remove the husk until she was left with a hard shell. Jesi did the same for the other two coconuts. Once the coconuts were husked, she held them one at a time in her hand, and cracked the hard shell with the back of a machete, allowing the coconut water to drip over a cup. The sweet water would make for an energizing drink.

Jesi could see Peter down the way a bit as he poured boiling water on the chicken.

"Håfa, you done?" Peter called up to her.

"Not yet, and don't worry, big brother, I'll clean your *kåmyo!*" Jesi said sarcastically, referring to Peter's coconut grater. Peter had carved a turtle, coconut crab, and *karabao,* or water buffalo, into the ifet wood he used to make the kåmyo. It was the only prized possession Peter brought with him to the cave when the Japanese invaded. The legs of the bench were the shape of latte stones and the seat looked somewhat like a pear with a very big bottom. The serrated blade was circular and sharp.

Latte stones were used as the base of support for Chamorro homes on ancient Guam. They were carved out of limestone or basalt rocks. Each latte stone had a *haligi,* or pillar, and a *tasa,* or cup. Haligis are wide at the bottom and narrow at the top. The tasa sits above the narrow end of the haligi. The floor of the home was built across the flat surface of the tasa. There are still a handful of places in the jungles of Guam that have bare, sacred latte stones.

Jesi watched her brother cut the chicken. Peter was several inches taller than Chief, taller than most Chamorro men. While Chief preferred his hair long and in a ponytail, Peter kept his hair short. That he had lost his thumb and two fingers didn't stop Peter from anything he had done prior. Except when it came to girls. He'd yet to have a girlfriend since his accident.

Jesi sat on the kåmyo then took one half of the cracked coconut and placed it over the blade. Holding the nut in place with both hands, Jesi rotated the coconut around the serrated edge. She did all six halves. In no time, the bowl was filled with shredded meat.

"I peeled a couple of taros," Peter said, as he walked up to Jesi.

"Do you want to make the milk while I wipe your prized *kâmyo*?" It was so much fun harassing him.

"Give me that." Peter smiled at his sister and took the bowl of grated coconut from her. He added water to the coconut and squeezed the mixture between his hands. He and Jesi carried the ingredients for their dinner back to the cave.

"You like him?" Peter asked while they sat in the cave eating their stew of chicken, taro, and coconut milk.

"What do you mean I like him?"

"Don't be dumb with me."

"I only just met him." Jesi kept her eyes on her *kâdo*. She spooned a piece of taro in her mouth.

"This is so good."

"Look at me, *fan*."

Fan means "please" in Chamorro.

Oh god, he'll know, he always knows.

"Fine, I think I like him, but don't tell mom and dad."

Peter was quiet, his eyes downcast.

"What are you thinking?"

"It's bad out there, Jes. Everything's bombed." A tear ran down his cheek.

She'd never seen him cry.

"Peter," Jesi started to put her bowl down and move toward her brother.

"I'm good." He wiped the tear and stood up.

Jesi stayed where she was.

"I never seen nothing like that. Worse than when the Japanese came." Peter looked toward the entrance of the cave, shaking his head. "The church is gone, the houses, Plaza de España. All ruined." He ran his hands through his hair. "Agana's gone. Sumay's gone. It's all gone." Peter turned around and stared at Jesi.

"You'll have a better life in the States, Sis."

"Peter, how dare you say that, I will never leave Guam! I will never leave Guam. And we will rebuild Peter, just like the Chamorros always have." Jesi could not believe her brother said that. She set her bowl down, too.

"You're old enough to make your own decisions now. You'll be twenty next month." A tiny smile crossed his face. "I know I've been very hard on you. We all have been strict when it comes to you. But it's for your own good."

"I've never really liked someone till now. Johan didn't tease me about my eyes, or my skin."

"If you like this man, I'll help you."

"I don't even know if he's still alive."

"I can find him."

"He probably doesn't even like me."

"Trust me, he likes you. I know."

"But I don't want to leave. Do you think he'll stay here on Guam? Why are you saying all these things to me?"

"The stuff I saw out there and I couldn't do nothing. If something happens to you like that, Jes, I don't know what I would do. I rather you be far away and safe."

"What kind of things?"

"Let me have your bones," Peter held his hand out for her bowl and walked to leave the cave.

"But, Peter, what kind of things?"

7

August 12, 1944 — Still in Pago Bay Cave

"JESI, PETER." JESI HEARD HER FATHER calling them.

"Wake up, you two," Chief said.

"You're back." Jesi got up from her guåfak. "Can we leave now?" This was Chief's second visit back to the cave since he left with Johan.

"It's safe to go home. Da Japanese haf loss and we're free again."

"Oh, Dad!" Jesi hugged her father.

"We can go home now!" Jesi turned to her brother and hugged him.

"Did they catch them all?" Peter asked.

"Dey tole us to still be careful. We can stay at da refugee camp, or come back home if we want."

"Mom and grandma, are they still in the camp?" Jesi asked.

"Ya, but dey want to come home."

"So we can go back home today?" Jesi's face lit up.

"Yes. Da tree of us will walk der today. Den tomorrow we can get mom and grandma."

Jesi was elated. She and the men straightened up the cave and stored away the nonperishables. They would have to come back here at some point to collect the rest of their stuff.

Jesi walked between Chief and Peter with Chief leading the way. She had found a calendar in one of the containers and counted seventeen days since Johan had left. They were long, torturous days. As much of a distraction as Peter was, she thought about Johan and prayed every night that he would be safe.

I wonder what he's up to right now? "Look, *salis*!" Jesi said in a low voice, pointing to the birds as they flew off. Chief was still taking them on the safer, "secret" path.

It seemed as if the army was his life, but then he said he hoped to see me again. Jesi was a mess of confusion and worry. "We're almost here," Jesi said. She started to run ahead of Chief.

"Wait a minute," Peter called to her.

"*Nangga nåya,*" Chief said.

Jesi stayed behind and watched as Chief and Peter made their way to the house. It looked the same as she remembered. Jesi smiled, recalling the nights her mom told stories about how her dad, Jesi's grandfather, built the house. He added one room at a time to the original structure. It was built of ifet, the strongest wood on Guam.

Chief waved her over.

"Nothing has changed." She admired the sturdy exterior of the house. Jesi felt like a kid again at grandma and grandpa's. She ran to the back.

"Dad! Peter!" Jesi tried to scream a whisper. "You two won't believe what's back here."

8

August 13, 1944 — Barrigada–Agana Road,
Central Guam

J OHAN SAT IN THE BACK OF THE SERVICE company's truck. It started to sprinkle, again. At least it would help with all the dust the truck stirred up. They were leaving their Barrigada post. He had tried to find out where the Taimanglos lived through the few natives that passed by, but no luck. *I've got to find her.*

The truck crept down the dirt road. They passed a refugee camp with pup tents set up. Johan thought about getting down and looking for her. Jesi's cave was more comfortable and clean than what these poor people had to live in at the moment. The truck slowed, getting Johan's attention.

"What the heck? Look at that, Calhoun." Johan nodded toward the natives and the animal in front of them.

"What is that?" Smithy asked.

A couple was riding on what looked like a cow pulling a cart. The driver waited for the animal to get to the side of the road. Johan caught a glimpse of the girl's hair flying in the wind. *Probably not,* he shook his head and turned away. The truck accelerated. And the sprinkles turned to rain.

"It's a cow with horns!" Calhoun yelled. "Cows don't have horns do they?"

Johan didn't pay any attention. *If I could just kiss her one more time.*

"Check out that girl. I'd love to get me a girl like her."

Johan glanced at the couple.

"Jesi!" Johan jumped out of the truck. She looked at him and smiled her big, beautiful smile.

"Yo, Landers. You're crazy man." Calhoun pounded the side of the truck. "Stop the truck, stop the truck!"

"Whoa, boy," Johan lifted both of his palms out in front of him, a little too close to the cow. He stepped sideways toward Jesi and Peter, and waited for them to get down.

"It's, Peter, right?" Johan reached to shake Peter's hand.

"Ya."

"I've never seen a cow with horns."

"Her name is Bonita, and she's a water buffalo," Jesi said.

Johan turned to her. She was prettier than he remembered. He wanted to take her in his arms really bad.

"Ah, I guess female buffalo have horns, too. You look great."

"I'm so glad to see you, Johan. I was worried."

"Landers, come on, man," he heard someone call from the truck.

"Just a minute," Johan said without turning away from Jesi. "I asked some natives if they knew where your family lived, but they didn't."

"You tried to find me?"

It was a downpour now and Johan couldn't stop staring. The rain had straightened her hair. There was no makeup running down her face, only a slight smile. She was in another white T-shirt and cutoff jeans shorts. And her eyes, it was always her eyes. She was even more becoming. He burned this picture of Jesi into his memory forever.

"We're far out in the jungle," Peter interjected, breaking Johan from his trance. "Where's your camp and I will come get you."

"Really?" Johan wasn't sure he heard him.

"Only if you and your men help us fix my auntie's house."

"Peter!" Jesi scolded.

"We need help."

"I'm sorry, Johan."

"Hey, man, you'll be walking if you don't get your ass in the truck."

Johan turned around. The driver stood on the door ledge, pissed. He knew the driver was worried about the truck getting stuck in the mud, for the third time today.

"One minute!" Johan yelled. He turned to face Jesi and Peter. "I'll be at the camp near Mount Alifan. Come get me as soon as you can." Johan looked at Peter. "Thank you." He shook Peter's right hand. *Damn that's tight.* Forget that he's taller than most of the local men he'd seen, but Peter was much stronger than his body portrayed. Peter would not let his hand go.

"On Guam, if you hurt someone, we all come for you. Brothers, cousins, uncles. *Komprende,* I mean you understand?"

"Stop, Peter," Jesi said.

"You understand?" Peter insisted.

"I do."

Peter let go.

"Jesi," Johan held his hand out to her. He pulled her into a hug and closed his eyes. He didn't care what Peter thought. "It's good to see you," Johan whispered into her ear. He unwrapped his arms and jumped back into the truck, keeping a straight face, but smiling inside.

"Wow, Sarge, you waste no time," Smithy said.

Johan ignored him and the other men making their comments. As the truck drove away, she waved to him. Then she held her arms out to her sides and turned around and around in the rain.

Jesi and Peter climbed back on Bonita. It was a short rain spell and the sun was out again. They continued to make their way to Agana.

"He couldn't take his eyes off you," Jesi heard her brother say. She sat in front of Peter smiling. Jesi closed her eyes, drifting back to her encounter with Johan. His uniform wasn't bloody this time and he looked as if he were carrying a thousand pounds of equipment on his body. A helmet covered his head and all Jesi could focus on were his lips. *Those wonderful lips.* And then he hugged her. It was so tight she couldn't breathe. *To have those arms around me again.* Jesi touched her left cheek, the scratching of his unshaven jaw still fresh on her skin.

Jesi opened her eyes and looked around her. She had dozed off. "Peter! Oh no."

"What, Jes?"

"Let me down, Peter. Let me down!" There were more Chamorros and military trucks on the road. Jesi cupped her hand over her mouth as she stood on the grass by the side of the dirt road. Tears welled up. Every which way she looked, the buildings were destroyed. The tin from most of the roofs lay all over the grass. There were power lines that dangled from wooden poles. Many of the buildings Jesi could see were missing a part of their concrete walls. Piles of wood rubble lined the streets.

"Oh god." It felt as if her ribs were choking the air right out of her.

"Come here, Sis. Breathe." Peter took her hand away from her mouth and wrapped his arms around his sister.

"How could this happen?" Jesi asked through muffled cries on his chest.

"We'll be OK. It's OK."

Jesi knew she had to pull herself together.

"Shh. We're strong. You're strong."

Jesi stepped back from her brother and wiped her eyes and cheeks. "Sorry. It's just—"

"I know, I know."

"You ready?" Jesi asked, exhaling through pursed lips.

"Ya."

Jesi and Peter climbed back on Bonita and made their way to Anigua, an area along the outskirts of Agana.

"How are we going to find them?" Jesi stared at the field in front of her.

"*Ai*, there's hundreds of people here," Peter said.

"You'll find them," Mames whispered.

Thank you. Yes, I will find them. "Stay with Bonita. I'll go," Jesi told Peter.

Jesi walked through the maze of refugees and tents. She paused for a moment, looking, and was so happy to see the people. A big lump formed in her throat, but she stifled her urge to cry.

Many elderly women wore their *mestisas,* or the old Spanish-style dresses. The younger women and girls had on American dresses. The men were in white T-shirts and pants. The boys wore shorts and T-shirts. It must have been lunchtime as people were getting in line and coming away from tents carrying food. Jesi continued walking and had to watch her footsteps. Mud puddles littered the ground.

"Jesi, Jesi!"

Jesi turned around. "Antonio!" Jesi wrapped her cousin in her arms and picked him up.

Antonio was only four years old when Jesi last saw him. They were cousins, but he was like a little brother to her. She used to watch him every time Auntie Julia came up to visit. Jesi's grandma and Auntie Julia were sisters.

"*Tan Chai* is over there," Antonio pointed across the field. Jesi's grandma was known to most people as Tan Chai.

Jesi turned to look and saw her mom, grandma, and Auntie Julia. She put her cousin down and they ran holding hands.

"Mom, oh, Mom." Jesi let go of Antonio's hand and held her mom tighter than she had ever held anyone. She sobbed on her mother's shoulder.

"Ai, my baby, ai *haga-hu,*" Mrs. T said. Mrs. T was a couple of inches taller than Jesi. They were identical in body proportions though Mrs. T was more voluptuous.

"I was scared. I missed you so much." Jesi was still crying.

"I'm OK. I'm here *Neni*, I'm here."

Neni is the Chamorro word for "baby," but is a term of endearment used by Chamorros when calling a loved one or a younger person.

Jesi felt Antonio hugging her legs. Tan Chai and Auntie Julia wrapped their arms around all three of them.

"Let me see you, Jesi." Tan Chai held Jesi's shoulders.

"I missed you, Grandma," Jesi sniffled.

"I know, my Neni." Tan Chai placed the fingers of Jesi's left hand against her lips, kissing them as she always did.

Jesi hugged Tan Chai. *Oh god, I can feel her bones.* She loosened her grip. *"Hu guaiya hao."*

"Hu guaiya hao *lokkue'.*" Tan Chai told Jesi she loved her, too.

Mrs. T took Jesi's cheeks in her hands. She kissed her forehead. *"Nihi."* Mrs. T told Jesi "let's go."

"Mom, where are Antonio's parents?"

"We haven't seen them yet."

"Then Antonio and Auntie Julia are coming with us right?"

"Of course, Neni."

"Antonio," Jesi squatted down, "you get to stay with me until we find your mommy and daddy."

"Yaaaay!" Antonio hugged her.

Jesi stood up and took her cousin's hand. She held her grandma's hand, too. Mrs. T helped Auntie Julia.

"Peter's waiting over there because dad wanted to stay home and cut wood."

Jesi led the women and the little boy toward her brother. When she could see Peter, she waved her hand at him. He ran toward them.

"Ai, my boy," Mrs. T said, hugging Peter and kissing him on the forehead.

"Hi, Grandma," Peter moved over to hug Tan Chai. "*Nora,* Auntie Julia." He held Auntie Julia's fingers in his hand and brought them to his nose as a sign of respect, then gave her a big hug.

"Hi, boy," Peter rustled Antonio's hair. "I'll help grandma and meet you guys over there," Peter nodded toward Bonita. He was very close to Tan Chai.

Once they reached the cart, Jesi and Peter helped Tan Chai and Auntie Julia settle in comfortably. The two sisters sat next to each other, across from Jesi and Mrs. T. The boys turned Bonita toward home then straddled her, Antonio sitting in front of Peter. They made their way down the dirt road.

"Mom, there's so much damage on this side."

"I know, Neni."

"Our house is still good. There's nothing broken or burned down. Bananas and papayas and sweet potatoes are growing all over the place. I guess the Japanese didn't go that far into the jungle." Jesi looked over at her grandma. Tan Chai and Auntie Julia were holding hands and had fallen asleep.

"You look good, Neni. You did OK in the cave then?"

"Yes. I think I even lost some weight, but when Peter came back I ate good."

"That boy can't go long without kådo."

"He made chicken in coconut milk, and shrimp in coconut milk, and breadfruit in coconut milk. He's gonna change into a coconut," Jesi chuckled.

"*Ai adai!*" Mrs. T turned sideways with a smile then gave Jesi a hug and a kiss on the cheek.

Jesi missed being with her mom.

"Your dad said a soldier came down to the cave at Ylig?"

"I thought he stopped following me, but then he just appeared out of nowhere."

"Why did he follow you?"

Jesi took a deep breath and peeked over at her grandma.

"Why did he follow you? Did he hurt you?"

"I went looking for you guys when I didn't find you at Ylig cave. I went to Uncle Kin's house to see if you were there . . ."

"And," Mrs. T encouraged.

"No one was home then these Japanese men started chasing me. I ran away very fast to the cave and I guess Johan stopped them because they didn't follow me." *Please believe me, please believe me.* "The next thing I knew, Johan was sitting on the ground and bleeding from his arm." Jesi watched her mom's face. She couldn't bear to tell her mom what the Japanese did to her. "I made the medicine to put on his skin. He went unconscious. I gave him the aspirin he carried since he had a fever."

"Dad said he was able to walk."

"Yes, after two days I think. His fever was short."

"Anything else?"

"No, but he did pass us on the road today with other military men. Peter asked him if he could help rebuild Auntie Julia's house."

"What did he say? Johan, right?"

Jesi nodded. "He told Peter to come get him."

"Neni, there's not much left of Auntie Julia's house in Agana. I think we're going to build her house up near ours." Mrs. T sighed.

"So they have to come up to Mangilao?"

"Yes."

9

August 16, 1944 — Orote Peninsula,
Central Guam, Western Coast

"**A**ND THANK YOU AGAIN FOR MAKING** those darned flies go away during the night," Calhoun prayed.

"Amen to that," Johan added, half joking.

Johan lay on the bed he had made using strips of bamboo. He could hear the humming of insects and the soft music emanating from one soldier's radio.

He wondered if Jesi had something to keep the flies at bay when the sun was up. Johan thought about the last time he saw her, in the rain. It felt good to hold her again. For that one moment, it was as if he were exactly where he was meant to be. Peter hadn't come looking for him. It was for the best, he would be gone soon anyway. Just one more time he wanted to kiss her, to take her in his arms. Johan closed his eyes and imagined riding his horse with Jesi. As impossible as it seemed, he longed to be with her there in the mountains, with his horses, even if it was in his head. *Damn.*

"Landers, man, wake up. There's a local here for you." Johan jumped out of his bed then walked out of the shelter.

"Peter," Johan reached to shake his hand.

"Hey, man, you said you can help build a house?"

"Yup, of course. Right now?"

"If you can. We'll collect wood, and tin, and whatever is left of the old house."

"Calhoun, Smithy, Miller, you guys wanna help build a house and get out of this place today?"

"Heck ya." Smithy said.

"All right, Sarge," Calhoun added.

"Grab whatever tools you have." Johan turned to Peter. "Give me a couple minutes to get ready."

"You want some bananas," Peter asked.

"Are they ripe?"

"Not yet, but almost. They'll turn yellow."

Johan picked up the biggest bunch of green bananas he'd ever seen. It was more than half as tall as Johan. He left it on a table in the tent then came back out with some tools.

"I don't see your buffalo, but I can take a jeep if you want," Johan said, as he and his guys walked toward Peter.

"Bonita is Jes's pet. I have my old truck," Peter nodded to the jalopy.

"Will Jesi be there?" Johan asked his eyebrows rose. He and his men climbed into the rusty old pickup.

"Ya, she's helping to make dinner so you'll see her. Just be careful around my parents."

"What do you mean? Isn't she of age?"

"Of age?"

"She's older than sixteen isn't she?"

"It doesn't matter on Guam with the girls. It's showing respect to the *manámkos*, the elders. My mom and dad have to like you first."

"And if they don't?"

"Just make sure they do, especially my mom."

"Your mom?"

"My dad's old-fashioned, but mom is the boss."

Johan heard Peter laugh.

"What's funny?"

"My parents. I hear crazy stories about my dad, how no one can order him around. I even hear that when he was going out with my mom, another boy looked at her. He just went over to him and punch his face." Peter imitated his father.

"Are you serious?"

"Uh-huh. And then I hear that when he married my mom, he got all soft."

"Why is his name Chief?"

"They said he's the one that start all kinds of trouble in the family. The leader of the pack."

"He looks like a spirited man."

"He works hard on the farm; hunting, fishing, and helping people build their houses. And it's been harder since the Japanese came."

"Can I ask what happened to your fingers?"

"I had an accident with the chain saw. Jesi helped take care of it."

"She did a good job healing me, too."

"Jes is my baby sister, man, if you know what I mean."

"I wouldn't hurt her."

"Good then."

They arrived at Auntie Julia's ruined house in Agana. After loading what they could fit in the back of the truck, Peter drove them to Mangilao.

"We used to play baseball and we even beat the American navy team."

"You play baseball here?" Smithy asked.

"It's our favorite sport."

"We have Christmas pageants and parades."

"With girls in them?" Miller jumped in. "I'd like to meet me an island girl."

Johan blocked out their voices. He couldn't wait to see Jesi, and wished he'd had something nicer to give her. Johan patted his pocket. *These will have to do.*

August 17, 1944 — Mangilao, Central Guam,
Eastern Coast, Taimanglo Land

Jesi heard Peter's truck pass by and knew he'd be heading toward the end of the property. She was glad most of the food was being cooked at her parents' home because everyone was over there. Jesi preferred to work in her grandma's backyard. It had the most breathtaking view.

She cleaned her hands and made sure her T-shirt and shorts were neat as well. Jesi let her hair down and picked up the tray. She had prepared a pitcher of månha juice, and a bowl of sliced star apples and ripe papaya. Butterflies danced in her stomach, and she couldn't stop smiling.

"Hi, Neni."

Oh no, Mom.

"You finished?"

"Yes. You're coming with me?"

"No, just checking on you. Can you bring the månha up to the house when you're done?"

"Of course."

"Don't take long because your grandma's waiting."

"Where's Dad?"

"He's getting tångantångan for the barbecue."

"I'll be fast."

Mrs. T headed back to the house.

Jesi turned and walked toward the men who were unloading stuff from the truck. They faced away from her, but Jesi recognized the shape of his body and his stance. Johan's hair was also darker than the others. As she neared them, the men turned to look at her.

No, no, no. Don't fall. She steadied the tray of food. *How embarrassing.* Even if that stump had a stop sign in front of it, Jesi wouldn't have seen it. She was glad she had good balance. Her heart raced, and apparently, her brain checked out of her skull.

"Hi, Jesi," Johan said as he walked toward her.

"Hi." She couldn't help but smile. "I've brought you all a little something to eat." Jesi put the tray on a cleared spot on the truck's tailgate. "We'll have dinner for you guys later," she said as she looked at the other men.

"Aren't you gonna introduce us, Sarge?" Calhoun urged.

"Jesi, this is Calhoun, Miller, and Smithy. Don't mind them."

He's got such clean teeth.

"Nice to meet you. Thank you for rescuing us from the Japanese. We are forever grateful," Jesi said, "if there is anything I can make for you to bring back to your family in America, please let me know."

"Thank you, Ma'am," the guys said in unison.

"Please eat," Jesi spooned fruit into a bowl and passed it to Johan. Once they each had their serving, all but Johan walked to sit under a tree.

"This is thoughtful of you," Johan said.

"It's kind of you and your men to come up and help."

"I have my selfish reasons."

He hasn't stopped smiling.

Jesi sat on the tailgate and Johan stood beside her, both facing the dirt road.

"It's beautiful out here, as if there was no war."

"I know."

"I couldn't stop thinking about you," Johan said, and then he turned to face her.

"I've been thinking of you, too."

He took both of her hands in his and looked into her eyes. "We're leaving for another mission soon, but I'd like to spend what time I have left here, with you."

Jesi watched as Johan looked down at her hands. He'd been stroking them.

"Would you like that?"

"Yes."

"You would?" Johan looked up at her again.

"Yes, I would."

He was about to hug her.

"Oh no, my mom's coming." Jesi jumped off to the side of the tailgate.

"My shirt." Johan pulled the shirt that hung from his waistband and put it on just in time.

"Neni, I told you to hurry," Mrs. T said. "Who's this?"

"I'm sorry. This is Johan, the soldier that rescued me."

"Good day, Ma'am. It's nice to meet you. You have a brave daughter."

"She is."

"I told my mom you stopped the Japanese men from catching me and that I was able to run from them thanks to you," Jesi interjected.

"Thank you for keeping those men away. She's my only girl, and my youngest. Her father and I would never forgive ourselves if anything had happened to Jesi."

"She saved my life, Ma'am. I am forever in her and your family's debt."

"Please, come join us for dinner when you're done. I'm Mrs. T by the way."

"Come, Neni, we need to get dinner finished."

"Oh, Ma'am, um, Mrs. T, I have something for you."

Jesi watched as Johan pulled a bag out from one of his pockets.

"It's just a few pieces of caramel. Jesi mentioned that your family hasn't had candy since the Japanese landed. It's from our rations, but they're really good."

"Thank you, Johan, I love caramel. I might even share."

"We'll see you at dinner," Jesi said. "And thanks again for helping to build Auntie Julia's house." She shot him a smile then turned to walk with her mom.

"He likes you."

"Mom!"

"And you like him."

"I don't like him." "It's OK, Neni." Mrs. T smiled. "Your dad almost came looking for you."

Jesi sighed.

"Dad's not going to be happy. Johan's not a Chamorro." Jesi's heart started to feel heavy. She didn't want to disappoint her father.

"You can't always please your father. You're not a little girl anymore."

"But, Mom, he'll be mad and he won't talk to me. He won't disown me will he?"

The day's construction was done. Johan, Calhoun, Miller, Smithy, and Peter cooled off sitting under the shade of a mango tree.

"She was checking you out you know," Peter said to Johan who sat beside him.

"Who? What?"

"My mom."

"Shit!"

"I think she's OK with you."

"How do you know?"

"She wasn't *muyo*ing, ah, frowning. I think she even smiled. That's a good sign."

"What can I do to make her like me more?"

"Nothing. She either likes you or she doesn't. But I know she wants some flour and sugar. That would make her happy."

"All right. I might be able to get some. They fed us homemade bread so I know somebody's got that stuff."

"Mom wants to make a cake for Jesi. She'll be twenty next month."

"What do you think your sister would like for a present?"

"She loves to read books and look at pictures."

"I can work with that."

"Let's go eat," Peter said.

The men donned their shirts and climbed into the truck. They reached Jesi's parents' house in no time. *What the heck?* He wiped his clamy hands across his thighs. Johan and his guys followed Peter to the back. Loud chatter filled the air. *Whoa.* Chamorros, at least thirty of them, mingled and gabbed in an outdoor kitchen.

"We have a big family, aunties, uncles, cousins, everyone," he heard Peter say.

"I see."

"Do what I do." Peter walked around and paid his respects to the elders. "*Ñot*," he said to the older men, bringing the fingers of one of their hands to his nose. "Ñora," he said to the elderly women as he performed the same gesture. Johan saw that Calhoun, Smithy, and Miller followed suit.

He felt uneasy, and spotted Chief watching him from afar. The older women pulled Johan into a hug when he *åmened* them.

"*Si Yu'us ma'åse'*," they said.

"Peter," Johan whispered, "what does that mean?"

"Thank you."

Johan nodded his head. He tried to shake the younger women's hands, but they all hugged him as well, a little too long. Then he got to her. He felt everyone's eyes on him. Jesi had changed into a yellow dress with colorful bird of paradise prints.

"You're lovely in a dress."

"Thank you."

"I meant to give you the candy, but the next thing I knew I was handing the bag to your mom."

"Thanks for thinking of me anyway." "Let's pray," he heard Chief announce from the door of the house.

"Do you pray?"

Do I pray? Johan shook his head.

"*Gi na'an i tata, yan i låhiña . . .*" He didn't understand, but saw that everyone made the sign of the cross. Johan shifted his weight to his left leg and took a peek at his men.

"Bow your head and look at the ground," she grinned, "sorry."

"It's OK," Johan whispered.

Johan stood beside her, and could feel her arm against him. The slight grazing of her skin assaulted his senses. *Christ Landers, they're praying and you're thinking of that.* She did the sign of the cross again, and the prayer ended.

"Come, Johan, you and your men eat first," Mrs. T said, appearing out of nowhere.

"We can wait, Ma'am."

"No, you're our guests. Jesi and Peter, show them what we have."

Jesi led Johan, more like pulled him first, to the table. Peter helped the other soldiers.

"It's not fancy," Jesi said as she handed him an old bowl and spoon. "We're blessed we didn't lose our house."

"It smells delicious, and reminds me of you." Johan smiled, remembering the coconut oil.

"You know what rice is right?"

"Yup."

"I hope you like seafood."

"Sure do." A grin spread across his lips. "My favorite is brown trout because my Pops used to take me fly-fishing in the Catskills, and we caught a lot of that kind of fish."

"You're a fisherman?"

Johan watched as she ladled fish, shrimp, and white broth into his bowl.

"I wouldn't go that far. I was mediocre on my best days. Pops was great at it. We'd come home with tons of fish."

They moved down the table.

"Sounds like you miss him."

"I do. He passed awhile ago."

"I miss both my grandpas."

In an instant, he saw the joy dissipate from her face. *Don't make her cry.*

"What is that?" *Jeez, I might have to eat it.* "If I eat whatever that is," he nodded toward the bowl of beans and something, "will it bring that pretty smile of yours back? I didn't mean to make you sad."

"It wasn't you."

And there it was. "You're smile is brighter than the sun."

"You make me smile."

"Any day now," Calhoun said from behind.

"Patience," Johan shot him a scowl.

"This is a coconut crab. I'll give you a big pincer."

"It looks like a lobster."

"Yes, it does. But it lives on land and can open a coconut with its claws."

"That's scary, but the beans are thick and green."

"They were in our overgrown garden. We were surprised."

"And that is?" Johan said as they moved closer to the charred, greenish object on the table. It looked similar to what he saw in a tree while on guard duty.

"*Lemai,* but its American name is 'breadfruit'. We barbecued a few today."

"The ones I saw in the jungle were oval."

"It's almost the same. The oval one is *dokdok.* It has black nuts inside that we eat, too."

"This is plenty of food. And it all looks and smells delicious."

"Thank you. Let's get water and sit down."

Johan watched as Jesi demonstrated how to crack the crab pincer with a rock.

"Looks juicy." He spooned a heap of coconut-milk-soaked rice into his mouth with some crab, then another, and another. He looked up at Jesi.

"You're really hungry."

"Sorry, we eat fast in the army, and it's very good."

"Thanks."

"Different, but great," Johan said as he chewed on a piece of breadfruit, "it's like a dense potato but more, more something. Can't put my finger on it. You still have food in your bowl."

"I was watching you."

I can think of other things to do to you.

"Want more? Don't be shy. You'll make my family very happy if you keep eating."

He followed Jesi back to the table. *Yes, I want more of—*

"You like our food, Johan?" Chief startled him from behind, ladling food into his own dish.

"Sir, yes, Sir. I hope you don't mind I'm having seconds."

"No, Boy, go head, and call me Chief. Jessica, fill his plate up." Chief walked away.

"Whew," Jesi said.

"What?"

"He's not mad. Thank God."

Johan and Jesi walked back to their table and sat down. He dug into his second helping of Chamorro food. Johan made a funny face as he watched Jesi suck the juices from the head of a shrimp.

"What? It's good. I dare you. A tough army soldier as yourself couldn't be afraid of these little heads."

"I'd rather have my lips around something else."

"Really?"

"Uh . . ."

"You're chicken!"

That was close. Johan reached into his bowl. All that was left was the head of the shrimp and the shells. He picked a head up.

"Put it in your mouth like this," Jesi said.

Johan kept his eyes locked on hers as he sucked, just as she did. *Man, that's real good.* He picked up another empty shell and sucked. And then another.

"I'm full." Johan grabbed at his gut.

"Me too. Let's wash up then I want show you the something."

"Mom, I'm going to grandma's backyard."

"OK, Neni."

"Take Antonio with you," Chief said from a few tables away.

"No, Hon, I need him to throw the trash. You two go ahead."

"Thank you, Mom," Jesi whispered to Mrs. T, then walked back to where Johan sat.

"Let's go, quick."

Jesi led him to the front of her parents' house, then down the dirt road.

"Where are we going?"

"My grandma's."

The butterflies in her stomach were up and about again. She could feel her cheeks warming. *I can't do this, but I want to.*

"You'll be fine," Mames whispered.

I'm glad you agree.

"Is this all your family's land?" Johan interrupted Jesi's wanton thoughts.

"Yes. My grandma says it goes back to even before her own grandmother's mother."

"That's ages ago."

"Next time, I'll have to show you the Pago Bay cave where I was hiding for most of the war. It's just above the cliff."

They stopped at the front of Tan Chai's house.

"I want you to close your eyes."

"All right."

"Promise not to open them until I tell you."

"I promise."

Jesi took his left hand. Her hand was tiny compared to his, and she could feel his rough, calloused skin. She stepped ahead of him and guided Johan to her favorite spot. The sun was setting and the tångantångan trees cast a soft shade across the yard. She could taste the salt in the breeze.

"Open your eyes."

Johan moved his head left to right.

"So?" Jesi asked.

"I, I've not seen anything like this."

"Isn't it beautiful?"

"It's gorgeous. And I thought the Catskills were grand, but this is . . ."

Jesi observed the emotions that played over his face.

"Tranquil, peaceful. I'd have never thought a place ravaged by war could hide such beauty," Johan finished.

"That is Pago Bay," Jesi pointed. "See how the land circles around the water to the left over there?"

"Yup."

"That's where my cave is, but you can't see it from here."

"Ah."

"And look at how the land juts out on this side," Jesi raised her hand to the right, "it makes me feel like I'm on top of the world."

Jesi watched as Johan stepped forward a few paces, closer to the edge.

"Not too much, you might fall over."

"Don't' worry."

After a moment, Johan turned and walked back. "Is there a way down?"

"Yes, but we have to walk a little farther. If you sit there, you can lean back against that rock." Jesi pointed to a large boulder on the grass. She waited for Johan to sit, then was going to settle beside him, when he reached for her hand.

"Sit in front of me."

Jesi watched as he spread his legs so she could sit between them. She hesitated.

"I won't bite."

She smiled at him, then sat and faced the water. "Doesn't it make you feel like you're far, far away? Like there's nobody in this world except you?"

Jesi felt Johan pull her back to lean against his chest. She closed her eyes and took slow breaths to calm her heart.

"You smell so good, it makes me—"

"It's the coconut oil."

"I know."

Jesi could hear him breathing hard. It was getting warm even in the shade.

"Sit facing me."

His voice was deeper.

Jesi stood, removed her slippers, and turned to sit on his thighs. He lifted her and brought her closer so that she was sitting very near that part of him. She could feel him grow and harden beneath her. She'd felt that for the first time when they were in the cave. His eyes looked different. Not crazed, not worried, not in pain.

Johan cupped one hand around her chin then pulled her toward him with his other hand. He pressed his lips hard against hers, not gentle as before.

"Ah," Jesi let out a gasp.

She kissed him back, pulling him with her arm around his shoulders.

"Jesi."

She could barely hear him between kisses. Something had come over her. Jesi was no longer apprehensive. She had no control over the need in her body. Some unrecognizable force was pushing her. Jesi felt him caress one breast through the cover of her dress. He was now kissing down her throat as she rocked her pelvis against him.

"I want you, Jesi."

The weird and pleasurable sensations filled her between her legs. She was the one that was now breathing heavy. There was this ache in her, and she only guessed at what it was.

"Oh god, Johan."

He had reached inside her dress and was fondling her nipple, pinching it between his thumb and finger. That feeling down there was spreading.

"Jesi, Jesi."

She could hear someone from afar. *No don't stop.*

"Jeeeeesiiiii."

The voice was getting closer. She felt Johan pull away, and finally opened her eyes.

"Oh no, it's Antonio."

Jesi got off Johan and fastened two buttons.

"It's my cousin. Do I look OK?"

"You're mighty beautiful." Johan stood up. "You feeling alright?"

"Yes, ah . . ."

"Jesi, hi, Jesi."

She picked up Antonio, gave him a big hug, and kissed him on the cheek.

"Johan, this is my cousin Antonio."

"Hi, Antonio," Johan reached out to shake the boy's hand.

"Why are you down here?" Jesi asked.

"The soldiers are leaving and Chief said to come find you."

"Go tell them we'll be right there."

"OK, 'bye."

Jesi set Antonio down and watched him run to the front of the house. "That was close." She looked at Johan and he pulled her into a hug.

"I lose my senses when I'm near you, Jesi."

"I have no sense when you touch me like that."

10

August 25, 1944 — Mangilao, Mrs. T's House

THE SOUND OF RAINDROPS ON THE TIN roof filled the kitchen. The flame from the lamps danced on the wooden walls. Jesi and Mrs. T just finished cleaning up from dinner and they were sitting down with Chief to eat ripe bananas in sweetened coconut milk.

"I like him," Jesi said to Chief.

"Jessica, you're too young for a boyfriend."

"*Asagua-hu,*" Mrs. T warned. It was a term of endearment for one's spouse. "She'll be twenty soon."

"Oh. I tought she's seventeen."

"She was seventeen before the war. Don't play dumb."

"Jessica, you're going to marry a Chamorro boy."

"But I don't like a Chamorro boy. I don't even know any Chamorro boys."

"Asagua-hu, stop being like that."

"Deb," Chief called his wife by her first name. "Why you're not on my side?"

"But they just saved us. Don't you think that's good enough?"

"I'm grateful, but dis is my girl. I cannat just do dat."

Jesi watched her parents' exchange. Her mom might appear to be quiet and disinterested to most, but that couldn't be further from the truth.

"He's very respectful and considerate, asagua-hu. Don't you remember how he àmened everybody? And he ate a lot of your food. Besides, there are plenty of *tai respetu* Chamorro boys." Mrs. T reminded Chief that Johan was more respectful than some native kids.

"What about when he leafs, Jessica? What den?"

Jesi stared at her father. "I don't know. I'll never know if you keep me locked up here. Don't you think I've been protected long enough? First, I couldn't have boyfriends then I had to stay in the cave forever. Please, Dad."

Jesi was scared, but determined. She had never spoken up against her father, but she wanted to spend as much time with Johan before he left. She lost her appetite.

"I'll think about it."

Do I have to jump off a cliff, too? Jesi thought about the ancient Chamorro legend of *Puntan Dos Amantes,* or Two Lovers Point, where the couple jumped off the cliff in order to be together.

"You'll think about it?" Jesi said in an incredulous tone. She never, ever challenged her father.

"Jesi," Mrs. T warned.

"Mom, it's not fair. All the boys got to go out and play and have fun. I want to have fun and be happy, too."

"I know, Neni, just calm down."

"Jessica, while you're liffing under my roof, you don't raise your voice to me." Chief slammed his fist on the table. All the plates and cups shook. It was raining harder, and thunder made loud clashing sounds outside.

"Fine. I'm going to stay at grandma's so I won't be *liffing* under your roof anymore!"

Jesi thrust her chair out from under the table and headed to her room. She could tell Chief was dumbstruck, but didn't care.

"Leave her alone, asagua-hu," she heard her mom say. "If you try to stop her, you'll make it worse."

Jesi found a bag and stuffed as much of her things into it as she could fit. She was crying and mad.

"Neni," Mrs. T walked into her room.

"I have to go. I can't stay here anymore. He's not being fair."

"I know. Go ahead and go to grandma's. You can get the rest of your things later."

Jesi turned to her mom to hug her. "Thank you, Mom," she said through her tears. "I'm so sorry to do this to you."

Jesi walked out of her room and past her dad. His eyes bore into her, but she didn't look at him. The dirt road was muddy. The thunder and lightning were fitting, but it was still daylight. Having reached her grandma's house, Jesi knocked on the door.

"*Håfa*, Neni," Tan Chai said, and pulled her inside the house.

"Oh, Grandma," Jesi dropped her bag and cried on her grandma's shoulder. "Can I stay with you, please?"

Jesi cleaned herself up then settled into bed. She pulled a blanket over her as the rain and wind made for a chilly night. Tan Chai's house had three bedrooms. One was occupied by

Auntie Julia and Antonio, and the other by Tan Chai. Jesi was glad she had a room all to herself.

She knew she was disrespectful, but couldn't help it. *What was wrong with wanting to spend more time with Johan?* Jesi closed her eyes. She could still feel his lips on hers, and his fingers on her nipples. And then there was that needy feeling in her pelvis. Her American friend, Suzie, had told Jesi about sex, that that's how babies were made. Jesi wondered what sex would be like with Johan. She knew he wanted her by the way he touched her. But sex before marriage was a no-no for the Catholic Chamorros. A big, big sin.

11

August 26, 1944 — Orote Peninsula, Central Guam,
Western Coast

"I **'LL BE GONE FOR THE DAY," JOHAN SAID** to
Calhoun as he placed the two boxes in the back of the
jeep. He tossed the map Peter drew for him on the passenger's
chair, hopped in, and was on his way to the Taimanglos'. The
sun was out and it was just past 0700. It should take him about
thirty minutes to drive there. Johan had been too busy guarding
the camp for the last week to get away. *You practically had sex*
with her in her grandmother's backyard. He could've kicked his
own ass for being so aggressive. The thought of being with Jesi
drove him mad. All control evaporated when he was next to her.
Her breasts, her hips.

"Christ!" Johan yanked the steering wheel to avoid running
into a banana tree. He had to focus if he didn't want to crash and
to make sure he spotted the turn. Street signs were nil on the
island. On his so-called map, there was a cross for "the church"
where he had to make a right turn then left at "the shack with
the very big cherry tree." Johan chuckled at the drawings, and
almost illegible writing.

Having finally reached the Taimanglos', Johan parked at
Jesi's house. "Hello, anybody home?" There was no answer.
"Hello," he called again then walked to the back. No one was
there. Disappointed, he returned to the jeep. Johan took a

chance that maybe they were working on the auntie's house so he started the jeep and headed toward the end of their land.

As he passed her grandma's house, Johan saw Antonio playing in the front yard. He stopped and waived to the little boy. "Hi, Antonio. Is Jesi here?"

"Yes, she's in the back."

Johan's heart rate went up by a thousand beats. With the jeep parked and turned off, he got out to retrieve the boxes.

"Hi, Johan," Jesi said.

That smile.

Johan moved from behind the passenger's door and scooped her up.

"I've missed you. I'm sorry I couldn't come sooner. Did Peter tell you?"

"Yes, he did. I've missed you, too."

"Is anybody home? No one was at your house."

"Just my grandma, Auntie Julia, and Antonio. I moved out of my house and into my grandma's house."

"Really?" Johan squinched his brows together.

"It's a long story. But now I can spend as much time with you as possible."

Johan smiled. He looked around. The boy had disappeared. He kissed her on the lips, his intensity making up for the week he hadn't been able to see her. Johan stepped back and held her hands in his. "I didn't cause any problems when I was here last did I?"

"No, it's just my dad. He's having a hard time letting me grow up. My mom's OK with you."

"Did you argue?"

"Yes, but—"

"I'm sorry." Johan laced his fingers behind his head, looked up, and took a deep breath. "I don't want to make trouble between you two. He loves you very much, I can see that."

"If I stayed there, I wouldn't be able to be with you before you leave."

"All right. I did bring some things your mom and grandma would like. I even bartered a saw and drill for your dad and Peter. Help me carry the boxes to the back?" Johan turned around then picked up the box of ingredients to give to Jesi.

"Thank you so much. You didn't have to."

"I know. I confess. Peter suggested I could win them over with a few things, especially your mom." Johan followed Jesi to the back of the house.

"Åmen my grandma, OK. Do you remember how?"

"Yup." Johan saw Tan Chai outside hanging clothes on a line.

"Grandma, Johan brought flour, sugar, and milk in a can, and some other foods, I think." Jesi set the box on a chair and Johan did the same.

"Hi, Boy," Tan Chai said.

"Ñora."

"There's also tools for dad and Peter," Jesi added.

"*Dankolo na si Yu'us ma'åse' låhi-hu.*" Tan Chai told Johan, "Thank you very much, my Boy."

"Grandma, we're going to take this inside the house then I'm going to show Johan around the property, OK?"

"Yes, Neni."

"Do you need me to do anything?"

"No, Neni, go ahead."

It appeared to Johan that Tan Chai had no reservations about him. As if Jesi going with him was as natural as a seed sprouting. In fact, it felt as if the old lady wanted them to be together.

Johan watched Jesi as she hugged her grandma then Tan Chai held Jesi's fingers up to her mouth and appeared to be kissing and smelling them. The elder's eyes were closed, holding Jesi's hand as if it were the most precious thing in the world. There was a bond between them that he recognized, that he missed. *Would my kids ever know that with my parents? I don't even have kids.*

"Come on, Johan," she broke his train of thought.

He followed her inside. "How old is your grandma?"

"She's sixty-eight. She lost a lot of weight since the war started. And she doesn't move around like she used to."

"She just needs time to recover. I saw a lot of older Chamorros in the refugee camps that looked as if they really suffered," Johan said.

"Can we talk about something else, please?"

"Sure. Is Peter working on the house? I thought I'd come up to help today."

"No, I don't know where they are at. But, how would you like to see the cave I'd stayed in through the war? It's a bit of a hike and it's beautiful out there, too. It's not very far from here."

"Sounds good. Is it OK for you to go with me?" Johan tried to hide his excitement.

"Now it is. Let me get some leftovers for us to eat while we're there."

Johan waited for her. She came back with a woven bag and they climbed in. He turned the jeep on and followed Jesi's directions. They weren't on the road for too long.

"Stop here."

"What is this place?"

"It's where we bring Bonita, the karabao, remember?"

"The buffalo?"

"Yes."

"Can you believe she not only survived the war, but she even had a baby? I found her in our backyard the first day we came home."

"Where are they now?"

"At another hole, a bigger one."

Johan got out of the jeep, looped his pack around his shoulders then grabbed his machete.

"We won't need that," Jesi said.

"So we're going to hike through all those blade-like leaves?" Johan nodded toward the jungle.

"Yes, just follow me," she shot him a smile.

"Lead the way," Johan grinned.

It was breezy and sunny. The birds were chirping, and there were plenty of them in the jungle.

"What time do you have to be back at your camp?"

"I have all day."

"We can also hike down to Pago Bay, too, if you want."

Johan was thrilled that he'd have her to himself for a while. "I guess you'd only see this path if you knew where to look."

"That's how Chief wanted it."

"Speaking of your father, are you sure you'll be all right?"

"He'll come around."

Johan continued to follow Jesi as she led him through the jungle. They seemed to be climbing uphill though Jesi didn't skip a beat. He could tell she was fit. Johan had a great view of her backside. He started to think of what he could do with those hips and that butt. *Get a grip.* He couldn't help himself. He was a man after all, not a saint. Johan could feel his erection growing. It was a constant torture since he'd met her.

"We're almost there," Jesi interrupted him.

"Great."

Johan began to see more light coming through the jungle in front of him.

"Don't go running ahead of me OK, or you'll run right over the cliff," Jesi said chuckling.

"You're just all funny aren't you, Jessica? And what's with you and cliffs?"

"It's Jessica now?" She turned to face him with an eyebrow raised.

Johan reached to pull her into a kiss, but she shimmied away.

"I don't think so. Is it Jessica or Jesi?"

"And if I pick the right one, what do I get?"

"I guess we'll see. You have a few steps to think about it."

Jesi turned and walked forward.

She wants to play does she? Johan laughed under his breath. Around her, he was always smiling, and laughing, and horny.

Jesi waited for him to catch up. "And you've decided what?"

"I've decided," he said. Johan was standing very close to her.

"You decided," she eked out. *I want to kiss those lips.*

"I like Jesi."

"Good." She stepped back. "Ready?"

"Ready for what?"

"Another gorgeous sight, you will never want to leave Guam." Jesi pulled the last bit of brush to the side so she and Johan could step through.

Jesi placed her hand over her heart.

"You weren't kidding. It's stunning up here."

"I know." Jesi stood to his right. The trees blocked the sun, it was cool from the breeze, and she could hear the waves rumbling below. "And to think it was just a few weeks ago when I was hiding and all I could hear day and night were bombs and planes."

"It's over now."

"One day I was at school and then I blinked and the Japanese were here. And then I blinked again and here we stand."

"Time does go on even if we're not ready. But hey, what is it with you and cliffs?"

"They have the prettiest views," Jesi managed a small grin.

"Can you see your grandma's house over there?"

"Not with all the trees. I've even tried with Peter's binoculars. No one can see us." Jesi was glad, her happy mood coming back. She reached behind her for her bag. "Here, let's put this blanket down then I'll show you the cave."

"Is it far?"

"Nope."

They anchored the blanket at the corners to keep it from blowing away.

"The cave's right here." Jesi pushed the wall of vines aside, exposing the entrance.

Johan stepped inside. "You stayed here for two years?" The pitch in his voice rose a couple of notches.

"Almost three. There's a space to wash up, to exercise or relax, and to sleep. They took turns staying with me." Jesi led him all the way to the back.

"Your brother?"

"And my dad."

"It's huge in here. How'd you keep from getting bored and going crazy?"

"Exercise. I read a lot, too. Once in a while we hiked down to the bay, but we had to be careful."

"That must have been fun."

"A lot of families stayed on their farms and ranches, but my dad wanted to keep me and my mom and my grandma away from the Japanese."

"You have a strong spirit."

She felt Johan take one of her hands in his as he stepped closer to stroke her cheek. His fingers sent lightning bolts down to that part of her. Jesi could feel his breath on her face. He bent his head down and took her top lip between his. She kissed him back. Johan started to kiss along her chin then on her ear. His hardening sex rubbed against her.

"Johan."

Jesi was caught off guard when he swept her off her feet. He carried her out through the wall of vines and laid her on the blanket. She watched as he knelt over her and took his uniform top off. *This is it. I'm really going to do this.* Jesi was excited and scared. His eyes were glistened over with desire. He lay on top, pressing his pelvis into her. She could feel his erection against the top of her vagina. As he kissed her lips, he unbuttoned her blouse. Jesi gasped when he cupped her right breast in his hand. She could feel the muscles along his torso flexing. He kissed down her throat, removing her blouse, and then her bra. Never once did he stop his assault of kisses.

Jesi moaned when Johan took her right nipple between his teeth. He moved to suck on her left nipple and teased her right breast with his fingers. Her hips arched forward and back, pulsing into him. She'd never felt such a strong desire to have sex.

"Not yet, sweet girl."

Jesi felt Johan's hand run down her tummy. He unfastened her shorts and ran his finger over her panty.

"That feels so good."

Johan rubbed her sensitive spot. *How did he know to do that?* Then he quit.

"Don't stop."

"Don't worry."

Jesi was in a dreamy state and didn't want to open her eyes. She realized Johan was lifting her buttocks and removing her shorts. He kissed and bit the inside of her left thigh until he reached her vagina. Johan stopped and moved over to her right thigh, sprinkling it with tenderness. Again, he stopped when he reached her womanhood. Finally, he kissed her on that one spot where all the sensations emanated. Even over her panty, it excited Jesi to no end. She clutched the blanket in her hands, needing something to brace herself against. As she pressed her vagina into his mouth, she felt him remove her panty. She lifted her butt as if it were the natural thing to do. Lying stark naked, Jesi opened her eyes.

Johan stood above her. She couldn't help but stare at his erection. *Is that supposed to fit inside me?* He bent down and bit the inside of her thigh, going back and forth from her left to her right. Every time, Johan moved a little closer toward her womanhood. She could feel his hands on her hips, holding them tight.

"Oh god, Johan."

He was kissing her there then he sucked on it. He ran his tongue in circles. And he kept on and on. His tongue went around and around on that one spot. That feeling was building. It was overwhelming and Jesi kept pushing her sex against him, against his magical, swirling tongue. Whatever he was doing, she didn't want him to stop. She breathed faster. It was getting so strong, that feeling. His pace intensified.

"Johan, oh Johan."

Jesi pushed her hips up against his mouth. Then it exploded between her legs.

"Johan, oh my god, Johan, I ah, oh god."

Whatever it was, it tore through her being. Her fingernails dug into her palms through the blanket. In the air, she was sure her nipples were dancing. Then it started to subside. She felt kisses on her vagina. Her hips relaxed and she loosened her grip on the blanket. She had never experienced anything so divine. Jesi opened her eyes.

"What was that?"

"You've never felt it?"

"Never. Is that what men do to women? I thought you had to have sex for that."

"You have a lot to learn, sweet girl. But right now, it's my turn." Johan knelt between her thighs, and paused.

"What's wrong?"

"You can say no if you don't want to do this."

"I want to." She closed her eyes as he kissed her from her tummy to her breasts. He reached her lips and devoured them, his erection, hard and long.

"It's going to hurt," Johan said, his lips just above hers.

"OK." The feel of his naked body against her bare skin would make her consent to anything right now.

"Tell me when you want me to stop. But you'll get used to me."

Jesi tried to make sense of her nerves, but she wanted him. She was anxious, and she still had this need. Johan lifted his chest off her and knelt right up against her buttocks. Jesi felt the end of him at the opening of her vagina. It hurt as he pushed into her then he stopped. He pushed in a little more, and it still hurt.

"Jesi."

She felt him push all the way in. It felt as if her tongue blocked her throat. *Don't you dare scream. Oh my god it hurts like crazy!* She held back a tear and let out a small gasp.

"I know, I'm sorry."

She felt him pause.

"Don't stop." Jesi held her breath and refused to cry. Johan pushed himself in and out of her. She could hear him breathing, and peeked at him. He looked right at her. *God you're gorgeous.*

He lay on top of her, sucking on her lips, biting them, teasing her tongue. Then he moved his mouth away. She opened her eyes again. His lips were parted, but his teeth were clenched together. Johan's breathing was getting faster. Jesi wrapped her legs around his hips and put her hands on the sides of his torso, pulling him closer against her body. The pain wasn't as bad. It felt like a massage, in and out of her.

"You're so wet and tight," he whispered.

The grazing of his skin against her flesh, his breath on her face, the sounds he made in his throat. All these feelings in her body and in her heart drove her mad.

"Jesi." His breathing was heavy and fast.

Jesi felt him thrust deep inside her, again, and again, unyielding and firm. He braced his weight on his left elbow as he clutched her against him with his right arm, pulling her chest closer with every thrust. Johan shuddered on top of her, groaning, much like she did when it exploded in her. Then his grip softened, and his thrusts slowed. Jesi still had that need burning between her legs. She wanted to feel that eruption of sensations once more, and opened her eyes. He stared down at her, still caressing the inside of her vagina with his sex.

"How do you feel?" Johan asked.

The look on his face was sincere, and encouraging.

"Out of my mind. Ecstatic. I don't think I can describe how I feel."

Johan bent down and took her lips in his, sucking and kissing.

"What part did you like the most?" His lips curved up into a smile.

"Everything. But when it exploded when you were—when you had your—"

"When I had my tongue on your clitoris?"

Jesi frowned as he pulled out and lay beside her left side.

"This little thing right here" Johan asked as he rubbed his finger on her sensitive spot.

"Mmm."

"You like that?"

"Yes." She was worked up again. Whatever he was doing to her, to her clitoris, it magnified all those good, happy feelings.

"Have you ever touched yourself down there?"

"No."

"Really?"

"I never knew."

"I see."

She felt him sucking on her left nipple. "Ouch." He bit her.

"Did you like that?"

"Yes."

Johan was still playing with her there. *How does he do that? God it felt incredible. You're going to hell, Jesi. You're not even married!* Jesi froze.

"What's wrong?"

"I'm going to hell!"

"What do you mean?"

"We're not married. I'm not supposed to have sex till I'm married, but I, it felt so good and I couldn't help it." Jesi sat upright and looked at him.

"Why are you smiling?"

"You're not going to hell."

"How do you know? I just sinned!"

"I'm sure even your people have had sex before they got married."

"No. Not if they want to go to heaven."

"Your parents told you that to keep you safe."

"Are you sure?" He was still smiling at her. "You promise?"

"Promise."

Mom's going to be so mad.

"You're very beautiful."

It dawned on Jesi that she was still naked.

"I, um, thank you. Where'd my blouse go?" She stood up. He smiled that naughty smile and pulled her back down on the blanket beside him. "But we just—"

"I know."

Johan was touching her clitoris again. Round and round he rubbed her. He sucked on her nipple, and pulled it with his teeth. Jesi arched her pelvis up as his fingers continued their torturous antics. That feeling was strong, and she was getting closer to that explosion of bliss.

"Do you like my playing with you?"

"Yes. Don't stop." *Please don't stop.*

Johan continued to massage her erotic nub.

Oh god, it's so good. He's so good.

She clutched the blanket and squeezed her thighs together, locking his hand in place.

"Johan, oh god, Johan."

He continued to makes circles on her clitoris.

"That's it, Jesi,"

"Oh god, I, I, I'm there."

She moaned, and screamed, and hoped nobody could hear her.

Jesi felt him cup his hand all around her vagina.

"Good girl."

"Mmm, god, oh my. Wow." After a moment, she felt him kneel between her legs. "Again?"

"Yes, again."

Jesi winced as he entered.

"Still hurts?"

"A little."

"I'll go easy."

Johan stayed on his knees while he pushed in and out of her. Jesi felt full in her womanhood and watched his face. His eyes glazed over as he bound her thighs in his hands. Johan started to push harder and faster.

"Do I make you feel good?" She knew her cheeks grew pink.

"You feel really nice."

That must have sent him over the edge. Johan gave one last, hard push and grunted. Jesi felt his grip lighten on her thighs. She never took her eyes off him, and even ignored her own sensations. He bent down to kiss her then lay on his back.

"What am I going to do with you, sweet girl?"

"What do you mean?" Jesi closed her eyes. Exhaustion took over. A sleepless night, the hike, and this glorious sex made her more than tired. Johan mumbled something.

Johan looked over at Jesi then turned on his right side and supported his head with his hand. She was sound asleep. "What am I going to do about you?"

Finally. It had been far too long since he'd had sex.

"You're not just another girl are you?" Johan ran his finger from the base of her neck, between her breasts, and down to her navel. *Firm and flat but not bony.*

"Damn!" Johan looked at her face. Jesi lay undisturbed. *You bastard. What if she gets pregnant?* "Christ." He forgot to grab the condom in his pack.

After putting his clothes on, Johan took the blanket he had in his bag and laid it over her. *Ugh.* There were bloodstains on the blanket beneath her. He walked to just a few feet from the edge of the cliff and crossed his arms over his chest. It seemed even more breathtaking. "What have you done, you ass?" It horrified Johan, yet at the same time it stirred something in him. He turned and walked back to Jesi. Johan eased himself down on his right side then ran his hand over the blanket that covered her belly.

"Hi," she said.

"I didn't mean to wake you."

"It was a good nap," Jesi smiled, "is sex always like that?"

"What do you mean?"

"Does it always feel that good?"

"Yup. And there's more to do, too, you know."

"More?"

She was so innocent it tugged at his heart. Johan watched as she sat up.

"Yikes, oh gosh."

Johan saw the squirm spread across her face. "Sorry, it'll go away. You should get dressed."

He was getting aroused again, against his better judgment. "And don't be alarmed. Since it was your first time, you bled some on the blanket."

"I bled?"

"It's normal."

The expression on her face softened.

"While I get dressed, would you get out our lunch in my bag?" Jesi asked.

"Sure."

"I'm just going to cover my blanket with yours," she said.

"OK."

They both sat facing each other then Johan handed the containers to Jesi.

"Did you make your bag?"

"Yes. It's made from leaves of the pandanus plant. Pandanus is akgak in Chamorro."

"Rustic and useful. This smells great whatever it is." He handed the container to Jesi and watched as she spooned something onto a piece of bread of sorts.

"Here."

Johan opened his mouth as Jesi fed him a soft disc topped with lemony chicken.

"This is tasty." He chewed and swallowed then opened his mouth again, waiting for more.

"You like it."

"Yup, what is it?"

"*Titiyas*, well, tortillas, made with nuts from the *federico* tree. The chicken is mixed with onions, lemon, and hot peppers, and salt. It's called *kelaguen.*

Johan reached for his own disc of titiyas and kelaguen, and stuffed his mouth. "I could live off this Guam food you've been feeding me."

"Ha-ha, you haven't tried anything yet."

Johan loved hearing her laugh. As he watched her eat, he sat quiet for a moment, not wanting to bring up the subject.

"Jesi, I need to talk to you about something."

"You sound serious."

"It is. I forgot to put a condom on."

"A condom?"

12

JESI HEARD THE ROOSTERS CROWING. IT was time to get up. She had been dreaming about having sex with Johan, and never imagined sex would be so remarkable. Johan called the moment that the sensations exploded inside her an orgasm, or climax. Jesi smiled. There was something about the way he looked when he was on top of her that excited her to no end. And that he could make her have an orgasm with just his fingers. Unconsciously, she ran her fingers over her vagina. Jesi closed her eyes and thought about his naked body on top of hers. She squeezed her thighs together, relishing the memories then jerked upright. *Oh my god, what if I am pregnant? I could be pregnant? It was just one time, OK twice. But I can't get pregnant already can I?*

Jesi lay backward and thought about the end of their day. The hike down from the Pago cave was uncomfortable. He held her hand, though, as he drove her home. Johan was quiet, but he hugged her before he left.

"Jesi, *kahulo*," Tan Chai called for her to get up.

"I'm up, Grandma."

"OK, Neni."

She stepped out of bed and was excited to make *guyuria*. The fried cookies were crunchy and lasted a long time. Jesi couldn't wait to share some with Johan since he seemed to like Chamorro food.

"Morning, Mom." Jesi hugged Mrs. T who had come over to help. It was an intergenerational affair when it came to making the cookies. More hands in the kitchen meant that they could finish rolling the cookies much faster, and it ensured that the art of making guyuria was passed on.

"*Buenas*, Neni. You want some *pan tosta* and coffee before we get started?"

"I get to drink coffee?"

Coffee was a no-no before. She watched as Mrs. T poured a cup.

"You're growing up. Get pan tosta from that can over there on the shelf. I made it yesterday."

"Where's grandma and Auntie Julia?"

"They are checking on the plants. I came looking for you to see if you wanted to help me make the bread, but grandma said you left with Johan."

Oh no, what am I going to say?

"He came up to help with Auntie Julia's house, but Peter and Dad weren't here." Jesi sat down at the kitchen table. The butterflies woke up in her tummy.

"Where did you two go?"

Jesi took a sip of coffee, avoiding her mom's inquisition. "Mmm, it's sweet and a little bitter."

"Coffee is good with dessert. So where'd you guys go?"

"I took him to Pago Cave to show him the view there." *You could have lied you know.*

Jesi took a pan tosta from her plate and broke the ring of hardened, sweet bread in half. She ignored Mrs. T, wanting to keep further questions at bay, and wanting to savor her first bite of coffee-soaked pan tosta. Jesi blew on the saturated bread to cool it then took a small bite.

"This is sweet, and soft, and oh so good, Mom." She took another nibble.

"Did he like the view up there?"

"Yes. He liked the titiyas and kelaguen, too."

It was quiet for a while. Jesi ate her pan tosta, and wondered what her mom was thinking about.

"You look different."

"Different?" Jesi stared at her mom. *I can't look pregnant already? Oh my god.* She tried to hide her alarm.

"I'm just tired. It was a long hike and I didn't sleep well."

"Jesi, *chule' magi fan i lechen niyok guenao guatu,*" Tan Chai said, as she and Auntie Julia walked into the kitchen. Tan Chai asked Jesi to bring the milk to her from over there on the counter.

Saved by grandma. Jesi got out of her seat to get the milk, but she could feel Mrs. T's eyes on her. Jesi waited for Tan Chai to wash and dry her hands. She poured the coconut milk over the flour as her grandma mixed the guyuria dough. Jesi glanced over at Mrs. T who got the pot of coconut oil ready. Auntie Julia set trays on the table.

"*Esta*, Neni," Tan Chai told Jesi to stop pouring the milk.

The dough was done. Jesi brought the bowl to the table. She grabbed a large chunk of the dough, covered the bowl, and tore small pieces of dough from her hand until there was none left. She and Mrs. T used the back of a fork to shape the small pieces of dough into little shells. Tan Chai and Auntie Julia used a traditional wooden board that had grooves all across it.

"Did you and Johan have sex?"

"Mom!" *In front of grandma and Auntie Julia?*

"Did you have sex, Jesi?"

She's so not happy.

"Yes."

"I didn't hear you."

"Yes."

The whole world heard that one.

"You better pray the rosary tonight, ten times *diablo*."

I can actually hear her breathing. She's huffing and puffing. Oh god, she's angry.

Jesi kept rolling guyuria, avoiding eye contact. She heard Tan Chai tell Auntie Julia to never mind, it's none of her business. Trays slammed around her.

"I'm sorry," was all Jesi could manage, "I'm really sorry." She fought to keep the tears from falling.

"I hope you're not pregnant, because he's leaving. I trusted you to be smart so you can have a little freedom, but look what you did. I'm disappointed in you."

"*Básta*, Debbie," Tan Chai told Mrs. T to let things be.

"No, Mom, because she already had sex and she needs to be careful," Mrs. T replied back to Tan Chai in Chamorro.

Mrs. T had never talked about sex with Jesi. The fact that it was a sin among the Chamorro Catholics was pounded into every kid in *eskuelan palé*, or religious school.

"Did he use protection?"

"No, but it was just my first time. Nothing can happen right?"

"Right."

Jesi could tell by the sound of her mom's voice and her scowl that Mrs. T wasn't convinced.

"Can I really get pregnant my first time?" Jesi had to know. She stopped rolling guyuria.

"I had Tommy my first time, but I was already married," Mrs. T said.

God.

Jesi was mortified. Not only did she have sex before she was married, but she could be pregnant as well.

"Do you know when your next period is?" Mrs. T asked.

"I'll give you a hundred bucks to take my shift today," Johan said to Sergeant Lucas.

"You're on, Sarge, but where'd you get that kind of money to throw around?"

"None of your business."

"Just wondering."

Unlike many men in the army, Johan didn't smoke or drink. He didn't even have a need to spend his money. Johan had to see Jesi today. He got in the jeep and headed to the Taimanglos'. Visions of making love to her yesterday permeated his thoughts. *Making love? Are you insane?* Johan wanted to hold her. He left without saying much and he didn't want Jesi to think all he wanted to do was have sex. *Does she feel the same way about me?*

It was an overcast day. Johan's heart raced as he pulled into Tan Chai's yard and turned the jeep off. Antonio wasn't outside, but Johan grabbed the toy anyway. He walked to the front door and knocked.

"I got it, I got it." Johan heard the boy yell from inside the house.

"Hi, Johan!" Antonio said after he opened the door.

"Hi, Antonio. I brought you a truck."

"Thank you, Johan, thank you!"

"Is Jesi here?"

"Hi, Johan." Jesi popped her head past the door.

"Hi, I was able to get away. I wanted to check on you."

"Antonio, go inside."

No smile? Johan moved backwards a few steps so she could come through the door.

"They know."

"They know what?"

"Yesterday, that we, you know."

"What? How did they find out?" Johan let out a big sigh.

"My mom guessed, and she was so mad. But then she said she was more disappointed."

"Jesi," Johan heard Mrs. T calling.

Oh Christ!

"We have a visitor. Be right in," Jesi said.

"I could come back later if it's better." *No problem fighting the Japs. Big problem facing Mrs. T.*

"Just amen everybody inside, and don't say anything about it."

"All right." *Gather up your courage, Landers.*

"It's not that we had sex, just that we weren't married before we had sex."

Johan followed Jesi into the house and whispered, "We can fix that—"

"Hi, Johan," Mrs. T said.

Not her normal, happy self. Great.

"Ñora," Johan paid his respects to Mrs. T, Tan Chai, and Auntie Julia.

"Sit and eat," Mrs. T pulled out a chair for him, slamming it against the floor.

Oh no.

The tension in the air was thicker than mud, and now he was trapped behind a table.

"Thank you, Ma'am. I ate, but it's hard to turn down your cooking." Johan couldn't help it. It smelled incredible inside the house. "What is it?" He watched Jesi as she set a cup of coffee in front of him, along with a round piece of bread.

"It's pan tosta. A hard bread that you dip in coffee."

"For a minute I thought it was a bagel."

"What's a bagel?"

A slight chuckle escaped his throat, and a smile. "It looks like this pan tosta, but soft. And you can cut it open for a sandwich or put butter and jelly on it. So, I dip this into the cup?"

"You have to break it in half first."

Johan did as instructed then dunked the hard bread into his coffee.

"Blow it so it cools off."

"OK."

"This is pretty good." He finished the half in two more dunks and started on the other piece.

"Thank you, Johan, for the flour. I used it to make the pan tosta," Mrs. T said.

She's hospitable. But Jesi is almost twenty.

"You're very welcome. If you need more, I can get some for you."

"Thank you."

Johan saw a hint of a smile emerge from Mrs. T's face.

"Lāhi-hu, malago' chagi guyuria?" Tan Chai asked Johan if he wanted to try the cookies. She set a small plate of the sugar-coated, shell-shaped treats in front of him.

Her grandma doesn't seem mad.

"Those are Guam cookies. They're crunchy, and they're made with coconut milk. I think you'll like them," Jesi said.

"Si Yu 'us ma 'äse', Tan Chai." *She smiled, grandma is smiling. I'm not doomed.* Johan was glad he remembered how to say thank you in Chamorro. He still thought he sounded funny, but made an honest effort to pronounce the words. "You and your mom and grandma sure like to cook." He wanted to get up off the chair and hug Jesi, but didn't dare.

"Yes."

"What do you have planned for today?" Mrs. T looked at Johan.

He set the cookie back on the plate. "Not much, Ma'am. I wanted to check if Peter needed help, and bring Antonio a truck. *Liar.* And check on Jesi."

"I see."

Here it comes.

"Jesi, finish coating the guyuria. Peter is taking us down to Uncle Kin's house to work on his roof."

No lecture?

"Yes, Mom. Shouldn't Antonio stay with me?"

"His dad is back home. Vicente was hiding in Umatac, not far from Fouha Rock."

Fouha Rock sits in Umatac Bay in the village of Umatac. The ancient Chamorros believed the goddess and god, Fo'na and Pontan, used their powers to create the world, and people. Fo'na, with permission from her brother Pontan, used Pontan's eyes, eyebrows, and back to create the sun and moon, rainbows, and the Earth. Fo'na gave life to Pontan's parts so the Earth could thrive. Fo'na also wanted to give life so she threw herself into the bay and became Fouha Rock. The first humans came out of Fouha.

"What about his mom?"

Johan saw Jesi turn to look at Antonio who was playing on the floor with his truck. He could tell she was worried.

"Rosa hasn't come home, yet." Mrs. T then looked at Johan. "Take care of my girl, ha."

"Yes, Ma'am." Johan stood up and åmened Mrs. T. She held on to his fingers for several seconds, squeezing them as one would squeeze pliers cutting through a ten-gauge wire. *Damn!*

"*Adiós* låhi-hu," Tan Chai said once Mrs. T released her grip. Johan stood still as the elderly lady held his cheeks between her hands. Her eyes bore into his. He swore she could see into the deepest holes of his heart. Then she turned and walked away. Johan felt uneasy, but let it go, and åmened Auntie Julia good-bye. Auntie Julia glared at him.

"My grandma really likes you, you know," Jesi said.

"How can you tell?"

"She's normally reserved and quiet. But she's given you food, and talked to you, and held you. I thought you had to work the rest of the week."

"I do. You're mom's not pleased."

"Nope. I'd rather she be mad, but instead I let her down."

Johan watched Jesi as she finished pouring a sugar syrup over the fried dough, and stirred everything together. She draped a cloth over the bowl then sat across from him at the table.

"I hope coming over didn't make things worse. I had to see you. I'm sorry I left without saying much. I was mad at myself."

"Don't be. I'm glad you're here. I was worried you might not come back."

Johan reached for her hands on the table. "I wouldn't abandon you, whether you are pregnant or not." Johan got up and pulled her into a hug. He clutched her against his body without saying a word.

"My mom said that if I don't have my period by the end of September at the latest then for sure I am pregnant."

He could feel her tense up and hug him tighter. Johan pulled himself away to look at her. "This is my fault."

"It's not a matter of fault. I wanted to be with you, too." She reached for his left hand and placed it over her tummy. "If I am pregnant, would you still want me and the baby?" Her hand was shaky.

"Jesi," he raised her chin to look into her eyes. "I love you, of course I'll still want you and our baby." He waited. It felt like forever as she stared back at him. "You have nothing to worry about."

"I love you, too."

That was all Johan needed to hear. He took her lips in his and kissed her. His heart was full of joy, and love. It opened up to her having been closed dead to the world for years. Johan felt his sex growing as he pressed his body into hers. *Cool it, you've already been warned for Christ's sake!*

"Come," Jesi said, "Follow me." She started to step away.

"I don't think that's a good idea." Johan stopped her. He had to exercise some restraint even though he was aroused.

"I heard Peter's truck. They've left and they'll be gone for a long time. No one will be here."

"Jesi, I didn't bring a condom, and—"

"Does it matter now? I may already be pregnant."

True.

Johan didn't need any more convincing as he followed Jesi then locked the door behind him. "I haven't felt this way in a long time," Johan confessed, pulling her close and looking into her eyes. "I do love you." He took her lips in his then she pulled back.

"I know. I love you, too."

"Every time you smile, it makes me want to kiss you." Johan nibbled on her upper lip, then her bottom. "Just like this." He engulfed her tongue, pressing his mouth on hers. After kissing her left ear, he planted wet ones down the side of her neck. Johan reached under her blouse and beneath her bra, squeezing her right nipple.

"Ah."

"You like that?"

"Yes."

She unbuttoned his uniform top and pulled his shirt off. The feel of her hands and lips on his skin was more than he could handle. Johan stroked his erection. Jesi looked down. He was surprised when she unbuttoned his pants and pulled at his zipper.

"I want to see it."

Johan closed his eyes. He reached under his briefs and pushed the material away, exposing his long, hard organ.

"Can I touch?"

All he could manage was a nod. *I've half a mind to take you right now.* Johan was enjoying her unfolding innocence. She touched the head with her fingertips then ran her thumb under his shaft. "Jesi," he choked when she kissed the head.

"Yes," she said and looked up.

"Wrap your lips around it." He was beyond taking it slow.

She glanced up at him and seemed unsure.

"Go ahead."

She looked at his erection, opened her mouth, and took him in. He nudged his hard-on into her a little farther then pulled back until his head was at her lips. The feel of her fingers digging into his thighs and pulling him closer to him was maddening. He pushed in again, this time deeper. Johan moved his erection through her mouth, savoring her warmth. "Jesi." It took every ounce of control to fight the urge to climax in her.

"Stand up."

"Already?"

"Not quite."

With a sly smile, he pulled her blouse over her head then took her shorts and panty off. "You smell so good." Johan knelt in front of her to kiss her sex. He stood up and lifted her to the bed then lay on top of her. Johan glided his erection over her vagina as he kissed her with such voracity he might have cut into her skin.

"Do you want me inside you?"

"Yes."

Johan lifted his hips just enough to enter her. He pushed all the way in. "You OK?"

"I'm fine."

He felt her legs constrict around his body. "Jesi, you're going to make me climax too early."

"What's another word for penis?"

Damn! He was breathing hard.

"I like how you feel inside me."

"Oh Christ, Jesi." He ground his hips into her and pushed deeper. She was so tight. Johan couldn't hold back. With one big thrust, he spilled his seed. Groaning and murmuring beside her ear, he slowed, caressing his sex with her wetness. "I never lose control like that." He stopped and studied her gray eyes. "I love you."

"I love you, too, but you still need to make me, um, climax, as you call it."

He felt her move beneath him. Johan lifted off and lay to her side. He sucked her left nipple and ran his hand down her tummy to her clitoris.

"You want to climax do you?"

"I want to feel that again, and again, and again."

"Do you want to try it with me inside you?"

"Yes."

Johan was hard once more. He got up between her legs. "Lift your butt up." Johan positioned a pillow beneath her then slid inside, his thighs against her buttocks. "Tell me if you want it faster, or slower, or deeper." Johan started his rhythmic assault. "Or even harder." He watched her. Her eyes were closed and her nipples swayed in the air with every thrust. She clenched the blanket. "I want you to pinch your nipples."

"You do it."

"Jesi, I want you to pinch your nipples."

"Fine."

"Ouch! What was that for?" Johan asked.

"Because I have to pinch my own nipples."

"You won't be complaining in a minute, sweetheart."

Johan concentrated on making her feel every bit of the pleasure he was giving. He tried to take his mind off how swollen and wet she was. Watching her face and her body language, he changed his speed and intensity. She was beautiful, sensual, sexy.

"Oh god, Johan, more . . ."

He obliged. Johan could feel her squeeze her muscles tighter around him. She was getting close. Her breathing was erratic and her pelvis arched up.

"Johan, oh god, Johan."

"That's it, Jesi, let it go."

The tightness was too much, and her moans. The feel of Jesi shaking beneath him broke open the dam. He pulled her hips against his pelvis, thrusting into her deepness, losing himself. The haze in her eyes matched his. Love. Lust. Satisfaction. Joy. Relief.

Once they settled down from their orgasms, he pulled out and lay next to her. "You're going to have to wash this sheet," Johan said.

"I know."

Johan stared at her. Her eyes were closed. "You're very beautiful. Your eyes, your lips, your nose, your cheeks, your forehead. Everything about you." He reached for her chin and turned her face toward him. She opened her eyes.

"I love you, Jessica Taimanglo."

She smiled her mesmerizing smile.

"I love you, too, Johan Landers."

"Much as I'd like to, we can't lie around here all day," Johan said.

"Ugh. I know."

"Is there anything I can do for your grandma? Your mom and dad, so maybe they won't hate me so much?"

"They don't hate you, it's just, I don't know. They are overprotective. My dad has this thing about marrying a Chamorro. And I did say that sex before marriage is a sin."

Did she just say marry?

"Still, you're of legal age, even if there's no such thing as legal age in your culture. It doesn't seem like your mom or grandma are prejudice."

"They're not. My dad has friends that are American, but, I don't know."

"In the eyes of the law, you can make your own decisions." *I hope you choose me.* "So what should we do?"

131

"My mom would love it if we picked *achoti* seeds for the rice. She hates doing it. I haven't talked to my dad yet, but I'll think of something."

"What's the *a-tso-tee* seeds?"

"They're tiny seeds inside a poky pod, and the seeds make your hands red, and then later, your hands turn yellow."

"So the rice turns red then yellow?"

"No, dark orange it's almost red."

"I guess we better get going."

Johan got off the bed and helped Jesi do the same. He pulled her in for a hug. *I love you so much.*

"Will you marry me?" *What the hell, Landers.*

"Did you ask me to marry you?" Jesi creased her eyes together.

"I'm sorry. I didn't mean to. I mean I did. It just came out of me. But—"

"You want to marry me?" She stepped away from him then reached for her blouse and started to put her clothes on.

"I love you, Jesi. I'm alive and happy when we're together. I've never felt like this before. Not even with Lily."

Jesi turned around, eyebrows raised. "Really?"

"I know we've just met, but I love you and I want to spend the rest of my days with you."

He loves me that much? She listened to him as he buttoned his pants. Jesi sat on the bed. Johan knelt in front of her and took her hands.

"I know it's unfair of me to ask you."

His eyes were sad, pleading even. Johan looked down, away from her, and took a deep breath.

"There's a rumor we have to ship out in six weeks. We're moving our camp to Orote in a few days to prepare to leave."

He looked up and Jesi could see his hesitation.

"I'll do my best to come out of this war alive. But if I don't, I'll die a happy, proud man if you were my wife. It's selfish of me to ask this of you. I didn't come here to ask you to marry me."

The thought of his leaving made her want to cry. *It can't be.* She didn't want to think about it. Jesi knelt down to hug him.

"I love you, too, Johan. Can't you get out of the army? The thought of you dying. . ." She tried not to cry, but the tears started to run down her cheeks. "Yes, I will. I will marry you," Jesi said, hugging him.

"You'll marry me?" Johan asked as he nudged her back to look at her.

"Yes."

"You've just made me the happiest soldier alive!"

He kissed Jesi then picked her up into a great big bear hug and spun her around.

"I love your hugs." Jesi smiled and laughed.

"I'm never going to let you go." He stopped turning. "I can't get out, but I will come back alive, Jessica Taimanglo."

Jesi accepted his kisses.

"I don't have a ring yet, but I can get you the biggest diamond ring a girl could have."

"I don't need a big ring. We can make them with whatever's around."

"Make a ring?" He looked at her funny.

"You always look at me like that. Why?"

"You're different in the best ways."

"Maybe you're the one that's different. Ever think of that?" Jesi challenged him.

"You have an inner strength, Jesi. There's some kind of force in you that shines, and I see it in your eyes, in your smile."

"I don't know what you mean."

"It's like you are happy and content. You don't have much in the way of fancy clothes or jewelry, but you are richer than any woman I've ever met in Manhattan. And I was around a lot of them with money."

"Oh." Jesi smiled back at him.

"We need to set a date, sometime soon," he urged.

"We can't get married!" Jesi stepped back away from him "Johan, you don't pray. Were you even baptized?" Jesi covered her mouth with one hand.

"Calm down," Johan took both her hands in his. "I was raised Catholic even if I've become a heathen. My parents baptized me. You know that you don't have to be Catholic to get married, right?"

"I didn't know that, but thank God. Should I even say thank God? You've corrupted me."

Jesi was relieved and smiling again.

"My dad, I haven't even seen my dad since I moved out. He'll never let me marry you."

Jesi's heart sank to the pit of her stomach. She sat on the bed, shoulders slumped.

"They won't let us get married in church, and you're supposed to ask my dad to marry me, and he'll never say yes, and you have to bring gifts to my parents. And you need thirteen silver coins . . ." Jesi rambled. "And he'll still say no."

She felt Johan sit beside her and pull her into a hug.

"Shhh, it'll be all right. We'll find a way, sweet girl. There's always a way."

"No, Johan, there's no way."

"Look at me."

Jesi tilted her head back to look at him.

"You have to believe there's a way. I want to marry you. And you want to marry me right?"

"Yes."

"Then we'll find a way. Or make our own way."

"There will be a way," Mames whispered.

She's always right.

13

JESI STOOD AT THE FRONT DOOR OF HER parents' house. Mrs. T had forgiven her, and was getting used to the idea of Jesi growing up, and having sex. *Thank God mom is back to her regular self. I'll need all the help I can get with dad.* It was Sunday morning, just after brunch. Jesi knew Chief would be home and he'd be in a decent mood. Sunday was his favorite day of the week. And she had baked him coconut cake, delivered by Antonio earlier in the morning.

"You can do this," Mames whispered.

Yes, I can, thank you.

Jesi took a deep breath and knocked on the door.

"Mom, Dad."

"Hi, Neni." Mrs. T opened the door. "You don't have to knock, this is still your house."

"Sorry, Mom." Jesi hugged Mrs. T and already had to fight back the tears. "Dad's home right?"

"He's in his chair."

Jesi walked into the living room toward her father. Chief stood up and opened his arms. "I'm sorry, Daddy. I'm so sorry." The tears came flooding. "I didn't mean to make you mad."

"I know, my girl, I know."

137

Jesi always felt loved in her father's arms. It was a familiar embrace, the only safe place she knew until she met Johan.

"I'm very sorry, Jesi."

She felt her father swallow. He rarely apologized. Most of the time he was right.

"If you wan him to be your boyfriend, you haf my blessing."

"Thank you, thank you for understanding." She kissed Chief on his cheeks and hugged him.

"He's leafing pretty soon dough right?"

Jesi stepped back from her father.

"I think so."

"If he's jus gonna be here for a little, den I'm good."

"Ombren laña' hao, asagua!" Mrs. T told her husband to go to hell.

Jesi could tell Mrs. T was infuriated with the man.

"What if he's here for longer?" Jesi's cheeks started to burn.

"Don't you raise your voice at me, Jessica."

Jesi looked at her father, heartbroken.

"You're a liar!" She yelled. "Why can't you be happy for me? He saved me. You should be grateful to Johan and you owe him." The memories of the Japanese men came firing back. *Don't tell them.* She closed her eyes, but the tears wouldn't go away. *Don't tell them, don't tell them.*

"What are you saying, Neni?" Her mom looked at her.

"Nothing."

"Jesi," Mrs. T persisted.

"It's nothing." She tried to calm herself down, and looked at her father.

"I love him. And we're getting married."

"Håfa, you leaf my house an you think you all grown up. Diablo. Over my dead body you're getting married." Chief spoke in English and Chamorro when he was incensed. *Håfa* means "what" in Chamorro, and *diablo* is a curse word.

Jesi gathered all the strength she could muster to look him straight in the eyes. She saw the blood pulse through the vein in his neck. In his state, even Mrs. T backed off. But Jesi wouldn't.

"Be strong," Mames whispered.

"I might be pregnant with his child," Jesi yelled. She wanted to hurt him as he was hurting her. In a flash, Chief held her by her shoulders and pinned her against the wall. Jesi closed her eyes and when she opened them, all she could see were the Japanese men. "No! Get off me. Move away, no!" She kicked and punched and cried. "Help me, God no!" She fought harder. Chief let go and moved away from her in shock.

"Jesi, Jesi, it's Mom, Neni. Jesi." She could hear her mom. "Jesi, I'm right here, Neni. It's Momma."

Jesi's heart was still pounding out of her chest. It took her a moment to realize it wasn't the Japanese men. She moved away from her mom.

"Do you know what they almost did to me?" She yelled at her father. "They took my pants off." She tried to stop crying. "They touched me all over, and they tied my hands." Jesi had to catch her breath. "Johan saved me. If he didn't stop them and kill them, they would have raped me and killed me just like Carmen!"

She was close to hyperventilating. Mrs. T tried to comfort her, but Jesi stepped away. She wiped the tears with the back of her hands, and looked at Chief who was stunned into silence. Now that they knew, Jesi was relieved. She stood still to take a couple of breaths, and found a new surge of courage and purpose.

"I'm not asking your permission. I am going to marry him. If you choose not to accept him, that's fine. But I will no longer be your daughter."

"Jesi!" Mrs. T scolded.

"I'm sorry, Mom."

Jesi turned and walked out of the house. Her heart started to race and the tears came back.

"You OK?"

She ignored Peter and ran.

14

"WHATCHA GOT THERE, SARGE?" CALHOUN asked.

They finished chow and had to get back to work in an hour.

Johan looked at Calhoun. He hadn't said a word to anyone yet. Their platoon was settled in Orote and he'd get to visit Jesi tomorrow.

"You really want to know?"

"What the hell, Sarge. You've been talking in circles since you last saw her. Spill it, man."

"I asked her to marry me."

Johan sat under the shade of a tent that was tied to the trunks of bald coconut trees. The sound of a plane taking off filled the air.

"What?"

Johan waited for the noise to dissipate.

"I said I asked her to marry me."

"What?" Calhoun heard him for sure.

"And she said yes."

"You mean to tell me that kind girl wants to marry the likes of you?"

"Piss off."

"Just messin' with you. But, uh, she does know you're leaving soon right?"

"Yup."

"I could put in a good word for you with the chaplain. It'd be a better idea if you'd show your face at the chapel tent."

"I know. Just find me anyone who'll marry us. And can you check with the locals where to get our marriage license?"

Johan took his eyes off the piece of metal he was working on. "I'll give them whatever they want, whatever it costs, Calhoun. I'm going to marry her before we leave."

"All right, Sarge."

"One more thing. Would you be my best man? You're the closest friend I have."

"Me? I'd be honored. Whatcha making?"

"A ring. Trying to anyway. She didn't want anything fancy. Can you believe that?"

"Seems like a genuine girl. She'll love it."

"I'm going to etch stars into the band." Johan smiled. "They remind me of how her eyes sparkle. Do you know that they change from gray to green when she's mad?"

"She's not some kind of island witch is she?"

"Christ, are you for real?" Johan saw the serious look on Calhoun's face.

"Sarge, I mean we're out in the middle of nowhere. Who knows what the local jungle people really are into. And didn't you say she practices witch medicine."

"You're messed up man. She's no witch, but even if she were, I'd still marry her."

"That's a good thing, Sarge, cuz here comes her brother and he don't look happy. I'm gonna check on that chaplain for you."

Johan looked up and saw Calhoun nod at Peter. Johan reached out and shook Peter's hand.

"Hey, Johan, thanks for the tools."

"You look upset? What's wrong?"

"It's Jesi."

"Is she OK?" Johan was alarmed.

"She and my dad argued yesterday and she hasn't come out of her room. I don't think she's eaten anything since."

"Another fight?"

"Ya."

Johan stood up and took the piece of metal with him. Peter in tow, he walked to his tent, set the metal down, and put on his uniform top. *It's time to call in that favor.*

"She's never been like this. My mom's worried and she told me to come get you."

"I need to see my commanding officer. Wait here and I'll be back." Johan walked away.

It took him a few minutes to find his CO and get permission. Covering for the officer when he was too drunk to see the error in his ways proved to be beneficial. Johan hadn't planned on using the incident against his CO, but he had to get to Jesi.

"I have to be back by six tonight. You good for that?"

"Ya."

Johan opened his pack to make sure the envelope he had prepared was inside. He and Peter loaded the boxes of gifts Johan had been collecting into the back of the pickup.

"What happened?" Johan asked, as Peter turned the truck and drove it out of the base.

"From what my mom said, she went to apologize to my dad, but then my dad made her mad. Jesi told him you two were getting married, and that she might be pregnant."

"I see."

"I'm good with you, but my dad, like I say before."

"I was going to ask for their blessing first."

"My dad's temper is bad and I don't know what actually they said."

"Do I have any chance with Chief? We're getting married with his approval or not."

"I don't know, but you have my mom's permission since she sent me down here."

"Take me to your parents' house first."

Johan sat without saying a word for the rest of the drive. He had been thinking of how to approach Chief and Mrs. T. There was no other way but to show them he was sincere, and that he could indeed take care of their daughter. All too soon, Peter stopped the truck in front of the house.

"Let me go first," Peter said. "I'll come get you if it's safe."

"All right."

Johan was apprehensive, but he had already decided that a signed marriage license, in the end, didn't matter. He was going to spend whatever free time he had on Guam with Jesi.

Peter walked back out.

"It's good to go in. I'll be out here just in case."

Johan got out of the truck then pulled the envelope from his pack. Mrs. T greeted him at the door.

"Thank you for coming, Johan."

"Ñora," he paid his respects. "Ma'am, I mean no dishonor to you and Chief."

"I know. Please come inside. He'll behave himself."

"Thank you, Ma'am." Johan took two deep breaths as he followed Mrs. T into the kitchen. He hadn't yet been inside Mrs. T's house, but it looked very similar to Tan Chai's. The table was long and could sit ten. The floor was spotless. There were no dishes in the sink. A big pot sat on the stove. And it smelled delicious. It always smelled like good cooking.

Chief was sitting at the table and looked up at Johan.

"You wan some donats?" Chief asked.

"No thank you, Sir. I don't want to disrespect you, Chief. I love your daughter. I wanted to ask your permission first, but I guess she beat me to it."

"Why you wanna marry my girl?"

"I love her more than I've ever loved anyone else." Johan paused. He wasn't sure if he should bring up Lily. "I was married years ago, but my wife died. I loved her very much, Sir, but—" Johan felt a pang of guilt.

"I'm sorry."

"Thank you, Sir. I love Jesi more than my own life."

"I beeleaf you."

Johan opened the envelope and took out a folded piece of paper. He put the envelope in his uniform pant pocket then gave Chief the paper.

"I can't guarantee I'll come out of this war alive. But should I die, I've instructed the army and a lawyer back in New York to

145

give everything I own to Jesi." Johan waited. "And our baby if she is pregnant. They will both be well taken care of."

"An what can a soldier, who don haf much money, gif my daughter if he don come back. All she haf lef is a heart break."

"It says there in that paper. It's a legal document that transfers my belongings to Jesi. I have over five hundred thousand dollars in cash and land."

"Das plenty money for an army man."

"I inherited it from my family, and I still own my grandparents' home in the New York mountains." Johan could see the confusion in Chief's face, and watched the older man open the letter.

"Is this real, or are you jus doing dis to marry my girl?"

"That's legal. It is a copy of the original, but it has the army stamp."

"Why are you in da army if you haf all dis money."

"I didn't like being a banker. That's what my family did. After my wife died, I joined the army and left that life behind me." Johan waited for a response. "Is that enough, Sir? Because I can't get out of the army until this war is over."

"She said she lufs you very much. An for her to be dat disrespectful, I beeleaf her." Chief paused. "You don haf to gif her all dis money. She tole me about dose Japanese men. I owe you my life, Johan."

"Sir, it was my duty to save any man or woman from the enemy."

"It don madder. You safe her. I didn't know dat till yesterday. It's true I wan my girl to marry a Chamorro boy, but she lufs you and you earn my trust."

"So does this mean we have your permission to get married?"

"Yes."

Johan was ecstatic, but maintained his composure. "Thank you, Sir, thank you so much.

"Stop calling me Sir, Boy. Call me Chief."

"Si Yu'us ma'åse', Chief."

"I'll be proud to call you my son," Mrs. T said. "And thank you for saving Jesi's life." She gave him a hug. He didn't expect that.

"If you'll excuse me for a minute, please."

Johan went outside.

"They gave permission?" Peter asked.

"Yup. I'm just going to bring these in then go to Jesi."

"Let me help you. I can pick you up around five, plenty of time to get you back. I have chores to do."

"Thanks, Peter. I appreciate all your help."

The men carried the boxes into the house and placed them on the kitchen table. Peter said good-bye and that he'd be back later.

"I also brought gifts, *tsen-tsu-lee*. Is that right?" Johan asked his soon-to-be parents.

"Yes, *chenchule'*," Mrs. T said. "But Johan, you owe us nothing. We're in your debt."

"Please, accept my offerings. It's not much, but I hope you like them." Johan wanted to make them happy. He nodded to the box, "There's more flour, sugar, and canned milk. I also brought canned meat. You just keep it on a shelf till you're ready to eat it."

"May I?" Mrs. T pulled out a can. "Spam. Is it good?"

"It tastes like ham. It keeps well without refrigeration so they feed us soldiers with it. We slice it and put it on crackers, or bread. And sometimes they fry it for us."

"Thank you, Boy. Asagua-hu, look, he brought me more candy." Mrs. T showed Chief a bagful of caramels. She was all smiles.

"I was able to get a few coveralls. They're good for going in the jungle." Johan handed Chief a new one.

Chief stood up and opened the folded uniform. Johan noted a softening in the older man's face. "I been wanting one of dis. Tank you."

"I could only get two new ones, but there are a few used coveralls, too. I hope they fit.

Chief put it up against his body. "Ill fit, Boy."

"There's a couple of other things in there. But if I may, I would like to go and see Jesi to tell her the good news."

"Tank you, Boy, OK go head," Chief nodded his approval to Johan.

Johan smiled at Mrs. T then turned and walked out. He ran the short distance from their house to Tan Chai's. He knocked on the front door.

"Hello, anybody home?"

Johan.

"Hello, Tan Chai? Jesi?"

"Johan." *Thank god I cleaned my face this morning.* Jesi got off the chair in her room, ran to the front door, and opened it. "Oh, Johan." She jumped into his arms, almost toppling him over.

"Jesi."

"He won't let us, but I don't care." Jesi didn't cry. She was done with all the tears. "I'm so glad you're here."

"Peter said you haven't come out of your room."

"I have, just not when anyone's awake."

"Have you been eating?"

"Of course. I'm not a girl who could starve herself." Before she knew it, Johan kissed her, and she kissed him back with the same need.

"I have to tell you something."

"OK." *He sounds serious.*

"Can we go inside to talk?"

"What's wrong?" Jesi led him into the kitchen and sat at the table.

"Nothing's wrong. They gave us their blessing."

"Really? How? When?"

"Peter came to get me. And we stopped there first."

"Oh." *I thought I'd die before Chief said yes.*

"You told them about the Japanese men. I think they felt indebted to me. I also brought chenchule' like you said. Your dad loved the coveralls."

"I'm so happy, but something's still bothering you."

Jesi watched as Johan pulled an envelope from his pocket. He took a piece of paper out and kept it in his hand.

"If I don't make it back—"

"Don't say that."

"Please, just listen. I need to tell you this."

"I'm sorry."

"We'll get married before I ship out. Calhoun is already working on a chaplain or minister or whoever can marry us. But if I die, I am leaving everything I own to you."

"I don't understand."

"I come from a rich family of bankers and investors. That life wasn't for me, but nevertheless, I have a lot of money, and my grandfather's homestead."

"I don't care about your money."

"I know. I want you and your parents to understand that I have the means to take care of you and our baby, if you're pregnant." He smiled at her.

"You're happy I might be pregnant?"

"I've been thinking about you and the baby you might be carrying. At first, I was mad because I'd be leaving you to raise a child on your own. But now I have hope. I have two reasons to live, a family to come home to. Before I met you Jesi, I just wanted to die."

She couldn't believe what she was hearing. *A family? A family!* Jesi beamed.

"This piece of paper," Johan unfolded the note and set it in front of her, "this tells the army and the lawyer that in the event of my death, everything goes to you."

"But Johan, I, I don't know anything about this kind of paper."

"You'll learn. I'll teach you. I want you to know for sure that you and the baby will have whatever you need or want to live a good life."

"What we will need is you."

Jesi stood up and walked to the window. She stared at the big flame tree with red flowers. Jesi had been on a rollercoaster of happiness and sadness. She felt Johan come from behind and wrap his arms around her. He kissed her head.

"I know, sweet girl. I'd give up every penny I own to come back to you." He turned her around to face him. "The best we can do is enjoy the time we have and believe that I'll return."

She leaned into his chest and listened to his heart.

"I love you, Jesi."

"I love you, too."

"Jesi, Johan," Mrs. T called to them.

"We're in here, Mom." Jesi unraveled her arms from Johan and walked toward the front door.

"*Ai,* my Neni," Mrs. T hugged Jesi.

"Are you OK?"

"Now I am."

Mrs. T pulled away and held Jesi's hands. "Grandma wants to see both of you at our house. Your dad is waiting, too."

15

September 13, 1944 — Tan Chai's House

"**F**INALLY," JESI SAID. SHE PICKED UP THE coconut husk and tossed it into a bucket on the back porch. Shining the ifet was the last thing she needed to do. It was strenuous work to rub the coconut husk across the floor throughout the entire house. Jesi spent all week cleaning the inside from top to bottom. The windows were all open, and the shower of sunlight made the floors glisten. The built-in empty shelves beckoned to be filled with books and photos. Other than her own bedroom and a few things in the kitchen, she had an empty canvas in which to paint.

Tan Chai gifted her house to Jesi and Johan as an early wedding present. She said it was getting too much for her to clean. Auntie Julia and Antonio went to stay with Antonio's dad until Auntie Julia's house was completed. A little less able to get around on her own, Tan Chai moved in with Chief and Mrs. T.

We have our very own house. And we will get to make love all day, every day. Jesi walked into her bedroom, grinning from cheek to cheek. It was bigger than the room Tan Chai had stayed in, so she opted to keep it as the main bedroom. She peeked at the clock. *Johan will be here in a little while.* Jesi changed out of her day clothes and put on a plain beach dress. She looked in her bag to make sure she had coconut oil, a canteen of water, and a blanket. *I've been dying for a swim.*

The trail down to her grandma's private cove in Pago Bay was not far from the back of the house. *Thank you, grandma.* Jesi put her fingers against her lips. She started down the gravel trail, ducked here, ducked there, avoiding tree branches. The cove was her favorite place to hide and relax. "Clank, clank, clank," the metal cans shook. They were her homemade alarms should someone come down the trail. Once she reached the bottom of the cliff, the trees gave way to a secluded area of white sand and crystal clear blue water. Jesi stood still. It was magnificent. Her lone coconut tree was still standing, tucked close to the cliff with a topful of leaves. The ripples of water crawled over the shore. It was so calm in the ocean today that the water looked like glass. There were a few puffs of white clouds studding the sky. Jesi walked to the edge of the path then took her slippers off. The feel of sand beneath her toes was exhilarating. After setting the blanket out under the coconut tree, she anchored the corners with her slippers, canteen, and bag. Jesi undressed and ran naked to the edge of the water. *Finally.* She waded into the ocean until it was just below her breasts then dipped under the water to wet her hair. Jesi turned toward the peninsula and began her laps. No one could see her as long as she swam within her imaginary boundaries.

Johan couldn't find Jesi in the house and there wasn't a family member in sight. He had to drop off a load of supplies for the wedding, but was two hours early. Johan remembered she said she might go for a swim down in the cove. He found the start of the trail and made his way. *I need to cut this for her.* The overgrown trees forced him to slow down. Just as he was about to make his next step, a sparkle from above caught his eye. He held his left foot in midair and looked up. "What the hell? Cans?" Johan backed off. He followed the rope with his eyes and realized it was a warning signal. A grin crossed his lips and spread to his eyes. Johan sidestepped around the cans and tiptoed down the trail.

There was movement in the water. He could see her arms comb through the ocean and was about to walk into the open when she stood up. The sight of her bare body aroused him. She sauntered toward the shore, wiped off with a towel then rubbed something all over her arms, increasing his excitement. Jesi dipped her fingers again in the container, and rubbed her breasts and abdomen. Johan ran his hand over his growing desire. She braced her leg up on the nearby rock to smear the stuff over her thigh and calf. He could see her mound from where he stood, and waited for her to finish the other leg.

"Don't put that on."

Jesi turned around, stunned.

"Johan, you scared me."

"I didn't mean to." He wrapped his arms around her waist and kissed her. "I was watching you," he said between kisses.

"I didn't hear the cans."

"I avoided them." He bit the right side of her neck, then the left.

"Sneaky."

He eased back just enough for Jesi to pull his shirt off then pulled her back against him.

"You're beautiful." Johan's breathing was strained. Jesi helped him remove his pants and briefs. The feel of her stiff nipples against his bare skin sent arrows down to his bulging erection.

"I can't wait."

"What?" Jesi asked.

"Sometimes sex is slow and loving," he said.

"And other times?"

"Other times it's hard," Johan pinched her nipple.

"Ouch."

"And a little painful."

"And," Jesi encouraged.

"And a lot of fun."

He picked her up and slid inside her.

"Johan."

"Did you like that?"

"Yes."

He held her against his body as he moved in and out.

"I've missed you. I've missed the feel of you around me."

"Harder, Johan."

He could hear the desire in her voice. Johan knelt on the blanket and lay her down without pulling out.

"Do you like it hard?"

"Sometimes."

"Do you like it hard right now?"

Johan buried his face in her neck.

"Yes."

"Tell me what you like, Jesi."

"I like it when you're pushing all the way inside me, Johan."

It drove him wild when she said his name. Johan rolled over so she was on top. Jesi's hair fell around her shoulders and nipples. He ran his hands along her thighs as he rocked his hips up and down against her sex.

"I want you to ride me." Johan pulled her down to ravage her lips. "Sit up and just follow me."

"I can feel you so deep this way."

"Good."

"Uh-huh."

"Put your hands on my chest," he told her. Johan watched as she closed her eyes. He increased his tempo.

"Oh god, Johan. Faster."

He did as instructed. Johan felt her muscles grip his sex, squeezing him. Jesi's fingers dug into his chest.

"I'm there, Johan, oh my god."

Johan sent his erection as far as he could push it into her. "Jesi, damn you feel . . ." Her quivering body and her moans spiraled him into an intense, long-overdue orgasm. He spewed unrecognizable words as he bucked into her. Her breasts heaved in front of him. Johan reached for a nipple with his right hand, pinching it.

"I like that," Jesi said.

Jesi lay down on him. Johan could feel her heart still racing. He held her in a vice against his chest. The fact that he loved her, that he'd be spending the rest of his life with her, made the sex even more exciting, more pleasurable.

"I love you, Jesi."

"Mmmm."

"How'd you like being on top?"

"Mmmm," she purred against his skin. "I loved it."

"I hope no one could see us down here, or your family might change their mind."

She laughed.

"No one can see, else I wouldn't have been swimming naked."

"So what do we need to do today?"

"What do you mean?" Jesi said.

"For the wedding?"

"Oh, I guess we should get up?"

"If we don't, I'd have to take you again and we'll never get out of here."

"All right." Jesi rolled off him.

"I'm using this towel."

"You're quite the mess there." She nodded toward the white goo covering his relaxed specimen. Johan cleaned himself then tossed the towel at her.

"That's dirty!"

"You need it, too." He looked at her crotch, and watched her wipe up.

"Have you touched yourself since the last time we were together?"

"What?"

Jesi stood over the pot of soup. She had prepared the coconut milk, ground corn, and fresh corn before she cleaned the house. Jesi had also chopped up the leftover barbecued chicken. In no time she was done making corn soup.

"God, woman, that smells damn good," Johan cuddled and kissed her from behind.

"You done?"

"Yup, your brother got home just in time to help me unload."

"There's soap and water over there to wash your hands."

"When I get back, we're putting running water in this house."

When you get back? Jesi's heart stopped for a second. *Don't think about it. Just enjoy the time you have left.* She filled her lungs with air then looked at Johan and smiled. Jesi ladled two bowlfuls of the soup and set them on the table.

"You did a great job in here. The house is immaculate," Johan said as he walked toward her. She was standing by the table.

"I know. I love that it's empty and we get to fill it with our own things and make it—"

He smothered her in such a passionate kiss that she encircled his neck and pulled his lips firmly against hers.

"You keep this up and we'll get soup all over the floor I just cleaned." *Who cares? Sex on the kitchen table.* She loved that he bit her bottom lip as he backed away and sat down.

"You drive me mad." He smirked at her.

"I've gone over the deep end already." Jesi walked to the counter and poured them each a cup of water.

"Have you had your period yet?"

Uh-oh. Jesi set the cups on the table and sat across from him. "No. My mom asks me every time she sees me. I think she secretly wants me to give her a grandchild."

"How do you feel about it, Jesi? You know you can be honest with me."

Jesi smiled at Johan then took a spoon of corn soup. "I'm hungry, sorry. At first, I was scared. I had helped my grandma a few times with women who were having trouble during their pregnancies. It was frightening. They were in so much pain." Jesi ate another spoonful. "But then I'd lie in bed at night and think about him, or her, growing inside me. I'd have a part of you forever."

"What's wrong?" he asked.

"Nothing." She didn't want to dampen the mood. "You're hoping I'm pregnant, too?"

"Yes. I think about you chasing a little boy or girl around the meadows."

"Meadows?"

"In the Catskills. I'd love to show you my grandfather's land."

"Oh." Something etched at her heart.

"Hey, I didn't say we'd leave Guam forever. Is that what you're thinking?"

She nodded yes. "I can't leave. I thought you wanted to live on Guam. You said it was so beautiful you could stay." Panic rose in her voice.

"Jesi, I'll live wherever you want to live. But I'd love to show you where I spent my summers."

"I'm sorry, I didn't mean to be silly." Jesi was relieved.

"I'd follow you to the ends of the earth, Jessica Taimanglo."

Jesi beamed. She liked the sound of her name as it rolled off his tongue. "You haven't touched your soup."

"Don't worry. You'll have to get me another bowl." Johan said.

She watched as he gobbled his food. "Slow down, there's plenty more."

"It's fit for a king. We don't get this kind of meal at chow."

"Chow?" Jesi watched as he continued to eat at a normal human being's pace.

"Mealtime. What's this dish called in Chamorro?"

"*Atulen elotes.*"

"Since you and your family have been feeding me, I can do more push-ups, pull-ups, and sit-ups," Johan bragged.

That's why you're hard all over.

"What you smirking at?"

"Nothing," Jesi replied.

"Uh-huh."

"Another bowl?" Jesi asked.

"Please. So I can't come see you till we're married? That's in ten days."

Jesi set a fresh bowl of soup in front of him.

"You can't wait that long?" She teased him.

"Can you?"

"Only because I'll be very busy."

"Doing what?"

16

September 23, 1944 — Orote Peninsula

J OHAN STOOD UP THEN SNAGGED HIS newly pressed uniform top off a hook. He was glad a local family provided laundry services, and that new uniforms were just given out. Jesi wanted him to wear his army clothes, not that he had much else to choose from.

"You ready man?" Calhoun walked in.

"More than ready. I never thought I'd do this again."

"Never?"

Johan shook his head.

"Got the rings?" Calhoun asked.

"Yup." Johan patted his pocket. "The guys all ready to go?"

"They're in the jeep. Got the marriage license?"

"Yup. Thanks again for tracking a commissioner down. And finding a priest to do this."

"The locals were so grateful they didn't have any reservations. And as soon as they found out her grandma's name, well, it was a done deal." Calhoun shrugged his shoulders.

"I'll have to get used to it," Johan said.

"What?" Calhoun asked.

"Praying. Church. They're very religious, the older ones especially."

"It's not so bad man," Calhoun added. "Helps me sleep at night. Keeps me going so that I make it back home to my wife and kids."

"Oh."

"Let's go, Sarge. We don't want you to be late."

"All right." Johan picked up a medium-sized box wrapped in newspaper.

"She'll love it, Sarge. And he's waiting in the jeep, too."

Johan followed Calhoun outside. "Thanks for coming guys," Johan shook hands with Smithy and Miller. "And Donnelly, I hope it wasn't an inconvenience." Johan shook the army combat cameraman's hand, too.

"Not a big deal, Sergeant Landers. It's kind of hard to turn down the cash."

"What's money without a good woman to spoil?" Johan grinned at Donnelly before getting into the jeep. Donnelly's job as a combat photographer was to record soldiers at war — in battle and respite. It was Donnelly's day off. Johan offered not just extra cash, but an opportunity to record a native wedding.

"Let's roll," Johan said.

Calhoun revved the jeep's engine and the men were on their way.

"Even with all the damage, it's still paradise isn't it?"

"Especially when you're in love," Calhoun responded. "But yes, I mean how many people in America get to drive along that big blue ocean out there?"

Jesi sat still with her eyes closed. She and Mrs. T were in Jesi's kitchen. Jesi took a deep breath to calm her nerves. It was making her a little sick.

"You OK, Neni?" Mrs. T asked, securing the last flower into Jesi's bun.

Jesi's hair was pulled back behind her head in a loose gathering. It framed her jawline and toned neck and shoulders. The lone white-and-yellow plumeria was nestled between two red hibiscuses.

"Yes, I just have butterflies all over my stomach."

"You'll be fine." Mrs. T walked to move in front of Jesi.

"Stand up."

As Jesi stood, she watched a teardrop roll down her mom's cheek.

"You're going to make me cry." Jesi reached up to wipe the droplet.

"You're beautiful, Neni. And your dress, you did a great job sewing it."

"I learned from the best." Mrs. T had been teaching Jesi how to sew since Jesi was five years old.

"And to think it was just an old sheet. You look like one of those Greek goddesses."

"I know I should have put some sleeves on, but I have always loved this style. Do you think he'll like it?"

"Neni, he's going to faint when he sees you. You even take my breath away."

"Thank you, Mom." Jesi paused. "I'm still a little scared. What if I'm not a good wife?"

"Nonsense. You'll be fine. You know more than I did when I got married. He better be good to you."

"He is." Jesi smiled thinking of Johan down at the cove.

"You made those, too?" Mrs. T nodded at Jesi's new slippers.

"I wanted to match my dress. Peter had a pair on at one time. That's where I got the idea."

"What did you use?"

"I saved one of the sacks that Johan had brought up and covered the top, see." Jesi slid one foot out. "I sewed the broken shells to the rubber straps."

"Can you make me one?"

"Of course. Peter said the Japanese call these *zoris*. It's a pretty name."

"He's here," Chief said.

The women turned around to see Chief at the entrance to the kitchen. Jesi stood frozen to the floor. Chief had cut his long hair and shaved his beard.

"I cannat give you away looking like a—"

"But there was nothing wrong with the way you looked."

"I wanna be clean for your wedding. Ill all grow back anyway."

Jesi ran to Chief and hugged him as if her life depended on it. "I'm so sorry I was disrespectful." She tried her best not to cry.

"Stop saying sorry, Jesi. I forgif you already."

"I know, but—"

"You don't want him to see your eyes all red so don cry."

Jesi felt Chief loosen his grip and push her back.

"Ai my girl, you all grown up. You look as beautiful as your mom when I married her." Jesi saw her father glance at Mrs. T.

"It's time to go," Mrs. T said.

Jesi nodded. She took a deep breath. And another. "I'm ready." Jesi followed her mom and dad out the front door. "It's a perfect day."

There was a gentle wind in the air and small white clouds in the sky. Jesi could see a military tent that was set up as a temporary chapel. It was erected between her house and her parents' house.

"There's more people than I expected, Mom. It was just supposed to be close family," Jesi said as they walked to the chapel.

"You know how it goes, Neni. I'm just glad we have enough chairs, thanks to Johan. He's very resourceful."

"Mm." Jesi could see several men in uniform. *There he is.* Johan looked at her. *Oh my god.* He was a man of men. His broad shoulders hinted of the muscle underneath. But it was his clean-shaven jaw – strong and square — and his intense eyes that captivated her. The flash of a camera caught her attention. *A photographer?* Finally, they reached the back of the chapel.

"I love you, Neni," Mrs. T hugged her, and Jesi saw that her mom had already started to cry.

"I love you, too." Jesi was still holding strong.

"Go ahead, walk slowly with your dad."

Jesi couldn't understand her mom. She was too distracted by the man waiting for her. They neared Johan. *Those eyes, it's as if he's peeling my dress off.* She had to hide her lust with a grin. *Why can't he stop staring at me? Well jeez, Jesi, stop looking at him.* Jesi was now standing by his side.

"God bless you, my girl," Chief said.

She hugged her father and was grateful he pecked her on the cheek or she may have very well balled like a child in front of everyone.

"You are the most magnificent, beautiful creature in the world. I've half the mind to take you right here," Johan whispered.

"Stop, Johan," Jesi retorted under her breath. She pinched his bicep as they walked closer to the priest. "You're looking quite handsome yourself."

"What are we supposed to do?" Johan whispered.

"Just follow the priest, and everyone else. They'll show us."

Jesi and Johan stood quietly as the priest began the ceremony. There was the first reading, the second reading, and the Gospel.

The priest started his homily. *We're only halfway through.* Jesi smoothed the front of her dress covering her thigh as they sat and listened. It was all she could do to keep from holding his hand.

"Everyone, please stand. Jesi and Johan, face each other," the priest said.

Finally.

"Jesi and Johan, did you come here of your own free will to give yourselves to one another in marriage?"

"We did."

"Do you promise to love and honor one another as husband and wife for the rest of your lives?"

"We do."

"Since it's your intention to marry, please join your hands and declare your agreement in front of God and your family."

Tears of joy spilled onto her cheeks. Jesi couldn't hold them back any longer.

"Johan, repeat after me," the priest said.

She somewhat understood Johan even though he spoke clearly. When Johan finished, the priest turned to Jesi and repeated what he wanted her to say.

You can do this. Jesi took a deep breath.

"I, Jesi, take you, Johan, to be my husband." *Breathe. Smile.* "I promise to be true to you in good times and especially in bad times, in health and especially in sickness." *Just let the tears go.* "I will love you always and honor you for the rest of my life."

The priest blessed the rings.

"Beautiful," she whispered as Johan slipped the ring on her finger. *He really made them.*

"Johan, take this ring, this precious ring you made, as a symbol of my love and of my fidelity. In the name of the Father, and the Son, and the Holy Spirit."

"You may kiss the bride."

Jesi looked at Johan. She hoped he would restrain his kisses somewhat though she could see the longing in his eyes. Johan bent down then kissed her, and just long enough. He pulled her into a hug.

"Out of respect, I'm not going to ravage you right now."

Jesi smiled from ear to ear. "I can't wait till you do."

The priest asked for the thirteen coins from Johan. He blessed them as symbols of Johan's pledge to care for her and provide for her.

After a few more prayers, Tan Chai pinned the *belo* – a lacy white cloth — over Jesi and Johan's shoulders. It took a little while, and her hands were shaky, but she did it. The cloth bound the couple together spiritually. Jesi wiped another tear that fell. She knew Johan couldn't understand what was being said in Chamorro, but the words touched Jesi's heart. It was time to receive communion.

Once communion finished, Auntie Julia walked up to Jesi. She was their godmother for the wedding. Jesi followed Auntie Julia to the statue of the Virgin Mary to present the saint with a bouquet of flowers. *"Hu nå'i hao, Nanå-hu as Maria . . ."* The elderly ladies continued to sing the offering song, and sent Jesi's emotions over the edge, again. Jesi took the napkin from Auntie Julia then made the sign of the cross. "Virgin Mary," Jesi stuttered between sobs. *Where was all this coming from? I'm getting married for Pete's sake, not at a funeral.* "I ask for your help, guidance, and strength," she wiped her eyes, "in my marriage to be an honorable and loving wife. Si Yu'us ma'åse'. In the name of the Father . . ."

"I love you, Neni," Auntie Julia said, as she walked Jesi back to her chair.

"I love you, too, *Nina*, thank you." *Nina* was the term for "godmother."

The priest said his final prayer.

"I now give you Mr. and Mrs. Johan Landers."

The newlywed couple watched as their godparents — Auntie Julia and Uncle Kin — came up to sign the marriage license. Uncle Kin stepped in as godfather since Johan didn't have any relatives on Guam.

"Shall we, Mrs. Landers?"

"Yes, we shall." She took his arm.

Jesi and Johan walked down the aisle smiling and thanking the family.

"We need to go to my parents' house first. The elders will come over and we have to ámen them."

"OK."

Jesi and Johan knelt on the pillows and waited in the living room. The new couple paid their respects to the older people, and listened to the advice they gave about marriage. Jesi did a lot of translating for Johan, which sometimes made him laugh. Once they ámened the last elder, Jesi and Johan stood up and were just about to leave the house.

"Sergeant Landers, Mrs. Landers, would you like to take some pictures outside?" Donnelly said.

"You up for it, Jesi? Do we have time?" Johan asked.

"Go ahead, Neni," Mrs. T encouraged.

"The family must come with us, Mom."

Jesi and Johan and the immediate family followed Donnelly to a space with a clear backdrop of Pago Bay. Donnelly posed the couple together, with close family, and then individually.

"Do we get to see them soon?" Jesi asked when Donnelly had finished.

"Yes, Ma'am. I'll develop them real fast and hand them over to Sergeant Landers."

Mrs. T got everyone's attention to head back to the house.

"Let's go, it's time to eat." Jesi said.

"You mighty eager there, Wife." Johan's big smile took over his entire face.

"Funny. Husband, I'm starving. I ate breakfast, but my god it's as if I'm eating for two I'm so hungry. Feed me."

"Holy heck!" Johan's eyes were as wide as golf balls when they walked into the food tent.

"Are we supposed to eat all this?"

"Not just us, but we always make a lot so that there's plenty of leftovers for family to take home."

Johan did the sign of the cross as Auntie Julia blessed the table. It was becoming less foreign to him, and even brought back distant memories of his early childhood years when he attended church services with his parents.

"She blesses us in our marriage, and for your safe return to Guam." Johan heard Jesi translate. He did the sign of the cross to end the prayer. Johan followed Jesi to the table.

"How hungry are you?"

"Ravenous!" He gave her a wanton look. "I'm starving for food, Jesi, for food," he teased.

"Uh-huh. Here's the red rice."

"It is very orange."

"You're just going to have to put a little bit of everything on your plate, OK."

"All right." *It's not all going to fit on this plate.*

"I'm so excited you brought a photographer."

"I wanted to capture everything about today."

"Thank you. I can't wait to see the pictures."

"You and your family did beautiful work here, setting everything up."

"I could have gone for something a lot smaller, but it truly is wonderful."

Johan put a piece of a sliced banana on his plate. "What is this? It smells like cinnamon."

"Bananas with coconut milk, cinnamon, and a little sugar, *gollai áppan agá*."

He nodded, still chewing. When Jesi turned away, Johan snuck another bite. "I couldn't help it."

"That's OK. The older people like to do that. And you're old right?" She smirked at him.

"Very funny. We'll see who's laughing tonight."

Johan pinched her hips.

"Hey, I almost dropped my plate."

"Almost doesn't count." Johan grinned back at her.

They reached the end of the table.

"You have to get a piece of this pig skin. It's crunchy."

"I've never seen one cooked like that."

"Here you go."

He waited for Jesi to fit the golden brown skin on his plate.

"Our table is over there."

Johan followed her to a decorated set of tables and chairs.

"My parents, grandma, and our godparents will join us."

"That means I have to behave?" Johan chided Jesi as they set their plates down.

"For now." She shot him back an amused smile.

"Jesi," he turned to face her before they sat down. "You are even more pretty today, and I didn't think that was possible."

"It must be my dress. Do you like it?"

"It's becoming."

"I made it myself."

"You can sew, too? I'm one lucky man, Jessica Landers."

"I like the sound of that."

"And I can't wait to peel that dress off you." Johan kissed his wife. "Now sit and eat."

"Look here, you two."

Johan turned to face Donnelly.

"Get closer."

"Don't forget to grab a plate, Mr. Donnelly."

"Thank you Ma'am, when I'm done."

Johan watched as Donnelly walked away. "I can't wait to see all the pictures," Johan said then looked at Jesi, "Do you have a camera?"

"Thank you again, mom and dad." Jesi hugged her parents. "It was a lovely wedding."

"You're welcome, Neni. Here's some cake and food for later."

"This was a beautiful display of love and family. Thank you for entrusting me with your daughter."

"I know you take good care of my girl, Johan, or you answer to me," Chief said.

"Daddy!" Jesi scolded her father, smiling.

"You two have a good night. Go, go already." Mrs. T chased them away.

Jesi gave her parents one last hug then took Johan's hand and walked toward their house.

"I don't think I've ever kissed so many people at one time," Johan said.

"I know," Jesi laughed. "That's just our custom. And there's going to be more of that in the future." Jesi couldn't feel her feet on the ground anymore. "Johan, put me down." Jesi giggled.

"You walk much too slow, sweet girl. I've been waiting forever to get you all to myself."

I'm in trouble. Jesi gazed up at Johan as he carried her in front of him.

"Your eyes are twinkling," he said.

"Are they?"

It was already dark, but the moon and the lanterns along the gravel road illuminated the night. They reached the front door of their house.

"Close your eyes," Johan said.

"What, why?"

"Just do it."

"OK." Jesi could feel Johan reach for the doorknob. She heard a gentle kick to the door, and it creaked as it swung open.

"Keep your eyes closed."

Jesi felt the pressure of his mouth on hers. She pursed her lips together, denying him access to her tongue.

"Really?"

"Might as well keep my mouth shut, too."

"We'll see about that."

Jesi felt Johan take a few steps in, and heard the door close behind them.

"I'm going to set you down, but keep your eyes closed."

She leaned back against his chest.

"You can open them now."

His lips were so close to her ear she could feel his breath. *Oh my god, what did he do.* Jesi stood speechless.

"You don't like it?"

"I, I . . ."

She unraveled herself from his arms and walked through the living room. Lanterns filled the house with enough light for Jesi to see vases and pots of flowers everywhere. Orchids, hibiscuses, plumerias, and wildflowers studded the hallway, tables, and corners.

"How did you do this?"

"I had help from my guys."

"When?"

"Since we started eating."

"I love it." Jesi walked back to Johan. "It's the most beautiful, nicest thing anyone has ever done for me." She kissed his lips. "And I see we'll have no problem finding our way to the bedroom." Jesi nodded toward the hallway that was also decorated with lanterns and flower petals.

"We'll have enough time to christen the kitchen," Johan said as he kissed her right cheek. "And the living room," he planted one on her neck. "And the hallway," he sucked on her left ear. "And the other bedrooms," he licked and bit the lobe of her right ear. "But tonight, I want you in our bed."

She felt him lift her off the floor. "All this sex talk is making me very excited."

"Horny, Jesi. It's making you very horny."

He set her down just in front of the bed. Jesi turned and stole a kiss.

"This dress," he said as he ran his finger along her neck and chest, "shows just enough and not too much." Johan traced her skin right down to the bottom of the V-neck. "Face the bed."

Jesi felt his hands on her shoulders. Then he kissed the back of her neck. *Oh god.* She didn't realize she was sensitive there. Johan kissed across her left shoulder. When he had nowhere else to go, he teased across her right shoulder. Jesi threw her head backwards and felt Johan's hand encircle her neck. He bit her right ear. "Johan," she whispered as she rocked her hips into him. He pulled her dress up over her head. She nearly crumbled to the floor when he pulled her back against him and ran his fingers over her womanhood. Even through her panty, his touch bore into her clitoris. Jesi felt his hands around her shoulders again, and his erection massaged her skin.

"You still have your clothes on."

"I know. These looked beautiful on your hair, but they're coming off."

Johan handed her the flowers. Their scent was as divine as what she was feeling.

His hands traveled to her hips then the front of her pelvis. Johan hovered on her tummy then moved upward. Her excitement rose knowing that he'd reach her breasts soon. Jesi dropped the flowers as she raised her arms to grab his hair.

"Do you like my touching you this way?"

"Yes." Jesi faintly answer him. *God, squeeze them already.* He was still caressing her tummy.

"Tell me, Jesi, what do you want me to do."

"Pinch my nipples."

"I don't think so."

What?

"You'll have to wait."

"Wait? No!" Jesi pressed her right thigh against her left thigh. *God.* Johan was biting the back of her neck again.

"Where's your coconut oil?" Johan squeezed her butt.

"For what?" Jesi was panting. Johan's fingers lingered so close to her clitoris, but he didn't touch it.

"Just tell me where it is."

"No."

In a split second, he scooped her up on the bed, lay between her legs, and held her wrists above her head, sucking and biting at her lips.

"Where's the oil?" Johan asked again.

Jesi felt him press his hips firmly into her, rocking it back and forth, back and forth.

"OK, OK," Jesi caved, anything for him to suck on her, to be inside her. "It's there on the dresser." She watched as he leaped off the bed. Johan took off his clothing except for the briefs. Jesi could not tear her eyes away from him massaging his bulge. She waited for Johan to discard his underwear, but he didn't budge. She looked up at his face. He was staring at her. His lips curved into a mischievous smile as he opened the jar and brought it over to the bed.

"Turn onto your tummy."

No.

Her body moved.

Don't do it.

It had a mind of its own. Jesi felt a dribble of oil along the middle of her back. He smoothed it along her spine, upward across her shoulders. Though he wasn't touching her clitoris, she was no less stimulated. Deft hands slithered along the sides of her ribcage and over her lower back. She arched her hips upward as he massaged her ass. Johan roamed to her left thigh. "Oh god." He squeezed the inside of her thigh, too close to her vagina. "God, Johan, I need you."

"Patience, sweet girl, patience."

Johan continued his tortuous massage down her left leg then on to her right. He straddled her and rubbed his erection against her butt.

"Your juices seeped through your panty."

"That's because you've been teasing me all day, all night."

He turned her over, slid her panties off, and sat between her legs.

"Spread your legs wider, Jesi."

Oh god.

She opened her thighs and watched as he ran his hand along the length of his penis.

"Feel how wet you are down there."

What?

"Jesi," he said in such a low, hot voice it sent shivers through every cell in her body.

"OK."

So wet.

Her fingers found their way to her sensitive spot.

"I could climax this way."

Johan grabbed both her hands and pinned them over her head again.

"Hey!"

"I didn't say you could feel that good."

In seconds he was in her, and breathing by her ear.

"You're very wet."

Jesi closed her eyes and concentrated on that sensation that had been building up.

"Faster."

And then he was out. She opened her eyes and looked at him.

"Turn over on your hands and knees."

"Why?"

"You'll like it."

"Promise?" She grinned at him.

"I promise."

Jesi turned. Johan stroked her butt cheeks as he ran his manhood between her inner thighs, gliding over her opening.

"Do you want me inside you?"

"Yes."

Without hesitation, he was in her, moving fast and hard.

It is much better this way.

"Jesi."

She could barely hear him. *Oh god, I'm almost there.* "More."

He did as he was told.

"Johan, I'm, yes, oh god . . ."

Jesi drove her hips backwards, her orgasm engulfing Johan's erection, and fueling his release.

"Jesi."

Johan shuddered behind her, over her.

He sounds so, so, like an animal, so good.

"I've been waiting for that all week," he said.

God, oh god, how could sex be so great.

"Don't come out yet."

"All right."

17

September 24, 1944 — Jesi and Johan's House

JESI TURNED TO LIE ON HER BACK. SHE opened her eyes. The sun peeked through the shutters and the thin curtains. She glanced to her left. They made love all night. Johan was sound asleep with his arm draped across her tummy. *I better see what I have to make for breakfast. Or is it lunchtime already?* Jesi crept from under his arm and sat up. She slipped into a nightdress then had to sit back down as nausea took over. *Oh god, I need a trash can.* Jesi bound across the room and made it to the trash just in time. She heaved out what was their midnight snack of leftover wedding cake. Jesi was so sick she had to kneel on the floor, and heaved again.

"Jesi!" Johan lurched out of bed and was by her side.

"I'm not feeling good." *Oh god.*

"Can I get you anything?"

"A towel." Jesi held on to the metal bin for extra support. "In the bathroom. I think I'm done."

Johan returned with a towel in no time.

"Water please." She wiped her mouth then lay along the right side of her body on the floor, head spinning.

"What's wrong?"

"I'm OK, a little dizzy. Just put the water down."

"Anything else I can do?" Johan sat on the floor beside her.

Jesi could sense the fear in his voice.

"I feel much better." She wiggled her head and shoulder onto his lap in a comfortable position. "I was suddenly sick when I got out of bed. I've never felt like that before." Jesi closed her eyes and rested for a minute. "I'm pregnant!" Jesi tried to sit up, but instead had to lean back onto his lap.

"What?" Johan crinkled his brows at her.

"My mom said if I didn't have my period or if I woke up sick, then I was pregnant."

"You're pregnant?"

"Yes." She beamed.

Johan scooped her into his arms in a great big bear hug.

"We're going to have a baby!"

She had never seen him smile so big.

"I'm still a little sick," she made a face.

"Sorry." He stood up and carried her back to their bed. "Should I get your mom, or grandma?"

"No, no, not yet. Could you throw that bag of trash out then come lie with me?"

"Of course, sweetheart. I'll be right back."

I'm pregnant. Jesi smiled. *We're going to have a baby.*

"You're still smiling so you can't be too sick," Johan said as he knelt in front of her. "You are mighty beautiful when you wake up, Jesi, even after you've been ill." He kissed her forehead then stood up and draped the thin blanket over her.

"Thank you."

"I have a surprise for you."

"A surprise?" Jesi watched as Johan turned and walked to get the box in the corner of the bedroom. "That wasn't there yesterday morning."

"I know."

"Your guys huh?"

"Yup, they're good men, as battle buddies and friends."

"I like them. They've been so kind to help us with Auntie Julia's house, and have always been respectful." Jesi scooted in from the edge of the bed and sat up against the wall.

"You all right sitting up like that?"

"I seem to be."

"Happy day-after-wedding day." Johan leaned to kiss her on her lips.

"I didn't get you anything."

"Jesi, you've given me my life back, and you don't even know it. Open the box."

She tore at the newspaper. *Take it easy.* "I'm sorry, I haven't had a present in a while."

"Nothing to be sorry about, sweetheart."

"I love you, Johan." Jesi leaned over to him. He bent his head down and kissed her lips.

"I love you too, now open the box already."

Jesi pulled at the cardboard flaps and removed the stuffed papers.

"A camera!" Jesi took the camera out of the box. "How did you get this?"

"I bought it off the photographer. Do you like it?"

"I love it. I never dreamed I could have my own camera. Thank you, thank you!" Jesi set the camera down on the safe side of the bed and hugged her husband. She could feel the tightness of his embrace. "I love your hugs. They make me feel safe."

"That's good because I love you more than anything, and I will keep you safe, always."

Jesi leaned back away from his chest and smiled at him. "Do you know how to work this?"

"Yup. May I?" Johan held his hand out.

Jesi gave him the camera. She listened as he explained to her how all the buttons worked, and how to hold it.

"Smile," Johan said as he pointed the lens at her.

Jesi did as she was told. She tilted her head to the side too, smiling. Then she started to make funny faces, and Johan clicked away.

"It's my turn."

Johan handed the camera to her. She positioned it as he had explained.

"You have to smile, Johan."

She waited.

He smiled.

"Now show me your serious army face." Jesi snapped a picture. "That's scary. Give me your, um, I-want-to-have-sex-with-you face." Jesi grinned behind the camera. "Mm, yes, that's the face."

"Oh really?"

"I'm not done," she said as she leaned back so he couldn't grab her. "Make a muscle with those arms."

After a few more pictures, she set the camera on the bedside table and moved all the packaging away. Johan was lying on his back, his legs hanging off the mattress, and his fingers laced behind his head. He was only in his briefs and she could see his erection. Jesi straddled his hips.

"I'm all excited now." Jesi leaned down to kiss his chest as she rocked her hips against his growing sex.

"You don't feel sick anymore?"

"No. I," she said then kissed the left side of his neck, "want," she made a trail of kisses to the right side, "to," she scooted lower on his legs and began kissing down his chest and abdomen, "lick," she slithered her tongue down his shaft, skimming his briefs, "you." Johan lifted his hips to push his erection against her mouth. Jesi pulled the material off his penis, releasing it to see his length in all its glory.

"*Hoe*', Jesi, Johan."

Jesi froze. "It's my mom again. She has the worst timing," Jesi whispered, and got up. "Just a minute, Mom."

"Everyone's waiting for you and Johan to open your gifts. It's two o'clock already."

"Sorry, Mom. I forgot. I'll be right out. Wait for me OK?"

"OK, Neni."

"Let's hurry up. I want to tell my mom the good news," Jesi said to Johan as she planted a kiss on his lips.

"Ah, Jesi."

Jesi followed Johan's gaze to his penis.

"Sorry." She frowned. "I promise to make it up to you tonight."

"Gonna hold you to it, sweetheart."

Jesi watched as Johan slipped his briefs over his erection and stood up. He pulled her into a hug.

"I can't wait," he said as he squeezed her butt.

"I'll meet you in the kitchen, OK."

"All right."

Jesi got dressed and tried her best to look presentable. She used the bathroom then washed her face and brushed her teeth. Taking a deep breath, she walked to the kitchen. "Hi, Mom."

"Hi, Neni," Mrs. T stood up to hug Jesi.

Jesi smiled. She couldn't help it. "Guess what?"

"What?"

"I'm pregnant!"

"You're pregnant?"

"I think so."

"Oh, Jesi!" Mrs. T hugged her again.

"How do you know? You haven't had your period yet?"

"I woke up very sick this morning."

"Oh."

"Like now. Mom, what did you cook? You smell." Jesi sat down and crossed her arms on the table to rest her head.

"I just made *eskabeche,* Jesi. You love that."

Eskabeche is a mixture of vegetables and fried fish that's flavored with turmeric and vinegar.

"Not any more. It's making me sick. Does the house smell like that?"

"Yes, we had it for lunch."

"I can't go over there. Oh god, I feel like throwing up again."

"OK, Neni. Johan, come, Boy. She's sick."

Jesi heard him rush to her side.

"How about you get back in bed?" Johan said more as an order than a suggestion.

Jesi nodded. He carried her back to their room, and Mrs. T followed them.

"I'll make you something for your morning sickness."

"Thank you, Mom. And go ahead and open the gifts without me."

"Ai, no, Neni."

"Please, Mom, I don't mind. I'm not going to make it."

"What do you feel like eating, anything?"

18

September 30, 1994 — Jesi and Johan's House

J OHAN POURED HIMSELF A CUP OF COFFEE then went to sit out on the back porch. *"Guella yan Guello, dispensa yu pot fabot sa bai hu gimen kafe."* He asked the taotaomo'na grandmother and grandfather to excuse him because he was going to drink coffee outside in the middle of the night. Johan learned that it was very important to respect the taotaomo'na, and to ask their permission, especially when it was still dark. It was just before 0500 hours, too early to wake Jesi. His CO allowed him to come back home every day after he and his platoon finished up their garrison chores. *Home.* It felt so right.

Though the war was still raging throughout the Pacific and Europe, Guam was secured and the 305th soldiers were waiting on the island for orders to their next mission. Other than helping cut brush, cleaning their campsite on Orote, and ensuring the men stayed combat ready, there wasn't much for Johan to do while he and his soldiers were in garrison. Some of the men even hunted for Japanese souvenirs, and made jewelry from Japanese aircraft debris.

Johan was happy beyond measure. He was committed to dying in this war until he met her. It tore at him that he'd be leaving Jesi and their unborn baby. Johan took a sip of his coffee then crunched on a guyuria. It was breezy and the roosters were waking up. The moon still cast a glow over Pago Bay. He stood up and walked to the edge of the porch. *No wonder she loves it back here. It's stunning even in the dark.* Johan finished his coffee, but left a few pieces of guyuria on the plate. One day he'll see what animal was taking his food.

Johan walked into the living room and pulled out a box from his pack. He brought the box into the kitchen and set it on the table. As he opened the big box, he put the smaller box to the side. The lamp provided enough light for him to see the pictures. Donnelly was quick to process the wedding photos and the photos from Jesi's new camera. Johan almost didn't recognize himself in the picture. It was of him and Jesi sitting behind the table after they had gotten their food. The man that stared back at him was smiling and overjoyed. Jesi was beaming, too. He flipped through the photos, still in shock of how his life had changed since he landed on Guam. When he finished, Johan placed the pictures, and the little box, back into the big box. He replaced the cover then tied the ribbon and looked at his watch. Mom would be here soon. As long as Jesi had her banana doughnuts for breakfast, the morning sickness wasn't bad.

Johan got up and walked to their room to check on her.

"Hi," she said.

"You're awake." Johan squatted down beside the bed. "Good morning, beautiful." He kissed her lips.

"Good morning."

"Good morning, baby. How's my girl, or boy?" Johan kissed her belly, and lingered there for a moment then sat beside Jesi. *"Biba Kumpleåños, Biba Kumpleåños."*

"You remembered? And you learned how to sing 'Happy Birthday' in Chamorro?"

"I would never forget. You can tell me if I have a terrible voice. I'm a big boy," Johan grinned at her.

"But I loved it." Jesi leaned up to hug him.

"How are you feeling?"

"No morning sickness so far."

"I know you didn't want a party or anything, but Mom will be here soon. I'm going to learn how to make *boñelos aga'* for your birthday."

"Really? You're going to cook?"

"I thought I should learn since you need it every day."

"Thank you, I can't wait."

"My pleasure, but you might change your mind once you taste my cooking."

"Mom's a great teacher so you'll have it down in no time."

There was a soft knock on the front door then it creaked open.

"Hoe', Johan." Mrs. T called.

Speaking of the angel. "Coming, Mom," he said, with his head turned toward the bedroom door. He looked at Jesi, "I have another surprise for you in the kitchen when you're ready to get up."

"Another surprise? You've done so much already."

"You'll love it. Besides, it's your actual birthday present." Johan kissed Jesi and gave her a hug then walked to the kitchen.

"Good morning, Mom," Johan ámened Mrs. T.

"*Buenas dias, låhi-hu.* How's she doing?"

"She seems to be fine."

"You ready?"

"Yes, Ma'am."

"Peel all those bananas and put them in that bowl then squeeze them with your hand."

Johan followed her directions.

Mrs. T poured oil into a pot and lit the gas burner. "You want to get your oil heated up before you mix the batter."

"OK," Johan said, looking at what Mrs. T was doing.

"That's good with the bananas."

"OK."

"I'm going to pour in sugar and you mix it together with that hand you used."

"Like that?" *The guys would be laughing at me if they saw what I was doing.*

"Yes. Taste it and make sure it's real sweet because when we add the flour, it will not be so sweet."

"All that will dissolve in here?" He asked about the flour Mrs. T put into the bowl.

"Yes. Add just a little bit of this baking powder. Just like that, OK?"

"OK."

"Have you been going outside a lot when it's dark?"

Johan looked at her confused.

"Keep stirring till it's all mixed together."

"I sit on the porch and drink coffee in the mornings, just like earlier this morning before you came. Why?"

"Yesterday, I needed to pick some leaves down a little bit from the side of your house. I always pick from there."

"And what happened?" Johan's guard went up.

"You know the taotaomo'na are real, right?"

"Yes." *I think so.*

"I'm sure Jesi has told you that if you ever see a clearing in the jungle, you need to leave it alone and don't mess it up. It's the taotaomo'na house."

"She did say that."

"They've made a clearing behind the tree that's on the side of the back bedroom. It's hard to see it, but it's there."

"Should I be worried?"

The sun started to peak in the sky and light was coming through the kitchen window.

"OK, that's done. Wash your hand and I'll show you how to fry them. You don't need to worry."

"That's a relief."

"But you need to respect that area over there. They don't usually like men."

"Oh."

"You see those bruises on your arm."

"Yes, and I can't remember bumping into anything, but I guess I must have. They are on my other arm, too." He showed Mrs. T.

"It's the taotaomo'na, they pinched you. Does that hurt?" Mrs. T pushed on a couple bruises.

"No."

"They like you so keep doing whatever you're doing. The taotaomo'na will protect you when you leave, too."

"Would they take guyuria or boñelos?"

"They could. Why?"

"Sometimes I leave my coffee and dessert out in the back because I need to go to the bathroom. When I return, it's gone, and I still haven't seen any animals around."

"Is the plate clean or does it have crumbs?"

"Clean."

"It's them. Just keep doing what you're doing, Johan. Don't change and don't be scared. They like you."

"OK." *That's scarier than a platoon of Japs with guns.* Johan was freaked out, but he didn't show it.

"That's interesting how you shape the boñelos." Johan had been watching Mrs. T take doughnut batter in one hand and plop some into the oil.

"It's your turn."

Johan reached into the bowl just as Mrs. T had done then squeezed batter an inch above the surface of the oil.

"Very good," Jesi said, walking up beside him. "The smell dragged me out of bed."

Johan moved his hand back into the bowl of batter then turned around to smile at Jesi.

"You are sworn to secrecy."

"My lips are sealed."

Johan accepted a kiss on his left cheek.

"Morning, Mom." Jesi hugged Mrs. T.

"Happy birthday, Neni." Mrs. T hugged Jesi back.

Johan watched as Jesi reached for a doughnut that was cooked.

"Mmm, these are very soft. You did a good job."

"Mom's a great teacher, just like you said," he smiled at Jesi.

"The taotaomo 'na like him, Neni. Look at all his bruises."

"Oh my goodness, Johan, they pinched you five times."

"I've been feeding them, too, apparently," Johan said.

"What do you mean?" Jesi asked.

Johan fried the last bit of batter leaving the women to talk about him and his taotaomo 'na friends. He turned the burner off then washed his hands and the dishes.

"Come over to the house, you two. Just a little lunch for your birthday, Neni," Mrs. T said, as she stood up from the table.

"OK, thank you."

"Thanks for showing me how to make doughnuts," Johan said, as he åmened his mother-in-law good-bye. He waited for Mrs. T to close the door behind her then turned to Jesi.

"Did you really like the boñelos I made?"

"Of course. I don't think I could have eaten even one if they weren't good. And look, I ate half the bowl."

Johan walked up to Jesi and wrapped his arms around her waist.

"So, what's my surprise birthday present?" Jesi asked.

"It's in that box over there with the ribbon tied on top."

19

"**J**OHAN, IS THE ENTIRE MILITARY HERE?**" Jesi was in awe of the massive numbers of vehicles and buildings. *In a little more than a week he'd have to stay here and wouldn't be allowed to go back home at all.*

Johan's unit was preparing to depart Guam. He had wanted to show Jesi where he would be. Jesi had never been on the peninsula as it was already occupied by the US Marines even before she was born. She tried to be attentive.

"Hey, you all right?" Johan asked.

"Uh-huh."

"Sad?"

"Yes."

"I know, sweetheart. I am, too. But, maybe you and Peter could bring me and the guys our lunch next week then you'd be able to come on camp?"

"Really?" She looked at Johan, hopeful. "Then I'd still be able to see you up to the day you leave?"

"I'm sure I can convince my CO."

"I'd love that." Jesi managed a half smile for him then looked out through her side of the jeep. She felt him squeeze her hand and she squeezed back.

They drove past fields of tents. The roads were paved and smooth compared to the rocky gravel roads outside of Orote. The roar of a plane caught Jesi's attention and she looked up. It was taking off.

"Will you be leaving in one of those?"

"Yup."

Jesi had to blink back a tear, and tried not to think about the inevitable, but it wasn't working. The jeep shook a lot when they reached a dirt road. Then it stopped.

Johan got out of the jeep and was coming to her side. He opened the door.

"Come," he said.

She took his hand and followed behind him. They walked a short distance on a narrow trail and he never once let her go.

"Just look straight ahead and you'll see them. They are always here at this time."

Jesi stared out in front of her. The ocean was a dark, beautiful blue, and there was a light gust of wind. "Oh my gosh, I see them. There are three." Jesi pointed to the dolphins that jumped through the water.

"A few weeks ago, there were only two. Here, look through these, and tell me what you see."

Jesi took the binoculars Johan handed to her and focused on the trio. "One's a baby!" Jesi squealed. "Oh wow, they're playing." Jesi felt a tear run down her cheek. She turned to hug him.

"I didn't mean to make you sad."

"I know."

"Let's sit over there."

She followed Johan to a big rock and sat in front of him between his legs.

"They give me hope, Jesi. When I come back, that'll be us and this little one." He rubbed her belly.

Jesi put her right hand over his and reached for the object around her neck with her left hand. It was her birthday gift, a promise "note." It looked similar to the dog tag around his neck except he etched, "I'll be back" on one side, and "Love, Johan" on the other.

"Let's name him or her," Jesi said.

"What?" Johan sounded surprised.

"Yes, I think we should come up with a name for our baby."

"Do you have one in mind?"

"I'd like to name him or her after you."

"Really?"

"Of course." Jesi looked sideways up at him. And even managed a big smile.

20

October 22, 1944 — Jesi and Johan's House

"STOP, STOP, JOHAN!" JESI WAS LAUGHING like crazy. He was tickling her to tears.

"You giving up?"

"Um."

He tickled her on her ribs again.

"I give up!"

"I win."

"You always win."

"I'm bigger and stronger," Johan said, as he lay along her left side.

"Thank you for this fluffy rug. It makes the living room so comfortable."

"Yup." He ran his left hand from her neck to her tummy.

"I want to ask you something, but don't be mad OK." Jesi had tried to find out about his family before the wedding, but Johan brushed off her inquiries.

"I can't ever be mad at you."

"You never talk about your family, except your grandfather." Jesi felt him tense up beside her. "This is our last night together, and I've been trying to figure out the best way to ask you." She turned to face him. "If you'd rather not, that's fine I guess. But I'd really like to know, just in case." A lump formed in her throat.

"I left New York very upset with my folks, and have not been in touch with them since."

"Did they try to get ahold of you?"

"I don't know. Both of my brothers are still in the family business. I left them on good terms, but haven't heard from them."

"No sisters?"

"No."

"Your parents still live in Manhattan?"

"Yup."

Jesi knew this was a sore topic.

"Just one last thing and I won't bring it up anymore."

"All right."

"Could you give me their address, please, Johan."

"I'm leaving you with some important papers in my file. There, you'll find their names, address, and phone number."

"Thank you." Jesi gave him a grateful smile.

He smiled back.

"Now," Johan said. He brushed his thumb over her lips. "As I recall, you have some very talented lips."

His teasing stirred those crazy sensations in her. Jesi opened her mouth and began to suck on his finger. She felt him harden beside her and reached to stroke his erection.

"No touching," Johan scolded as he removed his finger from her mouth and grabbed her other hand. He straddled her legs. Johan ran both of his hands along her ribcage and removed her blouse, exposing her naked breasts.

Jesi smiled. She loved the anticipation of what was to come.

"I'm going to teach you, and tease you tonight so you have something to think about while I'm away."

Jesi pushed her pelvis against him and watched as he removed his belt. The moonlight cast a glow across his husky, bare chest. The shadow of the lamp's flame danced on the ceiling. She could hear droplets start to beat against the roof, and the wind began to howl.

"You've been a very good girl," he said as he folded the belt, "so I won't spank you."

Jesi enjoyed everything he had taught her about sex so far.

"But I do want to tie your hands together. Is that OK?"

"Yes." *Tie my hands?* Jesi was intrigued. She allowed Johan to secure her hands above her head. "What did you tie me to?" Jesi asked surprised. She didn't realize her hands would be anchored in place.

"Just the couch. You want to change your mind?"

"Um, no." *Maybe, yes.*

"I can untie you."

"I trust you."

"All right."

Jesi watched as he pulled something black and white from his back pocket. It was a square piece of cloth. He placed it on her tummy then folded it from the corner up.

"What's that for?"

"I'm going to blindfold you. Close your eyes."

Her heart fluttered, and she was getting warm.

"You trust me, right?" Johan whispered into her ear.

"Yes." Jesi felt vulnerable, but quite aroused. She lifted her head so he could loop the cloth beneath her. He knotted the blindfold along her right temple. Jesi felt him kiss her left check, then her right cheek. She could feel him breathe on her lips, and longed for him to kiss her.

"No kiss?" Jesi chided him when he moved off her.

"Bend your knees so your feet are flat on the rug."

Jesi complied.

"Open your legs wide, Jesi."

"Mm." She mumbled.

"I'll be right back."

What? Jesi moved her head left and right in a futile effort to see where he was going.

"Just grabbing my pack."

Oh. She heard him put the bag down and unbuckle it. Metal clanked against metal. Something brushed against her tummy. She heard him strike a match, and the scent of smoke wafted across her nostrils.

"What are you doing?"

"You'll find out soon."

Then he was between her legs.

"Jesi," he said as he massaged the inside of each of her thighs with his hands. His touch sent shivers straight to her sex. She squirmed her hips upward, toward his voice.

"What do they call this in Chamorro?" Johan asked as he ran his middle finger over her vagina.

"Pånket."

"It's swollen and wet."

"Yes, it is," she said. Jesi tried to squeeze his hand against her with her thighs, but he wouldn't allow it. She felt him straighten her right leg in the air. *Oh god.*

He was biting along the inside of her calf, near her ankle.

"Do you like that?"

"Yes."

Once he reached her knee, he set her right foot down and began his teasing on her left calf.

"I want you," she said when he reached her left knee.

"I know."

He used both hands to massage the inside of her pelvis, just around her vagina. She writhed from his foreplay.

"Do you like how this feels?" Johan draped something over her deprived sex.

"That's the softest thing I've ever felt. Why are you covering me?"

"It's silk, and I'll take it off."

Jesi felt him scoot right up against her butt. His erection pressed against her, but she wasn't sure if he still had his briefs on.

"It's going to feel a little hot on your tummy, but it won't burn you."

Jesi tensed her abdomen, drawing her navel closer to her back.

She felt him dribble something on her skin. Johan made a trail of fiery drips to just between her breasts. *Oh god, yes.* Jesi tilted her chin up as she arched her back. She felt his tongue on her. He was licking whatever it was. It smelled familiar. She tried again to loosen her hands.

"When will you untie me?"

"Do your wrists hurt?"

"No."

"Not yet then."

"Uhh," she moaned when he drizzled the stuff on her right nipple. He sucked it off and nipped hard at her.

"That was unbearable!" Jesi said. "Again?" She felt him lather her left nipple with more of the hot goo. Jesi pushed her hips into his hard bulge. "Oh god, I'm about to explode!" She rubbed her clitoris against the soft material.

"No you don't." He moved to kneel on her left side, right next to her head. "I'm going to take off the blindfold."

Jesi turned and opened her eyes and was met by a long, hard shaft. She spread her lips to let him in.

He groaned.

She felt him squeeze her nipples. *Oh god, that feels so good.*

Johan pulled out of her mouth and shoved his thumb between her lips.

Coconut syrup.

He switched to his index finger.

She stared up into his eyes as she sucked then watched as Johan smeared the syrup on his erection. He grasped her hair to control how he moved in and out of her mouth.

"Do you want me in your pånket?"

"Yes."

Johan untied her hands. He removed the silk sheet covering her vagina and knelt between her legs. "Give me your right hand."

She complied.

"Use your middle finger to massage your clitoris."

Jesi closed her eyes and copied the way he had fondled her. *Ah, finally, that feels so good.*

"Johan." She arched her hips.

"That's it, Jesi."

He's rubbing my other hole. It feels good, too. She circled her clitoris faster. "Oh god, Johan, I'm going to—" Her self-satisfying orgasm coursed through her body. Jesi called his name again, and again. She cupped her hand against her climaxing sex, and squeezed Johan between her thighs.

"Umm, that was, I can't even say." Jesi moaned while he caressed her thighs. She opened her eyes and saw him smiling at her.

"Can't even say, huh?"

"Yeah," she smiled back at him. "I didn't know I could do that. Can you do it?"

Johan chuckled.

Jesi watched him as he encircled his manhood with his hand then slid it into her.

"Now it's my turn."

21

November 3, 1944 — Orote Peninsula

"LAST BAG, MAN," JOHAN SAID TO CALHOUN as they loaded the jeep with the remainder of their belongings. He looked at his watch. "She should've been here awhile ago," Johan mumbled to himself. The 305th was getting ready to permanently leave Guam for their next mission.

"She loves you, Sarge. It's the morning sickness that's keeping her."

"Probably." *But she hasn't been sick for the last few days.*

"We've got thirty."

"All right. Plenty of time. I'm gonna sit tight here."

Johan leaned against the jeep with his arms crossed in front of his chest. He looked down the road, waiting for her. With his eyes shut, Johan could see her, turning in the rain, standing near Bonita. The sight of Jesi as she walked down the aisle took his breath away. Her laughter on the rug as he tickled her melted his heart. *I'm going to miss you, too, Johnny.* A hint of a teardrop threatened to fall when Johan realized that he would no longer be able to rub Jesi's growing tummy.

"Here you go, Sarge," Calhoun held a sandwich out to him.

"Thanks, man."

"Hard to believe we've been here for over three months," Calhoun said.

"Tell me about it." *And what a three months.*

"Do you know what she named our baby?"

"What?"

"Johnny. Whether it's a boy or girl." Johan unwrapped his sandwich and took a bite.

"Sounds right. She's crazy in love with you."

"I hope she gets here soon."

The two soldiers finished their lunch in silence.

"It's time to go, Sarge," Miller called from the driver's seat.

Fuck! Johan hit the back of the jeep so hard it made an indentation. He shook his hand off. *She's not coming.* Johan's heart dropped a few inches. *Farewell, my love.* He tipped his helmet off in the direction of the entrance to Orote. *Until I come home.* His heart ached for her, but he knew hers was breaking. She couldn't look at him yesterday when she brought lunch. "I love you, Jessica Landers," he whispered before he turned and walked to the passenger's seat.

"Let's roll, Miller," Johan said and pounded on the outside of the jeep's door.

"Sorry, Sarge."

"Don't worry about it." *It's better this way.* He rubbed his wedding ring.

"Hurry, Peter! Can't this truck go any faster?" Jesi was hitting the door.

"Are you sure that's him?"

"Yes."

"But we're too far away."

"It's him."

"Johan, Johan!" She screamed at the top of her lungs.

Peter was honking his horn now. The jeep in front of them stopped.

"Take it easy, Jes, you gonna fall out!"

Peter's warning was useless. Jesi opened the door and got out just as the old pickup came to a stop. She jumped into Johan's arms while he was walking to her.

"I'm sorry, I'm sorry I'm late!" Jesi said and started to cry. "My heart broke into a million pieces and I didn't want it to break into a million more."

"I know, sweetheart. It's OK."

"I wasn't going to come, but I had to see you." His hug was almost suffocating. *Don't let me go!* His strength bore into her. She felt him swallow. *You have to be strong Jesi, just like he is showing you.* Jesi took a deep breath, filling her lungs even under the pressure of his hug. She squeezed him as tight as she could then leaned back and wiped the tears from her eyes.

"I'm sorry. I didn't want to cry."

"Don't be. I would cry, too, if they weren't looking," Johan nodded toward the jeep. He stroked her cheek and held her chin. It made Jesi smile.

"Now that's what I want to see."

"I was thinking of when we were first in the cave. The very first time you held my chin. Did you want to kiss me then?"

He smiled back. "I wanted to do more than kiss you."

Before she could say anything, his lips were on hers. He cradled her chin in his palm. Jesi savored the sensation, his tongue probing her mouth. She felt his need to have his way with her, to have a kiss that would last for a while.

He stopped and knelt down.

Jesi watched as he removed his steel helmet and pressed his ear against her tummy.

"Your belly hasn't grown much, but I can feel it has changed." Johan stayed there, motionless, as if to listen for something.

Don't you dare cry, Jesi.

" 'Twinkle, twinkle, little star, how I wonder what you are.' " He kissed her belly just as fiercely as he kissed her lips.

A tear rolled down her cheek. *I'm such a mess.*

"I hate to rush you, Sarge."

Jesi heard someone call out.

"Last minute," Johan replied.

"I almost forgot." Jesi said as she reached into the seashell purse that hung at her side. "This is a pin of Saint Joseph, the patron saint of families. Can I attach it somewhere?"

"Ah, it can't show."

"OK, how about under this pocket?"

"That's good."

"I had a priest bless this, for you to come home safely." Jesi swallowed the lump in her throat. "I will pray for your safe return every night." She could see unfallen tears cover his eyes. "You better go before I crumble right here. I want you to see me standing strong when you leave."

"You are strong, Jesi, don't forget that. I'll write every chance I get."

Johan pulled her into another embrace. She hugged him back with every ounce of strength she had, searing the impression of his body onto hers.

"I love you, Johan."

He pressed his lips against the top of her head.

"I love you more, Jesi."

Johan pulled away from her, but held on to her right hand.

"See you soon, sweet girl!"

Her hand hurt as he squeezed it good-bye. *Just smile, Jesi, smile!* Tears blurred her vision.

"Stand strong, girl, you can do it," Mames whispered.

Wave back. Jesi lifted her arm. It was as heavy as a concrete block.

Johan blew her a kiss and she caught it. Jesi put her hand against her heart then watched until his jeep disappeared down the road.

22

November 6, 1944 — At sea

Dear Jesi,

I miss you like crazy and it's only been a few days since I left. The guys are loving life on the ship with freshly made food and no mosquitoes to swat at. For me, I miss your delicious cooking and your smile. Please excuse me if my writing is poor. I don't even remember the last time I wrote a letter.

It wasn't so long ago that I was on one of these ships and I was looking forward to battle. Now all I can think of is you. We're supposed to be heading to a rest area. It's some island where the Japanese have already been driven out. Maybe that's why I miss you terribly. I don't know what the mission is yet. Well, I miss you because I love you. Can you love a baby so much even before he or she is born?

Don't laugh, OK. No, yes laugh. I miss your laughs. So I have asked Calhoun to teach me how to pray. Calhoun says prayer works for him. I need it to work so I can come home to you. And to keep you and Johnny safe until I get there.

By the way, if words are blacked out, it's because our letters are censored. They don't want us to write anything about our location or mission.

On a more personal note, I think of your sweet body every night. I miss lying next to your nakedness, and, never mind, I don't think I want to give the censor guy too much to read.

I bought a money order since we can't mail cash. It's most of my pay. Use it for anything.

I hope this letter gets to you. We were told to address it as best we can and it will get delivered to Guam eventually.

I'm looking forward to getting a letter back from you. Just write to the address on the envelope. I'm not in San Francisco, California, but that's how our mail is sorted. I hear mail can be very slow, as long as several months. Don't worry so much if you don't get a letter for a while. And if something does happen, you'll be getting a telegram.

Well, my sweet girl, it's almost lights-out. I used to wonder why the guys were so engrossed in sending a letter, and even more excited to get a letter back. Now I know. I am looking forward to hearing all about you and the family. Say hi to everyone for me.

I'll be dreaming of you! Tell Johnny I love him, or her!

Your husband,

Johan

23

December 5, 1944 — Jesi and Johan's House

JESI PLACED THEIR WEDDING PICTURE next to the statue of Saint Joseph. It was the photo of her and Johan sitting at their table ready to eat. It was his best smile. Jesi just finished setting up a prayer area on her dresser.

"That's beautiful, Neni," Mrs. T said, when she walked in. They both sat on the edge of the bed.

"Thank you. I'm glad you packed all your statues good."

"Me, too, next year, when Johan's home, it's going to be your turn to do the *Nobenan Niño*."

"I'll be honored."

"Mom, do you ever hear this voice?"

"What do you mean?"

"When I was little, I had a friend in the jungle."

"I remember. You said she was nice to you."

"Yes. Then she went away. But when we were hiding in the caves, she came back."

"Really?"

"I asked Peter once if he heard her. He just said I was hearing things."

"Is she still here?"

"She talks to me. I never see her, but I call her Mames because she smells like the sweet yellow flowers in the jungle."

"Ai, my Neni." Mrs. T pulled Jesi into a hug. "You are the chosen one. It skipped your grandma. You're not just a suruhåna, you're *le'an*, too, because you can talk to the spirits."

"Mom, but that's, that's for special people. I can't be. I'm too young and I'm not even full suruhåna, and I'm just a regular girl."

"Your great, great grandma was le'an. Neni, it's a special gift. There's not many like you."

"She helped me when I was scared in the caves, when the Japanese attacked me, and even when Johan left. She tells me I can do things I don't think I can do."

"Yes, Neni. It's a gift. And you're not just regular; you're the best daughter I could have. When Johan comes home, you guys can't leave Guam now. I need to go tell your grandma."

"He said he likes it here on Guam."

"Good, Neni."

"Wait, Mom." Jesi reached for Mrs. T's hand. "In a few days it will be December 8 again." Jesi's chest started to tighten.

"I know."

"All day today I've just been crying. I miss Johan. I'm worried about Tommy. And I just keep thinking about the things that happened to our people."

"Ai, Neni. We should be getting mail soon. We couldn't get Tommy's letters when the Japanese were here. I'm sure they'll start coming again."

"OK. Johan said he'd write. There's probably going to be a lot of people at mass."

"Your dad and Peter helped put some tents up already. After Peter gets off working at Orote today, they are going to hunt and kill deer."

Kill. "All those stories are true aren't they?"

"What stories, Neni?"

"The Japanese forced people to go in to caves then threw grenades at them," Jesi paused, "and cut their heads off if they were still alive."

Mrs. T nodded.

Jesi laid her head on her mom's lap and put her legs up on the bed, crying as Mrs. T stroked her hair.

"Is that what happened to Rosa?" Jesi asked between sniffles. Rosa was Antonio's mom and she hadn't come home yet.

"I don't know, Neni."

Jesi felt teardrops fall on her temple.

"They killed lots of people. There are so many graves," Mrs. T mumbled.

"What's going to happen to all the people who can't go back to their ranches and farms?" Jesi asked.

"I guess they have to rebuild somewhere else. They have family in other villages."

"We're very blessed, Mom. Grandpa was watching over us this whole time."

"He was, Neni."

The heartbreak in her mom's voice was overwhelming.

"Jesi, Jesi!"

"That's Peter." Jesi got off the bed and wiped her eyes as she rushed to the front door. Mrs. T followed behind her. Peter stood just inside of the doorway.

"You've got five letters from Johan!"

"Five?" Jesi took the envelopes from Peter and flipped through them. "November 9, November 13, November 17," she read. "Some have the same date. San Francisco? He's in San Francisco, California? He's safe then!"

"No letter from Tommy?" Mrs. T looked at Peter.

Oh no. Jesi's heart dropped to her stomach.

"His ship is out at sea, Mom, I'm sure we'll get some letters soon," Peter said.

"I hope so." Mrs. T turned to hug Jesi then nodded at Peter. "Let's go so she can read in private."

Jesi walked into the kitchen and sat at the table. Tears were already streaming down her cheeks. She had been so worried and scared. Once her tears were spent, Jesi got up to wash her face over the kitchen sink then dried off with a clean towel.

Jesi took a deep breath and walked back to the table. She arranged the envelopes in chronological order and opened the one marked November 9. She smiled and tears welled up again, but she blinked them away. Once she finished the fifth one, she was happy. She went to the living room for pen and paper.

December 5, 1944

Kisses for you, Johan!

I just finished reading all your letters. Can you believe five got here at the same time? I'm so happy you've been out of harm's way and I pray that you stay safe on your newest mission. Now

I can write back to you! I love you so much and I miss you. I miss your touch and—everything.

Some words were blacked out. I hope the censor guy has a wife to go home to! I don't know if I'm brave enough to write like what you wrote in your last letter.

I miss you, too, so much! Johnny is growing because my belly is growing! It's not really big yet, but it's getting larger. I can't fit into my shorts anymore so I just wear dresses.

When I go to sleep at nights, it's when I really miss you. I miss making love to you . . . and having sex with you . . . it's your fault. You wanted to know if I've been naughty? I'll tell you when you come home.

I've been keeping myself busy by making zoris. Remember what I wore on my feet when we got married? I make them nice and pretty and give them to the women and young girls that don't have anything good to walk in. I've also been making more seashell purses. I told Peter to just give them to the military men to send home to their families. Oh, he works down there now doing all kinds of things. The men want to pay him for the purses, but he tells them instead he'd trade them for things he can't get here. Sometimes they even give him more ingredients, and that Spam. We all love that Spam!

Peter has been staying with me to make sure I'm OK at night. He's so excited about his work. He was about to join the US Navy like Tommy, but then the Japanese invaded us. So he's happy to work now and doesn't want to join the navy. Chief has been making good use of all the tools you gave him and he really loves the coveralls. He tells me often to tell you thank you when I write to you. Grandma and mom are making lots of coconut oil, but grandma has to rest more than she used to. I massage her with the oil, and it makes her feel better for a little while. It makes me sad that she is getting older.

Do you know how many things a pregnant girl is not supposed to do? Oh my gosh!! I can't eat my favorite fish, tataga', because then our baby will be born smelling like sea food! Tataga' look like unicorn fish because they have that horn thing sticking out from their head. I can't even go out to pick leaves for medicine anymore. I guess I'm OK with it all because I'm making our house ready for you and Johnny. I'm sewing a blanket from whatever material I can find in grandma's things. Peter brings me some really nice fabric, too. He said the men get gifts from the States and their families use the fabric to wrap the gifts.

Gosh, I'm going on and on. I'm just so excited that I can finally write to you. I made you something for Christmas, and for your birthday. They have been wrapped and ready to go, but I just needed your address. Peter said to send only things you can use immediately and that don't take up room for you to carry.

It sounds like you are eating well on that ship. I'm happy you miss my cooking though . . . I miss cooking for you! I eat with mom and grandma often so I'm not so sad eating alone.

I hope you and your men have as good a Christmas as you can. Please say hello and Merry Christmas to them, especially Calhoun, Miller, and Smithy.

It's dark now and I can't see what I'm writing! I'm going to finish this letter so I can put it in the box and Peter can mail it tomorrow.

I'm sorry my thoughts are all over the place. I love you, Johan Landers, and I can't wait for you to come home!! I'll be waiting!!

I love you always.

Your wife,

Jessica Landers

PS I don't think it's funny that you are learning to pray. Now we have double the prayers for your safe return.

PSS You write just fine.

24

December 26, 1944 — Matagob, Northern Leyte,
Western Coast, Philippines

"MERRY CHRISTMAS, MAN," JOHAN SAID to Calhoun. It was actually the day after Christmas in the Philippines, but they were too busy fighting enemy stragglers and securing the area on the twenty-fifth to do any celebrating. Today, however, was the day their commanding general chose to celebrate Christmas with a turkey dinner.

"Yeah, it's Christmas in the States now. When's Christmas on Guam?" Calhoun replied.

Johan took a deep breath. "Yesterday, I think. I'm pretty sure it's about the same as this damn place."

"Yeah," Calhoun agreed.

"At least we get some turkey, huh." Johan sat on a stump beside his friend. He was grateful for the reprieve in the fighting. It had been nonstop since they landed on Leyte, Philippines, on Thanksgiving Day.

"You all right, Calhoun?"

"Yeah, Sarge, we've been fighting it seems like forever."

"A month now," Johan added. "I hope Smithy is doing good and all fixed up."

"His leg looked bad. This shit's even worse than Guam."

"All that training is paying off, Calhoun."

"Thank God, Sarge. I've not had a minute to think about my wife and kids."

"May be a good thing in this hellhole. We need to stay sharp," Johan said.

"We were lucky yesterday."

"Tell me about it. It was the weirdest thing. I felt as if someone were pushing me to the side. My legs just moved."

"It's not your time to go, Sarge."

"Damn right. I've got that beautiful girl and a baby waiting for me. I wish we'd get some mail. Probably not for a goddamn while."

"These Japs are more crazy here than the ones on Guam," Calhoun said.

"There's talks that tomorrow night we're to pretend we're celebrating and drunk to trick them into a banzai attack. Then we can kill a bunch of them at once." Johan relished the idea.

"That shit sounds like a damn good thing to do. We should do it."

25

January 20, 1945 — Mrs. T's House

"**A**I NO, NO, NO!"

Jesi heard the horrible screams coming from the front of her parents' house. She set the pot of custard on the counter, and ran as fast as a pregnant woman could toward her mom.

"Ai Yu'us, not my boy!"

Jesi made it just in time to hold her mom who fainted. The navy chaplain and the Chamorro boy that came with him helped Jesi guide Mrs. T to a chair.

"What's wrong, Jessica?" Chief was by his wife's side, having heard her from the backyard.

Jesi couldn't find the words. She looked at Chief and stared.

"Sir, I'm sorry to bring you sad news," the chaplain said, "We've received a telegram that your son Thomas died when the Japanese bombed Pearl Harbor."

Jesi saw no expression on her father's face other than the nod of his head. His muscular arms were wrapped around Mrs. T who was wailing.

"Jesi, leaf us for now. I come check you later. You gonna be OK?"

"Yes." She turned to the navy man and the Chamorro boy. "Thank you for letting us know."

"The navy's deepest condolences, Ma'am." The men walked back to their jeep.

Jesi stood by the doorway and looked at her parents. Her heart broke for them. She stepped out of the door and closed it behind her. As she walked to her own house, it dawned on her that she was relieved it wasn't Johan. A blanket of guilt covered her heart.

She went to the bedroom and sat at the edge of the bed. Tears rolled down her cheeks. "Tommy, you were protecting us, too, weren't you?" Jesi looked up, as if talking to her oldest brother. She got up to light the candle on her dresser, and picked up her rosary beads. Jesi prayed for Tommy to be at peace, for strength for her parents to bear their pain, and for Johan to be safe and protected, wherever he was. Tommy had wanted to travel beyond the horizon. He loved being in the middle of the ocean. It didn't matter to Tommy that he could only be a mess attendant.

Jesi lay on her side, and wept into her pillow, longing for her oldest brother.

January 29, 1945 — Mrs. T's House

"Thank you, Neni, for all your help," Mrs. T said to Jesi.

They were sitting at Mrs. T's kitchen table. Their family and friends had left. Jesi was exhausted after nine days of praying the rosary for Tommy, and feeding people, but she wouldn't dare show her mom. It was her duty to take care of the family when they needed her most. There were still nine more days of rosary for the immediate family.

"Mom, of course! I wouldn't do any less."

"I know, but you're pregnant, Neni. You're not supposed to work so hard."

The sun was setting and its rays flooded through the kitchen window. For the first time, Jesi saw that her mom was aging. *Oh, Mom.*

"Cooking and cleaning don't bother me even when I'm pregnant."

"I hope they can bring his body back home someday. Come here, Neni, come stand in front of me."

Jesi got up and stood near her mom.

"Ai, my Neni Girl, or Neni Boy." Mrs. T stroked Jesi's belly and talked to Johnny. "Grandma can't wait to hug you." Mrs. T kissed Jesi's tummy. "I already knew in my heart Tommy was gone, even before those men came."

26

February 12, 1945 — Tarragona, Central Leyte,
Eastern Coast, Philippines

Dear Jesi,

I'm sorry I've not written since who knows
how long ago. We've been in very heavy combat.
And I have to be honest; I came close to death
a couple of times. Every which way we turned,
we were fighting the enemy. This is the first time
we've had to rest since we got off that ship. I'm
sorry, that was back in November. It's been three
months since I last wrote to you? I'm very sorry
Jesi but please be understanding. How's my
Johnny doing? Tell him or her I love him, or her.
I haven't gotten a letter from you, but we haven't
had any mail delivered either. We've been fight-
ing a never-ending war. I'm happy to tell you
that Calhoun and Miller are still alive. Smithy
got hurt badly but they rescued him. He might
be all funny, but he's one of the bravest men I've
known. I'm sure he's recovering, I hope. Too many
of our men have died, but we've killed more of
the enemy. Hooah USA. I'm in a hell of a mood
aren't I? I'm sorry. They said we should be getting
mail in a few days. We haven't been in one place
long enough since we've been here. I wish I could

tell you where we are, not that it matters, but I'm not so far away.

The only thing that keeps me sane through all this chaos and death are my thoughts of you — your smile, your laughter, and your body that fits so perfectly beneath me, around me, and on top of me. The last time we made love on the rug was the best. You seemed to like all that extra play we did. Would you want to try a few more different ways to make love? I think about our afternoons at the tip of Orote. My lunch breaks were never so exciting. I could tell you loved it, too, Jesi. I still have much to show you. If I continue, I'd be in a bind with no way to relieve myself.

I'm in a much better mood now. I miss you like crazy. I love you even crazier. It's time to get some chow and I'd rather have hot food instead of canned rations.

I love you forever,

Johan

PS You probably didn't get my last letter yet so I'm still waiting to hear if you'd like to try some new ways.

27

March 5, 1945 — Jesi and Johan's House

"**P**ETER, PETER!" JESI YELLED FOR HER brother.

"What, Jes?" He came running to the kitchen.

"Come here, give me your hand." Jesi was sitting by the kitchen table drinking *champulado*, a thick, hot, chocolate drink made with ground corn.

"*Ai laña*, Jes, he kick me. Or she kick me!"

Jesi hadn't seen Peter smile so big in a long time.

"Wow, Sis, that's strong kicks."

"I know."

"Take it easy on your mom, Johnny. Uncle Peter has to go to work, but when I get back, we can play one-two punch." Jesi grinned as she watched her brother "box" with the baby.

"You're funny. But can I ask you something before you leave?"

"Uh-huh," Peter said as he stuffed a *buchi buchi* in his mouth. "Mom makes this pumpkin turnover so good."

"Will you be the nino?"

Peter looked wide-eyed at Jesi and chewed faster.

"Of course, Sis. I'll be happy to. Cuz if you ask someone else before me, I'll never forgive you."

"Thank you, Peter." She hugged her brother tight.

"Johan have any good news?"

"No. They are resting because ever since they got there, they've been fighting."

"Ai, Sis, hang in there, OK. He'll be home. You just have to pray."

"I know." Jesi took a deep breath.

"Kay then, I have to go. 'Bye."

"*Esta*." Jesi acknowledged her brother and watched him leave.

"Your daddy loved the picture we took for his birthday. We need to take him a new one since you've grown so much Johnny." Jesi rubbed her belly. "I don't know what I would do if it were just me by myself, if I didn't have you. At least I can talk to you all day, every day." Jesi closed her eyes and thought about the first time she and Johan made love by the cave. She smiled. *That's when you came along.* "Want another buchi buchi?" Jesi felt Johnny kick again. "I'll take that as a yes." She grabbed a second fried turnover from the table and took a bite. *This is even better cold.* Once she finished her pastry, she got up for a cup of water then went to the living room to get pen and paper. "We're going to surprise your daddy. He's so brave fighting those terrible men I can be brave enough to write him a letter he'll enjoy."

28

March 7, 1945 — Tarragona, Leyte, Philippines

Good Morning, Sweetheart,

Thank you from the bottom of my heart for all the letters and my gifts. I love the pictures. Please send me more pictures of you and your beautiful belly. You write very good English by the way. It's as if I am there when I read your letters. Tell Johnny I sing, "twinkle, twinkle, little stars" at night and think of him, or her.

The guyuria made it here in great condition. It was a good idea to seal it in a twist-cover can. The ants seem to get in to our boxes from home, but not mine thanks to your smart thinking. We finally got the mail on Valentine's Day. Do you do Valentine's Day on Guam? Well, it was the best Valentine's I ever had, even if we're apart. As you might guess, it's morning here in the jungles of, well, I can't say. But they've been working us like crazy which is why I haven't been able to write to you. I'm glad we're not fighting, but we are getting ready for our next mission. We're digging equipment out of mud and all kinds of fix-and-break type of jobs.

These last few weeks have been a bit of relief from constant battle. While there might be enemy stragglers hiding, we've pretty much secured this area. So my mind is not busy thinking ahead of the enemy.

I never thought I could miss someone so much. It's a good thing the army has been keeping me on my toes else I'd be out of my mind. If I can remember right, I asked you some personal questions in one of my letters. I guess you didn't get the letter by the time you mailed the box. I'm looking forward to your responses.

The platoon is ready for another day of grind in the rain and sludge so I need to stop for now. I miss you and love you like crazy, Jesi.

I love you forever,

Johan

29

March 24, 1945 — Jesi and Johan's House

"I **FEEL LIKE A KARABAO, MOM!" JESI SAT** up in her bed and leaned against the wall. She had just awaken from an afternoon nap a few minutes ago and was getting ready for her pregnancy exam.

"Neni, but you look beautiful."

"My belly is huge." Jesi still wondered how the big ball of a baby inside her was going to come out from down there.

"It's bigger than mine when I was pregnant with you guys."

Knock, knock, knock. "Hoe', si, Rita, este." Auntie Rita was Jesi's *pattera*, or midwife. She has been checking in on Jesi since the start of her pregnancy to make sure Jesi and the baby were healthy.

"*Maila' halom*, Rita," Mrs. T called for the midwife to come in.

Jesi sat up to åmen Auntie Rita.

"*Håfa tatatmanu hao*, Neni?" Auntie Rita asked Jesi how she was doing.

"*Maolek ha yo'*, Auntie" Jesi said she was good. All older adult women were addressed as auntie even if they were not related by blood.

"Håfa tatatmanu si nanå-mu?" Mrs. T asked Auntie Rita how her mother was doing.

"Maolek ha' lokkue'." Auntie Rita said her mother was fine, too.

Mrs. T and Auntie Rita talked a few minutes more in Chamorro about their aging mothers before Mrs. T turned to Jesi.

"I'll be in the kitchen, Neni," Mrs. T said as she left Jesi's bedroom.

Jesi scooted down on the bed for her routine checkup. "Is this baby going to get bigger?"

"Yes," Auntie Rita replied.

"It's a miracle it can fit." Jesi had some idea of what would happen. She read about how a woman gives birth in one of Suzie's father's books. Suzie's dad had shelves and shelves of different kinds of books in their house. But Jesi was still in disbelief now that she was actually about to have her own baby.

"I love your hair, Auntie. It's so long and the braid reminds me of the strong rope my grandpa used to make." Jesi could still remember Chief's father making rope from *pågu* fiber, the dried wood strippings from the wild hibiscus tree. Chief's dad was a farmer, and he was well known for the ropes he made.

"Hoe'," Jesi heard another female voice call.

"Maila' hålom, Auntie Julia. *Gaige yo' gi kusina.*" Mrs. T told Auntie Julia to come in, and that she was in the kitchen.

"OK, Neni, *esta monhåyan yo',*" Auntie Rita told Jesi she was done.

"Do I still have to drink that tea?" Jesi asked in Chamorro. She did not like the concoction, but it was supposed to help make it an easier delivery.

"Hunggan." Auntie Rita said yes, and left the room.

Jesi got off the bed then removed the top blanket and placed it in the laundry basket. She fixed her hair and clothes then sat back on the bed with her back against the wall. "I hope your daddy likes my new body, Johnny. I look as big as Bonita for sure." Jesi smiled. She liked her appearance. *And the blanket tightened around my tummy after you come out will make my stomach small again.* Jesi thought Mrs. T's tummy was still nice and flat even after four births. "I wish he were here, Johnny." Jesi closed her eyes and tried to remember what it was like to have Johan's arms around her, to hear his heartbeat with her cheek against his chest, to feel his lips pressed against her head when he'd kiss her in the mornings before work.

"Here, Neni, Auntie Rita had to go," Mrs. T said as she walked back into the room.

Jesi took the cup of not-so-yummy tea from her mom.

"Auntie Julia is still here. She brought fresh *kàddon mànnok* and fresh eggs from Uncle Kin. She also made *potu.* When you're ready, come out and eat OK?"

"Thanks, Mom. I should get pregnant more often with all this spoiling," Jesi chuckled.

Visiting relatives had been bringing all kinds of food for Jesi to eat. Jesi loved the smell and the taste of potu, a sweet, steamed rice cake. The pungent aroma came from *tuba,* the fermented sap of a coconut tree that was used to make the potu. She drank the tea and made a face, but smiled knowing she had dessert waiting. Once she finished it, she set the glass on the nightstand and reached for the envelope that came yesterday. The sun was now flooding the bedroom with bright light.

Jesi took Johan's letter out and reread it. A smile spread across her entire face. *I'm sure he got my reply by now.* She wondered what else they could do in the bedroom. Jesi had at least one idea since Johan had alluded to it. Jesi didn't know making love and having sex could be so exciting, so fun, and so consuming. Her parents never told her anything except "keep your legs closed." Even Mrs. T was uncomfortable saying anything other than "It's what a husband and wife does behind closed doors."

Jesi shut her eyes. She recalled that letter she wrote to Johan describing what she wanted to do to him, and what she wanted him to do to her. Every time she thought about making love to him, it stimulated sensations in her pånket.

30

March 28, 1945 — Zamami Shima Island, Kerama-Rettō,
Twenty Miles Southwest of Okinawa, Japan

"**C**ALHOUN, YOU GROWING FINS YET?**"** Johan
asked in a low voice trying to lighten the mood.
They were talking about all the islands they had shipped out
to since their prewar training in Camp Stoneman in Pittsburg,
California. Guam was the only island he cared about. *Not now,*
Landers. He refocused on the trail in front of him.

"Sarge, I've got gills, too!"

"How much longer do you think we've got in these
hellholes?" Miller asked.

"Don't know, but we're only about twenty miles from the
motherland," Johan replied.

Johan and his men continued to trudge through the mud
toward the southern end of Zamami Shima, an island just a
stone's throw from Japan.

"At least it's not raining," Calhoun added.

It was an overcast day, but it rained much more on the
Japanese islands than it did on Guam. As Johan's platoon
neared their assault positions, they quieted down. Two days
ago, a reconnaissance patrol came under fire along the beach.
Most of the patrol made it back to camp for reinforcement, and

now several companies from the Second Battalion were preparing for an attack.

"It's almost go time," Johan whispered. He stood between Calhoun on his right and Miller to his left. A corporal replaced Smithy on the squad. The corporal stood to Miller's left. Johan still had his grandfather's watch. It was just past 1415 hours and the ground troops were waiting for the navy to finish their barrage across the hills that faced the beach. The sounds of the big guns eroded away. The go command came through the radio.

"Let's go, let's go!" Johan yelled. They made their way closer to the beach.

"Sarge, the Japs are still shooting from the caves."

"Goddamn it, they should have been taken out by now," Johan cursed. As soon as Calhoun was about to peer from above the brush, Johan saw a flash not far from them. "Get the fuck down," Johan said. He lunged to the right at Calhoun, tackling him to the ground. Shots were still firing off from above their hiding place as Johan lay on his friend.

"Holy Christ, Sarge," Calhoun yelled. "You all right, Landers?"

"Goddamn son of a bitch," Johan cussed as he rolled off Calhoun. Johan touched where the pain was coming from and looked at his hand.

"Landers is hit!" Calhoun said.

Miller crawled over to them. "Goddamn it!" Miller looked at Johan. "Sarge, got feeling in your arms and legs?"

"They fucking hurt!"

"Can you crawl, Sarge?" Calhoun asked.

"I don't fucking know, but we gotta move." Johan took a deep breath. He could hear Miller calling for a medic.

"Let me patch one up, Sarge. Ya got a bleeder." Miller hustled to bandage the hole on Johan's leg that oozed plenty of blood.

"We gotta move, Miller," Johan said. *Ah hell!* Johan's left side hurt all over. He couldn't move his arm. Blood was everywhere. His ass was on fire.

"Done for now, Sarge."

"Start crawling," Johan ordered the corporal. It took everything Johan had to move his body. He used his right arm and leg to crawl. His left side might as well have been asleep. Bullets still whizzed above him. An image of Jesi popped into his head. She caught the kiss he blew. Then she was standing in the backyard with her bigger tummy. *Johnny.* Johan grunted. *Crawl you bastard, crawl.* Johan moved his body. The pain was excruciating, shocking, as if fire were scorching every nerve in his body. Still, he crawled. And when he thought he couldn't bear the pain anymore, he crawled just an inch farther. Johan heard some mumbling and tried to keep his eyes open. They lifted him off the ground. "Jesi," he called. "Jesi." He could see faces above him. Their voices faded. The pain disappeared. *Jesi.*

31

April 2, 1945 — Jesi and Johan's House

"OH, JOHNNY, YOU'RE VERY ACTIVE TODAY," Jesi stopped sweeping the front porch with the *eskoban ñuhot*. It was a broom she learned to make using the rib of each of the little coconut leaves. She put both hands on her belly where Johnny was kicking.

The sound of a vehicle got her attention. Jesi looked up and saw that a military jeep was coming toward her. Her heart sped a thousand miles. She took a deep breath, and pursed her lips to let the air out. Johnny was still kicking. The jeep stopped in her front yard. A man dressed in uniform and a Chamorro man got out of the jeep. *Oh god!* Jesi shook her head left to right.

"Hello, Ma'am. We are looking for Mrs. Jessica Landers. Is that you?"

Jesi nodded her head. Her hands trembled.

"Everything is OK, Ma'am. Your husband, Staff Sergeant Johan Landers is alive, but he was wounded. He's coming on a medical ship back to Guam and should make a full recovery."

"He's alive? He's OK?" Jesi wasn't sure she heard the navy man.

"Yes, Ma'am. The ship should be pulling into Guam soon."

"What happened?"

"There's no specifics, Ma'am, just that he was wounded in action and will be home soon."

Jesi breathed a sigh of relief. "Please wait here one moment, Sir."

"We do need to get going, Ma'am."

"Please, just one minute, I have something for you." Jesi walked into the house then came out with a gift for each of the men.

"I made these purses while my husband has been away. Please give them to your wife or loved ones. Thank you for bringing me good news." She gave each man her handicraft.

"These are very beautiful, Ma'am. My wife will love it," the officer said.

"Si Yu'us ma'åse'," the Chamorro man replied.

The men bid their farewell. Jesi watched as they drove away.

"Daddy's coming home, Johnny." The tears ran down her cheeks. She was so relieved. *I haven't cried in a long time.* For a minute there, she had feared the worst. She worried about Johan's injuries, but she was so grateful he was alive. *He's coming home. I have to get everything ready.*

Jesi wiped her tears and looked down on her tummy. "What are we going to do first, Neni?" Jesi wasn't expecting Johan to be home so soon. She went back inside, got paper and pen from the living room then settled down on the kitchen table and made a list.

To do:

-finish the curtains

-buy coffee

-restock drinking water . . . ask Peter

-wash and iron dresses

-ask grandma for more coconut oil

-get hair trimmed

-dust and clean

Jesi set the pen down and scooted away from the table. She rubbed her tummy. *God I'm so big.* "Ouch! Oh my gosh!" Jesi leaned over in excruciating pain. "Oh god."

32

April 23, 1945 — US Hospital Ship, Just off Guam

"**S**IR, YOU STILL NEED A CHAIR, YOU'RE** not a hundred percent," the army nurse said.

"I am not having my wife see me wheeled out of this ship, Miss." Johan said. Cora was with the Army Nurse Corps stationed on the hospital ship and had been tending to him since he first woke up onboard.

"Will you take the crutches then?"

"No," Johan said with finality.

He thought he'd recovered well enough. The ship would be entering its port on Guam any time now. It hurt to walk, but he wouldn't have to go too far. The nurse said he was very lucky. If the bullet had moved just a bit to the right, it would have missed his bones and gone straight through his heart. He'd have been dead. Never mind the ones they dug out of his ass and his forearm. If the one that grazed his back had gone through his body, he would have been paralyzed. *Saint Joseph.*

Johan remembered that he put the pin in his pocket. "Would you kindly place this under the flap of my breast pocket? I think it kept me alive all this time." Johan handed the pin to Cora.

"Saint Joseph. Indeed he was watching over you, Sir."

Him and the taotaomo'na.

"Why the long face?" Cora asked.

"My body is torn up." Johan thought about all his scars, and the nightmares that woke him up every night. *Would she still want me?*

"You've been at war, Sir."

"I know, just—" Johan sighed, and his shoulders slumped.

"You're wondering if she'll still love you?"

"Yes, well, no. Will she still want me? I'm scarred everywhere." Johan pictured her touching his body and being repulsed.

"Sir, your wife will be thrilled that you are home alive. Period. No matter what your condition."

"I hope so."

"You're one of the lucky ones, Sir. You have both arms and legs, and you can walk. Sure, you're not healed, but you will be just fine in a few months. And the scars on your body, think of all the lives you saved."

Johan grinned. It was just what he needed, a little bit of reassurance. "Thank you, Cora, you're great at your job."

"Why thank you, Sir."

A voice came over the intercom. They were about ready to dock.

"You have two choices, Sergeant," Cora was no longer sympathetic. "You can use at least one crutch, or I'll have you wheeled out of here in a chair."

"Fine. I'll take the crutch."

"Glad you agree. I'll be by your side until we find your wife."

Cora helped Johan up to the deck. Men and nurses were busy shuttling the critically wounded off the ship, followed by the not-so-critically injured.

"Can we stand by the railing and look for her first?" He wanted to have a line of sight straight toward Jesi. He was already tired and in a bit more pain from climbing the stairs. Johan watched as stretcher after stretcher came up the ship empty only to leave the ship with an injured comrade. It was a sea of broken bodies. They hadn't even started to unboard the men who died.

"Heartbreaking isn't it?" Cora said.

"You know, when I first joined back in 1942, February, I had nothing to lose. When I left Guam this past November, I feared losing everything." Johan was glad it was sunny and breezy. It put him in a more hopeful mood.

"You're lucky to have gotten married over here. That's frowned upon these days."

"Believe me, I wasn't looking for it. But I woke up one day, and there she was. I thought I was dreaming. I was injured then, too."

"Do you see her?"

"No. But if you see a short, beautiful pregnant girl with hair past her shoulders, it's got to be her." Johan continued scanning the crowd. He couldn't find her. He looked to the right. Johan thought he heard someone calling his name, a man's voice.

"Peter!" Johan waved back.

Jesi lay on her left side on the bed. She had been having contractions for a few weeks now and was starting to dilate. Auntie Rita had ordered her to stay in bed because she still had another six to eight weeks before the baby was full term. Lying around made her sad and depressed. She wanted to get so many things done before Johan got home. He still wasn't here and she was worried about him.

"Hi, Neni, how are you feeling?" Mrs. T asked.

"Like a big fat cow!" Jesi just wanted to cry. Peter said a hospital ship was supposed to come in today because it was following behind another ship that came in yesterday.

"Can't I get up, Mom, please? At least to shower and put on a new dress?"

"No, Jesi. You don't want to have the baby right now do you?"

"Then maybe I can sit up and you can help me wash my hair. I can just lean over the bed?" Jesi looked at her mom with such pitiful eyes.

"OK, Neni. I'll be right back."

"Thank you." Jesi prayed Johan would be home today, but she wished she looked prettier. She felt puffy and fat all over.

"That's a big bucket," Jesi said. Mrs. T was back in the bedroom.

Jesi got comfortable on her side and let her head hang off the bed. Mrs. T. used a cup to pour water over Jesi's hair then lathered the shampoo.

"I'm scared, Mom."

"Of what, Neni?"

"He won't like me anymore. My body is not like it used to be."

"Ai, Neni, you're feeling normal. He loves you and he's going to think you're the most beautiful girl in the world."

"I don't think so."

"I felt the same way with Tommy. After your first one, you get used to it."

"I miss Tommy." *He'll never get to see Johnny.*

"I miss him, too." Mrs. T finished washing the shampoo out of Jesi's hair then wrapped a towel around to soak up the water.

"Here's a washcloth to wipe up. I'll hang your dress on this chair. Call me if you need any help."

"It's good to see you, Peter!" Johan said as he shook Peter's hand and gave him a hug.

"Better to see you, Johan. My sister has missed you a lot."

"Hello, Sir," Cora held her hand out to Peter.

"Peter, this is Cora, my nurse who took exceptional care of me."

"*Håfa Adai*, Miss Cora. That's 'hello' on Guam."

"*Haa fa day*, Peter. Was that right?"

"That was very good, Miss Cora," Peter said.

Smile at the girl, Peter. Johan didn't dare say a word.

"My ship will be here for a few days. Maybe you could bring some island fruit?"

"Oh, um, um."

"If you have no time, that's OK."

Damn, she likes him.

"He just needs to drop me home, Miss Cora, then Peter can come back with lots of island fruit." Johan nudged Peter in the ribs.

"Oh, um, yes, Miss. We have plenty growing." Peter shifted his weight.

"Thank you, Peter. I must get back to the injured, but I look forward to seeing you later." Cora looked at Johan, "Sir, I'm glad you are home safely."

"Me too. Thank you, Miss Cora."

Johan watched as Cora smiled at Peter then turned to walk away. Peter stared as she disappeared into the crowd.

"I think she likes you, Peter."

"Nah, man, she's just being nice."

"OK, well, make sure you come back and bring her fruit, because she's just being nice."

"Ya," Peter replied.

"Now, if we could please go so I can see Jesi."

"My pickup is right there," Peter nodded over his shoulder. "You can make it?"

"Yup."

"Let me have your bag."

"All right." Johan limped beside Peter toward the old truck. *I thought I was more healed than this.* His left butt cheek was still sore.

"How's Jesi?" Johan saw Peter take a deep breath and hesitate.

"Something wrong, Peter?"

"She has been in bed for a couple of weeks."

"What?"

"She started having contractions and the pattera said she was starting labor so she better stay in bed cuz it wasn't time yet."

Johan stopped by the passenger's door. "But she's OK?" He looked at Peter with a serious, intent face. "Get in, Peter, and drive fast." Johan got into the passenger's side. It hurt, but he was concerned and uneasy about Jesi's condition.

Peter turned the jeep on and headed toward the gate. "She's OK. She's been eating good and not having any more pains. Johnny is a big kicker. He or she moves around a lot."

"Oh yeah?" Johan managed a small grin.

"So Jesi's really OK?"

"Yea, she's tired of lying down. She can only get up to go to the bathroom."

"Oh." Johan was quiet the rest of the way. He berated himself for being disappointed that Jesi wasn't at the port.

"Will a doctor deliver the baby? Are there even doctors here, other than the patteras and suruhånas?"

Peter looked at him confused.

"Sorry, Peter, the Chamorro medicine helped me to heal, but what if something goes wrong when she has the baby? So many things can go wrong."

"But the pattera has delivered a lot of babies and she knows what to do."

"Peter, I did not survive those Japanese islands to have something happen to Jesi and the baby. I just want to make sure we have a doctor there in case we need one."

"Oh," Peter said.

Johan had been so worried he hadn't realized how close they were. "This place is even more beautiful than what I remembered."

"Ya, lots of plants and trees are growing and flowering. Jesi did the house up nice. I have to move my things out today."

"Do that later, remember, you have a date today."

"OK."

Johan looked at Peter. "Thanks for taking care of her."

"She's my sister."

"Stop here. I want to surprise her."

Jesi was sitting upright on her bed and enjoying the breeze as she stitched the blanket. It was a quilt of squares from the material she had collected. She set the blanket and needle down on the chair beside her bed. The sun was setting on the other side of the house so it was cool inside her room. Jesi closed her eyes and leaned her head against the wall. *This baby is going to come out jumping and doing cartwheels.* Johnny had been moving around all day. Jesi took a deep breath, and then another.

"Hey, good looking!"

The voice startled her.

"Johan!" She screamed. He was leaning against the doorway.

"Don't get up, Jesi, that's an order."

Jesi stopped midmotion and watched as Johan hobbled over to her. She sat up straight and moved her legs to hang off the edge of the bed. "You're still hurt! Are you OK?" She held her arms out, and the tears started to build in her eyes.

"I'm fine now that I'm with you." Johan moved the chair aside then eased himself down to kneel on the floor between Jesi's legs.

"Johan, are you really here? Or am I dreaming?" Jesi blinked her eyes to make sure she wasn't imagining him in front of her. She covered Johan's hands with her own as he cupped her chin. He drew her lips toward his and kissed her. *He's really here.* Jesi kissed him back, as if he would disappear any second. Johan pulled his lips away from hers. He leaned against her belly with his arms wrapped around her lower back.

"Whoa there, baby!" Johan flinched and smiled up at her. "He kicked, or she kicked!" Johan smiled even wider. "Daddy's back, Johnny, I'm home to stay." He kissed her belly.

"Yes, you are home," Jesi said. Johan looked up and stared into her eyes. "I've missed you so much, Johan."

"I know, sweetheart. I've missed you so much, too. I didn't mean to come home limping and all."

"I don't care if you're limping or missing a leg. I just prayed to God that you would come home alive."

"Do you think it's OK to lie beside you?" Johan asked.

A huge smile spread across Jesi's face. "Of course."

Johan stood up and walked to the other side of the bed. He removed his button-down top then started to untuck his T-shirt.

"Why did you stop?" Jesi asked.

"I have a lot more scars, baby. I—"

"Johan, I've waited a long time to listen to your heartbeat."

"OK."

She watched as he pulled his shirt over his head. "Oh, Johan." *What did they do to you?*

"It doesn't make you ill?"

"No, it makes me love you more. You're home." She waited for him to lie back on the pillow then she lay on her right side with her head propped up on her hand. "Johan," she looked into his eyes, and familiar sensations stirred through her body. "If I wasn't pregnant and you weren't hurt, do you know what I would do to you?" She watched as a huge grin lit up his face.

"Jesi, sweetheart," he pulled her head down for a quick kiss, "if I wasn't in pain, I know what I would do to you even while you're pregnant."

33

A Week Later — Jesi and Johan's House

"MILLER, MILLER," JOHAN CALLED INTO the night. He shifted in bed and felt her warm body next to his. The bad dreams were becoming less intense since he'd been home. Miller made it out alive on their last mission, so far as Johan knew.

He turned to look at Jesi. His heart rate started to calm down, and his breathing slowed. She was lying on her side, facing him with her hair every which way. Johan reached over with his right arm and pushed her hair off her face. He remembered the first time he watched her sleep in the cave. *You're even more beautiful now.* Johan lowered the blanket just enough to expose her tummy. He lifted her shirt then placed his opened palm on her belly and was amazed at how large it was. He hadn't known many pregnant women, but this was by far the biggest growing baby he'd ever seen. She was half-naked beside him with just a panty and one of his old T-shirts. He sighed, frustrated.

Johan lay back on his pillow, not wanting to disturb her. He closed his eyes and willed his hard-on away. Sex was forbidden for Jesi lest it induce labor. Johan suddenly felt a hand on his erection, massaging it, stroking it. Lips were leaving wet trails on his arm.

"Jesi," he opened his eyes. "We can't do this," Johan swallowed. He watched her. A man could only exercise so much restraint. His pain tamed his desire over the past week, but now . . .

"Johan," he heard her whisper, interrupting the reasoning he tried to invoke.

"I don't want to hurt you or the baby." His voice was strained, and he tried to move her hand away. Instead, desire took control, and he tightened both of their grips around his erection.

"You don't have to make love to me to make me feel good," Jesi reminded him.

"Oh really?" Johan was caving. "What about me?"

"Mmmm," Jesi said as she nipped at his chest.

"I can think of something old," she bit him, "and something new to try with you."

"I've missed you, Jesi," Johan recalled what she had written in her letter. He brought her chin up and leaned down to take her lips. Johan lifted his head. Something moved and caught his attention. "Jesi!" Johan's eyes widened in disbelief, and he was paralyzed for a moment while he processed the thing in front of him.

"What, Johan, what?"

Johan eased out of bed and tiptoed to the closet for his knife.

"Johan, what is it?"

"Sh, don't move." He still had his eyes trained at the doorway.

Jesi followed his gaze. "Ha-ha-ha, are you scared of the baby lizard?" The faint light of dawn exposed the visitor.

"That is no baby lizard!" Johan was dumbfounded. She should be scared. *That thing could bite a hand off.*

"Don't hurt him, or you'll have to answer to Peter. It's his *hilitai*, ah 'monitor lizard.' "

"That *ha lee tie* is a pet?"

"Yes, and his name is Tommy. Peter said it was just a baby when it crawled on his lap the day they told us Tommy was dead."

"I'm sorry, Jesi." Johan felt bad he was not here for her when she got the news.

"Ha-ha-ha."

"What in god's name are you laughing at now?" Johan saw where she was looking, and bent his head down. Even in a somewhat relaxed state, he was quite endowed.

"Don't tempt me!"

"First, you should go get Peter, or you can push the hilitai into the other bedroom for now."

"I'll get the lizard . . ."

"Hilitai," she reminded.

"I'll get the hilitai into the other room." He shot her a piercing gaze. "Then I'll be back to finish what you started."

34

ESI SAT WITH HER FEET UP ON THE COUCH in the living room. The oil lamp cast a beautiful glow. It was still dark outside, and she was finally able to get out of bed and back to life. She had to beg her mom and Auntie Rita, telling them that the baby was almost due anyway. She sipped on her champulådo and watched as one gecko chased after another gecko. The tiny creatures were good to keep around the house because they loved to munch on bugs. The chirping sound they made was soothing.

"You're going to have lots of fun trying to catch those things." Jesi smiled at her belly, remembering how she and Peter would chase after the geckos when they were young, sometimes breaking off a part of their tail. "But don't worry, the tail grows back." Jesi set her cup on the side table.

"I never got around to telling you about how the hilitai got its split tongue did I?" She grinned, rubbing her belly. "You should have seen your daddy. He was so scared it was kinda funny." Jesi started to tell Johnny what she could recall from her childhood memories with Mrs. T. "When it was time for the hilitai to paint the Guam rail, the hilitai splattered paint all over the bird, covering the Guam rail with speckles of color. The hilitai didn't paint in any nice pattern. The Guam rail got very mad and chased the hilitai all around the jungle floor. In a quick moment, the bird struck the hilitai on the tongue and caused the end of tongue to split into two sides. This is how the hilitai got its funny tongue, and it's how the Guam rail got its spots."

"That's a great story, Jesi. I'd love to hear more," Johan said.

"Buenas, Johan. It's a Guam legend," Jesi smiled, "And the bird can't even fly. Can you believe that? I think I heard someone say it's found only on Guam." Jesi started to rise.

"You shouldn't get up." Johan gave her a kiss on her head.

"Oh, no you don't," Jesi replied.

"Good morning, Johnny." Johan bent down to kiss Jesi's belly.

"I'm finally able to walk around. I'm getting up."

"That's right," Johan said.

"What are we going to do today?" Jesi kissed and hugged him from behind. It was still dark outside.

"I don't know, what do you feel like doing?" Johan turned around.

Jesi looked up at him. "I feel like myself again, like all is right with the world now that you're here and I'm off my big butt."

"It's not big, Jesi, it's perfect."

"Mmmm," Jesi moaned, as he squeezed her butt. "I can think of something that would be perfect to do right now." She ran her hands over his chest.

"By the way," she tiptoed to kiss his lips, "I was a little naughty while you were gone." She slid her left hand under his briefs.

"What are you doing, Jesi?"

"Oh, I forgot to tell you," she knelt down and wrapped her lips around his erection.

"Jesi!"

"We can have sex now." She continued sucking on him.

"What?"

Jesi stood up. "You heard me."

"Really?"

Jesi saw the relief come over him. "It'll help start my delivery."

He pressed his lips against hers and bit it so hard it hurt. She needed him. And she knew he needed her, too. He backed her up against the arm of the couch.

"Turn around and lift your arms."

She focused on his hands as he ran them along her hips, her waist, and her arms, removing her dress.

"No panty? I've been waiting forever." He kissed along the base of her neck. She could feel his sex pressed hard against her backside. Jesi pushed her hips into him. She felt his fingers kneading her nipples. It was painful and pleasurable all at once.

"Kneel in front of the couch."

He moved behind her. He glided his shaft over her sex, massaging her clitoris.

"Stop teasing me!" Jesi wanted to feel him deep and hard inside her.

In seconds, he was in.

"Oh god!" Jesi braced her arms on the cushion. *God it's been so long. Yes, just like that.*

"Jesi."

The sound of his voice drove her crazy. She pushed against the cushion, forcing her hips into his thrusts. *Oh god, faster, Johan.*

Without her saying a word, he knew what to do.

"I've missed you, baby," Johan muttered.

Jesi concentrated on him pushing inside her. Everything was more sensitive than ever. Her orgasm was building. Johan started to rub the other hole with his thumb.

"Johan, Johan, oh god, Johan!" Her climax singed through her body. Every muscle in her pelvis and abdomen contracted. She moaned with such relief, as if it had been an eternity.

"Oh, Jesi."

She heard him. She felt him. He grunted and growled. And then he pulled out.

"Jesus!" Johan said, "I think I'm ready for a nap."

"Good idea." Jesi waited for Johan to lay a blanket down then arrange the pillows. She grabbed the other blanket on the couch to cover them. Jesi lay on her side, with her back against his chest.

"Well, Mrs. Landers, that was the best sex we've had in a very long time."

"I know." Jesi closed her eyes. She was happy, very happy, and satisfied. She hadn't felt this good since he left. *What was that?* She was fluttering between consciousness and dreamland. "I know this is a stupid question, but you didn't just pee on me did you?"

"No, but that is a kinky idea."

"What?" Jesi's eyes shot open. "It can't be that fast!"

35

Later That Day — Jesi and Johan's House

"I 'M DONE JOHAN," JESI SAID AFTER SHE finished washing herself in warm water, her dressed rolled up. The contractions were not too close together, but they were painful.

"Hang on to me."

"Thank you."

Johan stood beside her and helped her out of the shower.

"My pleasure," he smiled at her. "Now what?"

"Rub coconut oil on my back, oh god, it's starting again." Jesi closed her eyes and turned to hold on to Johan.

"I'm right here, sweetheart."

"God it hurts." Jesi cringed and leaned over, pressing her hand against her belly hoping to push the pain away. *Why would a woman do this over and over again?* She took another deep breath. "It's over. Just put oil on my back then my stomach."

Johan followed her instructions.

"I can still walk for now." Jesi unraveled her dress.

"Are you sure?"

"Yes. Is Auntie Rita here yet?"

"Yes. She's with grandma and Auntie Julia. They are starting to make chicken kâdo."

Jesi nodded.

"And they told me not to eat any. They even scolded Antonio for trying to sneak that sweet stuff wrapped in banana leaves."

"I told you so," Jesi said as they walked to the kitchen. "What woman would be hungry in all this pain?"

"I thought you were kidding."

"You want something to drink, Neni?" Mrs. T asked as they entered the kitchen.

"No thank you, Mom. I'm fine." Jesi âmened the three elderly women then went to sit by the kitchen table.

"I covered your bed with plenty of mats and clean blankets, Neni."

"Thank you."

"Neni, let me take your blood pressure first," Auntie Rita said. Auntie Rita had also been trained in the navy hospital before the war.

"Thank you, Auntie," Jesi extended her left arm out on the table and watched as Auntie Rita inflated the cuff, something Auntie Rita had done many times throughout Jesi's pregnancy.

"Ai, Neni, sa' it's high. Let me try your other arm."

"OK." Jesi straightened her right arm out on the table. She saw Johan cross his arms in front of his chest.

It's nothing. Jesi tried to comfort herself and Johan with a reassuring grin. *Other than lying in bed, I've had a very healthy pregnancy.*

"Your blood pressure is high, Neni."

"What do you mean? It wasn't before."

Jesi closed her eyes. *What did I do wrong?*

"I know nai, Neni, *lao* it's high now. I check both arms."

"Is she OK?" Mrs. T asked.

"Her blood pressure is high. I think she should go to the military hospital."

"What's wrong?" Johan asked, his voice louder than normal.

"The baby is in a good position. I need to check her dilation, but since her pressure is high, it's better to go to the military hospital just to be safe."

"Then we're going to the hospital." Johan was stern.

"But Johan, everything is ready here and . . ."

"No, Jesi!" He cut her off.

"Please, Johan." Jesi did not want to leave her house. She wanted to have Johnny here, in her own bed.

"Jesi, you need to be reasonable." Johan knelt down so he was level with her. "I know how much you've been looking forward to this, but I will not risk your life, or Johnny's."

A few hours later — Orote Peninsula, Military Hospital Tent
"One more push and he's out, Jesi." Johan said.

Shut up, shut up, shut up! "No, no, I can't."

"Look at me, Jesi."

He seemed to loom over her.

"One more time, sweetheart."

Oh god!

"You can do this," the navy doctor was between her legs, waiting. "Come on, Jesi, when I count to three you need to push really hard and your baby will be here. One, two, three."

Just this one last time. "Puuuuuuuuuuush," Jesi screamed. She pulled on her thighs and scrunched forward against her stomach.

"It's a boy." She thought she heard the man say.

"It's a boy, Jesi, it's a boy!" Johan smiled at her.

She wanted to smile back but she was tired.

"Do the honors, Sarge," the doctor handed Johan a scissor.

Jesi took a deep breath. She could hear the baby crying. Jesi opened her eyes and tried to sit up somewhat, but couldn't.

"They're just checking on him and cleaning him," Johan said. "You did great. I'm so proud of you."

"He looks good so far," she heard a woman say.

Jesi turned in the direction of the voice. It was the nurse.

"Oh god!" Jesi screamed. "It hurts, it hurts again. Johan!"

"It's OK, it's just the afterbirth," the navy doctor said. He was still between her legs.

"No, no, no, it's like before." *Oh god, oh god, I need to push again. Push, Jesi, push.* She gripped her thighs and scrunched against her stomach.

"What the hell!" The doctor sounded very surprised. "You've got another one coming!"

"What?" She could hear Johan.

"I'm tired, Johan. I can't, I can't do this again." Jesi started to cry. She heard something about blood pressure, got to do it now.

"Jesi, Jesi," Johan called her. She felt his hand on her cheek.

"Jesi, look at me. You are the strongest woman I have ever met. I know it hurts really bad now, but I know you can do this. You are much stronger than I am, sweetheart."

She opened her eyes. "It's starting again." She didn't want to cry, but the tears streamed down her eyes.

"You can do it. You are very strong. You are Chamorro," Mames whispered.

"I need her to push in one, two, three."

"Push, Jesi, push," Johan said.

One last puuuuuuush. Jesi held her breath and pulled on her thighs. She pushed as hard as she could push. And then the pain was gone. All the pain.

36

May 16, 1945 — Orote Peninsula, Military Hospital Tent

"**I**N THE NAME OF THE FATHER, AND THE Son, and the Holy Spirit," Johan did the sign of the cross while he knelt by Jesi's side. He placed his hands together. His heart was heavy. The hospital was quiet.

Mrs. T, Tan Chai, and Auntie Julia sat behind him.

Please Lord, I know I'm still new to this, but please don't take my Jesi. I need her. We need her. I've killed many men in this war, but it was in the name of war. Please spare Jesi. She should not be punished for my wrongdoings. He picked up her hand in both of his, and held it against his lips. *Please come back to me, sweet girl, don't leave me!* Johan could bear it no longer. He broke down by her side, as if he were a little boy who had lost his puppy.

"Johan," Mrs. T laid her hand on his shoulder. "Would you like to pray the rosary with us? We can say it in English.

"Yes, Mom," he nodded. He wiped the tears from his eyes and got to his feet. He leaned over and kissed her forehead. *I love you, Jesi.* He looked over Jesi's pale, still body. He'd never seen her like this. Jesi had yet to wake up since her delivery.

37

JOHAN SAT ROCKING HER. THE BABIES slept in his bedroom, next to his bed. She was born a bit smaller than Johnny, but she was catching up. "Oh, Kat, you remind me so much of your momma." The moonlight illuminated the bedroom. He cradled her in his arm and traced her chubby cheeks.

Whereas Johnny took Chief's darker complexion, Kat had Jesi's lighter skin. He looked at the mattress beside him, grateful. Johnny was asleep. He was calm compared to Kat. Kat needed a little coercing to settle down.

Johan closed his eyes and thought about that night. He was so upset that the pattera did not know Jesi was carrying twins. He had prayed as he never prayed before. The doctor said having two babies come through the birth canal was like suffering from a traumatic car accident. Jesi's body had gone into severe shock.

It was a year to this day when he first landed on Guam, ready to fight and die. The Germans surrendered in May, but the Japs were still at it.

I hope you never have to live through one, Sweetness. Johan caressed Kat's cheek with his thumb.

He knew better. There will always be those who believe that their way is the only way, that there exists only their God, that their race is the pure race. And so there must always be those ready to defend and protect America, and the freedom and opportunities she offers.

Once a heathen with nothing to lose, he was now a praying man with a life worth living. Becoming a parent also softened his heart toward his own folks. "I'm going to have to contact your other grandparents, Sweetness. They will fall in love with you two just as I have. And we'll have to visit them someday, too."

She tried to be as quiet as possible as she leaned against the doorway to their bedroom. Jesi loved watching Johan soothe the babies to sleep. *I can't believe a year ago today I was hiding in that cave, all by myself. I could have been killed if it wasn't for him.*

Her heart ached that Tan Chai was no longer able to treat patients. She had difficulty walking without help. Jesi thus had to fulfill the role she had been groomed for all her life. The weight of being not just any suruhåna and le'an, but also Tan Chai's granddaughter, was overwhelming. Jesi forged the strength and the courage to be who she was meant to be. *For my grandma.* Her love of swimming, and teaching children how to swim, would have to wait. *Or, I'll figure out how to do both someday.*

Johan walked toward her with Kat asleep in his arms.

"You're so good with them," Jesi said, smiling. She kissed Kat's forehead, inhaling her was more like it. *Hu guaiya hao, Neni.*

"Done?" Johan asked.

"Yes, I needed that soak. The tub has been a blessing." Having twins was more work than she ever imagined.

"Let me put her down."

278

Jesi watched as Johan laid Kat beside Johnny. She still couldn't believe she was pregnant with twins and didn't know it. Jesi knew she was lucky to be alive. Johan had said she was unconscious for two days.

"You smell so good." Johan wrapped his arms around her.

She kissed him back. He slid his hands under her dress and squeezed her butt. Jesi moved backwards to accommodate his forward steps.

"You taste good," Jesi said. She continued to kiss along his neck. She was getting very aroused and excited. She and Johan had finally been able to figure out a routine with the twins. They could make love now without rushing. Jesi lifted her arms so Johan could remove her dress. He sucked on her nipple and she gasped. His lips always felt intense around them. Jesi closed her eyes and tossed her head back, needing him to take the other breast. She could hear him fumbling for something behind her. She felt him slide it between her legs.

Jesi opened her eyes and looked at Johan.

"Something new I got for you. Calhoun sent it to me from New York."

"Oh god."

She loved him, and she wanted him. It was love and it was sex. He had helped conquer the Japanese and rid them from Guam, but she had conquered his heart.

PLEASE AND THANK YOU

I hope you enjoyed this story. Please consider leaving a review on Amazon.com. I would sincerely appreciate your comments. But don't stop flipping the pages yet! There's more: a map, a couple of recipes, a glossary, and a list of names, characters, places, and references.

Thank you,

Paulaq

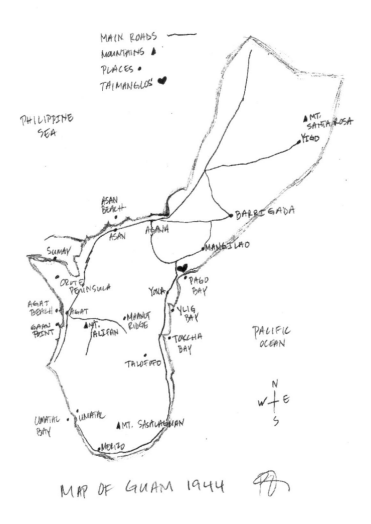

MAIN ROADS ——
MOUNTAINS ▲
PLACES •
TAIMANGLOS ♥

PHILIPPINE
SEA

▲ MT. SANTA ROSA
• YIGO

ASAN BEACH
ASAN   ASANA   • BARRIGADA
SUMAY   • MANGILAO

ORUTE PENINSULA   YONA   • PAGO BAY

AGAT BEACH   • AGAT   • MAANOT RIDGE   • YLIG BAY   PACIFIC OCEAN
GAAN POINT   ▲ MT. ALIFAN   • TOKCHA BAY

TALOFOFO

N
W + E
S

UMATAC BAY   • UMATAC   ▲ MT. SASALAGUAN
• MERIZO

MAP OF GUAM 1944

BOÑELOS AGA'
[BANANA DOUGHNUTS]

This will yield a small batch of boñelos, which should be quite soft even after it has completely cooled. Making boñelos aga' requires minimal adjustments to the dough depending on how much water is in the bananas. Do not add more flour than listed.

Makes about 40 doughnuts.

INGREDIENTS

SET 1

    3 cups overripe, smashed bananas (previously frozen and thawed to room temperature is best)

    1 cup sugar

    2 teaspoons vanilla

SET 2

    2½ cups flour (¼ cup more may be needed)

    2 teaspoons baking powder

SET 3

    Vegetable oil for deep frying

Tools: large pot, ladle with holes, medium bowl, colander, napkins, long butter knife

DIRECTIONS

Fill the large pot halfway with oil. Heat the oil on medium heat.

While it's heating, combine the smashed bananas, sugar, and vanilla in a large bowl.

Add 2½ cups flour and baking powder. Mix thoroughly.

Depending on the ripeness of the bananas or if they were previously frozen, you may or may not need the remaining ¼ cup of flour.

Check the thickness of the "cake mix-like" batter. The batter should be a bit thicker than cake mix, but not at all like bread dough. Take a scoop in your hand. Drop it into the rest of the mixture. The scoop should retain some of its shape without completely blending into the mix. It will flatten out, but you should be able to see the outline.

If you are not sure, leave out the extra flour for now.

Test your "batter dropping" technique. Scoop a small amount of batter into the palm of your dominant hand. Make a circle with your thumb and fingers. Turn your "circled fingers" to drop some batter back into the bowl. This takes a little bit of practice. If you can squeeze the batter out and let the trail of batter fall onto itself in the oil, your doughnuts have a good chance of turning out round. If not, and the boñelos has a tail, more crunchy parts to eat! You can always use two small spoons, or a small cookie-dough scoop.

When the oil is hot, drop about a teaspoon of batter into the oil. The dough should turn into a puffy ball. The batter may fall to the bottom of the pot, but rises as it cooks. It will only stay at the bottom a few seconds. If it sits longer, the oil is not hot enough. Use a butter knife to tease the doughnut from the bottom of the pot, and discard. Wait five minutes for the oil to continue to heat.

Test a bigger doughnut. Scoop enough batter in your hand to form one doughnut. Position your hand about an inch above the surface of the oil then squeeze the batter through your thumb and fingers. If the batter falls to the bottom of the pot, let it cook for two minutes. If it doesn't rise after two minutes, nudge it free with a long utensil.

The oil should be hot enough to cook the center of the boñelos and brown the outside of the doughnut within 15 minutes.

Cool the larger test doughnut on a napkin. Open the doughnut and check to see if it is cooked. Check carefully as there will be chunks of banana in the boñelos. If in doubt whether there is enough flour, go ahead and add the remaining ¼ cup of flour. Mix this very well.

Continue to squeeze batter into the oil without overcrowding the pot. The entire first batch of doughnuts may need nudging from the bottom of the pot.

The doughnuts in the remaining batches should float to the surface of the oil on their own.

Drain doughnuts in a colander then transfer to a napkin-lined dish.

A video for this recipe is available on paulaq.com. Select the tab for "Remember Guam."

GUYURIA

Yields 2 1/3-gallon freezer bags, or about 7.5 pounds of guyuria. The recipe may be halved, but use a good scale to measure the flour, or purchase a 2½ pound bag of flour.

INGREDIENTS

DOUGH

SET 1

> 5 pound bag of all-purpose flour, preferably a name brand such as Gold Medal
>
> 1 stick unsalted butter, softened

SET 2

> 4 – 13.5 ounce cans thick coconut milk*

*If the milk has separated into a solid and liquid, empty all of the cans into a bowl and whisk together to form a homogenous mixture.

Tools: large bowl, plastic wrap, large pot, slotted ladle or spider strainer, colander, 4 – 11 x 17 or larger cookie sheets/ cake pans with rims, small pot

DIRECTIONS

Pour the entire bag of flour into a large bowl.

Chop softened butter over the flour. Use your hands to mix until the flour resembles coarse crumbs.

Add enough coconut milk to form a soft, nonsticky dough.

Knead slightly. Divide the dough into seven equal portions and wrap each portion with plastic wrap.

Preheat a large pot of oil to between medium-low and medium heat, or about the 7 and 8 on the face of a clock.

Work with one portion of dough at a time. Pinch off a large ball of dough from this first portion, about what you can grab with one hand. Wrap the remaining dough. Pinch pieces of dough off the ball that are small enough to spread over the back of a fork. Fill a large dinner plate with these pieces, finishing the dough in your hand.

Roll the tiny pieces of dough off the back of the fork, pinching the edge of the dough with the pointed tines of the fork. Place the shaped dough on a dry cookie sheet. Fill two cookie sheets before you begin frying the dough.

Load a large slotted ladle or spider strainer with the shaped dough. Load the ladle OVER THE COUNTERTOP NOT OVER THE POT OF OIL.

Stir the guyuria so they cook evenly. The guyuria should not brown as soon as you put the dough into the oil.

Adjust the heat as necessary so that the guyuria cook inside before getting too dark on the outside. Fry the dough till golden brown

Each batch takes about 25 to 30 minutes to cook properly. If it browns too much before 25 to 30 minutes, it will not be crunchy on the inside.

Remove the first batch and drain in a colander then pour into a large cake pan.

Continue to pinch, roll, and fry dough until you have fried the last batch.

SYRUP

SET 1

5 cups granulated sugar

1 cup water

Tools: *small pot*

DIRECTIONS

In a small pot, combine the water and 2 cups of sugar. Heat the mixture on medium until it simmers.

Stir to dissolve most of the sugar. Remove the pot from the stove then add 1 cup of sugar.

Place the pot in the fridge until the mixture is completely cooled, stirring every now and then.

Remove the pot of sugar from the fridge then add 1 more cup of sugar. Stir.

Pour just a little bit of syrup over the guyuria and stir the cookies. Pour only enough syrup so as not to leave a thick layer of syrup on the bottom of the pan.

Dry the coated cookies for one hour. Add a little more syrup and sprinkle some dry sugar over the guyuria. Stir thoroughly.

Allow the sugared guyuria to dry completely.

Store cookies in two layers of Ziploc freezer bags.

Videos for this recipe are available on paulaq.com. Select the tab for "A Taste of Guam."

GLOSSARY

achoti (*a-tso-tee*). A type of plant, annatto, *Bixa orellana*

adai (*a-day*). For goodness' sake, or an expression of politeness

adiós (*a-dyos*). Good-bye

ai (*eye*). Wow, oh

Ai Yu 'us, Ai Yu 'us (*eye-dzu-uws*). Oh Jesus, oh Jesus

akgak (*ak-gak*). A type of plant, pandanus

amåntes (*a-mon-tis*). Lovers

åmen (*ah-men*). Bringing an elder's knuckle area of their fingers to your nose, or kissing the cheek of an elder

amko' (*am-ku*). Elderly

åmot (*aw-mut*). Medicine

asagua (*a-sa-gwa*). Spouse

atulen ilotes (*a-too-lin ee-low-tis*). Corn soup

båsta (*baws-ta*). Stop

belu (*be-lu*). A wedding ceremony veil

betbena (*bet-be-na*). A type of plant, *Heliptropium indicum* or scorpion weed

Biba Kumple Åños (*bee-ba coom-plee aw-nyos*). Happy Birthday.

boñelos aga' (*bo-nye-los a-ga*). Banana doughnuts

buchi buchi (*bu-chee bu-chee*). Pumpkin turnover

buenas (*bwe-nas*). Greetings

bunita (*bu-knee-ta*). Pretty

chagi (*tsa-gee*). Try, taste

Chai (*chai*). Chamorro nickname for the proper name, Rosa

champulado (*cham-poo-law-do*). Hot chocolate drink made with corn masa.

chenchule' (*tsen-tsu-lee*). Gift, money, donation

chule' (*tsu-lee*). Take or grab

dánkolo (*dung-ku-lew*). Big, large, extreme

diablo (*dyab-blue*). Curse word, devil

dias (*dee-as*). Day

dokdok (*dok-duk*). Type of plant, *Artocarpus mariannensis* or breadfruit without seeds

dos (*dos*). Two

eskabeche (*es-ka-be-tsee*). Fried fish and vegetables in turmeric and vinegar sauce

eskoban ñuhot (*es-ko-ban nyu-hewt*). A broom made from a bunching of ribs from individual coconut leaves.

eskuelan pale' (*es-kwe-lan paw-lee*). Religious school

esta (*es-ta*). Already

fan (*fan*). Please

fanohge (*fan-o-gee*). Everybody stand.

fo'na (*fogh-na*). To be first or in front, also name of Chamorro creation goddess

gaige (*guy-gee*). Here

gi (*gee*). At, in

gof (*gof*). Very

Gollai áppan aga' (*gogh-lie aw-pan a-ga*). Bananas cooked in coconut milk until the liquid evaporates

guáfak (*gwa-fak*). Woven mat

guaiya (*gwai-dza*). Love

guella (*gwe-la*). Grandmother

guello (*gwe-lu*). Grandfather

guenao guatu (*gwen-now gwa-too*). Over there

guyuria (*gu-dzu-ree-ya*). Fried, shell-shaped cookies

ha' (*ha*). Still, really still

háfa (*haw-fa-day*). What

Háfa tatatmanu hao? (*haw-fa tatat-man-nu how*). How are you?

haga (*ha-ga*). Daughter

hagon (*ha-gon*). Leaf

haligi (*ha-lee-gee*). Pillar

halom (*haw-lum*). In, into, inside

hao (*how*). You

heggao (*heg-ow*). Coconut husker

hilitai (*ha-lee-tie*). Iguana or large monitor lizard

hoe' (*hoy*). Hello or calling for someone at the door

hu- (*who*). I

-hu (*who*). My

hunggan (*huung-gan*). Yes

i (*ee*). Definite article

ifet (*ee-fit*). Ironwood tree

kådo/kåddon (*kaw-do*). Soup

kahulo' (*ka-who-lu*). Get up

kåmyo (*come-dzu*). Coconut grater

kao (*cow*). Indicates a question is being asked.

karabáo (*ka-ra-bow*). Water buffalo

kåtne (*kawt-knee*). Beef

kåtre (*kaw-tree*). Bed

kélaguen (*ke-la-gwen*). A dish in which raw beef, deer, or seafood, and partially cooked chicken is mixed with lemon juice, salt, hot pepper, onions, and coconut. The lemon and salt cook the raw protein.

komprende (*come-pren-dee*). Understand, comprehend

kusina (*ku-see-na*). Kitchen

låhi (*law-hee*). Boy

laña' (*lan-nya*). Expression for feelings of rage from surprise to disgust

lao (*low*). But

le'an (*lay-an*). Clairvoyant

leche/lechen (*le-tsee* or *le-tsin*). Any kind of milk

lemmai (*le-my*). Type of plant, breadfruit without seeds

lódigao (*low-dee-gow*). A type of plant, seaside clerodendrum

lokkue' (*lok-qwee*). Also, as well

lommuk (*lome-muck*). Pestle

lusong (*lew-song*). Mortar

månnok (*maw-nok*). Chicken

mågi (*maw-gee*). Here

mailá (*my-la*). Come

malago' (*ma-la-gogh*). Want

mames (*ma-mis*). Sweet

man- (*man*). Makes the subject plural

manåmko' (*man-um-ku*). More than one elderly person

månha (*mawn-ha*). Young coconut

maolek (*mau-lek*). Good

måtto (*maw-to*). Arrive or come

mestisa (*mes-tee-sa*). Traditional dress or blouse with high, elegant sleeves

monhåyan (*mon-ah-dzan*). Done, finished

-mu (*moo*). Your, yours

Mumutong sapble (*moo-mu-tung sawp-blee*). A type of plant, *Cassia occidentalis*

muyo' (*moo-dzu*). Pout/pouting

na (*na*). Connects a noun to its modifier. *Gof bunita na palao'an.* Very beautiful girl.

nai (*n-eye*). Where, when

Nåna (*naw-na*). Mom

nannga (*nang-ga*). Wait

nåya (*naw-dza*). For a while

Neni (*ne-knee*). Baby

nihi (*knee-he*). Let's go, let's do something.

nino (*knee-no*). Godfather

niyok (*knee-dzuk*). Coconut

ñora (*nyo-ra*). An expression for kissing a woman's hand; a sign of respect

ñot (*nyot*). An expression for kissing a man's hand; a sign of respect

ombren (*owm-brin*). Please, having already been asked or told

pàgu (*paw-gu*). Type of plant, *Hibiscus tiliaceus* or wild hibiscus, used in making rope

palao 'an (*pa-lauw-an*). Female

pan (*pawn*). Bread

pan tosta (*pan toss-ta*). Toasted bread

pattera (*pat-te-ra*). Midwife

pontan (*pon-tan*). A ripe coconut that fell from the tree, also the name of the Chamorro creation god

potu (*po-too*). Rice cake

punta/puntan (*puwn-ta or puwn-tan*). Point, peak

ramas (*ra-mas*). Twig

respetu (*ris-pe-too*). Respect, veneration

sa' (*sa*). Because

sàli (*saw-lee*). Micronesian starling bird

si (*see*). This is.

Si Yu 'us ma 'àse' (*see dzu-uws ma-aw-see*). Thank you.

siña (*see-nya*). Can or be able

sinamomu (*see-na-mow-moo*). Type of a henna plant, leaves are made into an ointment to treat wounds and bruises.

suruhàna (*sue-ru-haw-na*). Medicine woman

tai- (*tie*). None, to not have

tala' (*ta-la*). Dry

tan (*tan*). Term of respect used to address older women or older female relatives

tàngantàngan (*tawng-an tawng-an*). Type of plant, *Leucaena leucocephala* or wild tamarind, wood good for barbecue

tano' (*ta-nu*). Land

taotaomo'na (*tauw-tauw-mogh-na*). People of the before time

tasa (*ta-sa*). Cup

tataga' (*ta-ta-ga*). Type of fish, Naso unicornus or unicorn fish

tinalan kàtne (*tee-na-la kawt-knee*). Dried beef

tinanom-mu (*tee-na-nom-moo*). Your plants

titiyas (*tee-tee-dzas*). Tortillas

tosta (*toss-ta*). Toast, dried, cooked to a crisp

tres (*tres*). Three

tuba (*too-ba*). Fermented coconut sap

un (*un*). One of something

ya/yan (*dza* or *dzan*). And

yanggen (*dzang-gin*). If or when

Yo' (*dzu*). I

Yu'us (*dzu-uws*). Jesus

NAMES AND CHARACTERS

American GI radioman. The character in the story resembles the historical radioman who eluded the Japanese, George R. Tweed, during the occupation of Guam, surviving in the jungle and providing the US armed forces with info in recapturing Guam; the Japanese soldiers in the story believe the family of Jesi's friend Carmen were hiding him and retaliated by raping and murdering Carmen.

Army Nurse Corps. United States Army Nurse Corps, Miss Cora, who takes care of Johan on the hospital ship.

Antonio. Jesi's young cousin was only four years old when she last saw him before the Japanese invasion; he was like a little brother to her; he interrupts Jesi's and Johan's foreplay at her grandmother's house on the day the soldiers came to help with the building of Auntie Julia's house; his parents have gone missing in the occupation and he has lived with Auntie Julia and Tan Chai; when his father Vicente returns he goes to live with him along with Auntie Julia; his mother is called Rosa and has disappeared in the war.

Bonita. Name of the water buffalo Jesi and Peter ride to Agana, when they meet Johan's unit and then pick up Auntie Julia and Tan Chai; she's Jesi's pet; she had a calf during the occupation of Guam.

Calhoun. Specialist Calhoun, an army buddy of Johan's; a bit of a daredevil; a few years older than Johan and left behind a wife and two kids in the States; he helps work out the wedding arrangements for Jesi and Johan by finding a chaplain.

Carmen. Jesi's childhood friend on Guam who was assaulted, raped, and nearly beheaded by the Japanese; the Japanese thought her family was hiding an American radioman; Jesi still has nightmares about her; in arguing with Chief she taunts him with the fate of Carmen and how Johan saved her from a similar tragedy with her Japanese attackers.

Chamorros *(cha-mo-rro)*. Name of the native ethnic people on Guam.

Chief. Jesi's father, Dad; Hon; he's called Chief because he was the one to start trouble in the family, also known as the leader of the pack; was protective of Jesi and wouldn't let her go out with boys in high school; prefers to wear his hair long in a ponytail; punched another boy in the face when he was dating Jesi's mother; Jesi bakes him his favorite coconut cake to make up with him after they argue over Johan; he has a quick temper; Jesi is tiny when compared to him; Johan asks Peter if he'd have a chance with Chief in asking for Jesi to marry him; Chief cuts his ponytail and shaves his beard for Jesi's wedding; his father was a rope maker; he speaks in Chamorro and English when he's mad; he's hidden his family in two separate caves during the Japanese occupation; his grandson Johnny has Chief's dark complexion.

Cora. Name of an army nurse on the ship attending the wounded Johan back to Guam; she and Jesi's brother hit it off when they meet.

Deb. Debbie, Jesi's mother's first name, and what Chief calls his wife.

Donnelly. A combat photographer, teamed with Johan's unit; he comes to take photographs at Jesi's and Johan's wedding.

Fo 'na *(fogh-na).* Guam goddess.

Marine Major General Roy Geiger. In charge of the operation to retake Guam.

Grandma. Also known as Tan Chai; she's sixty-eight; Jesi's grandmother and the most respected medicine woman on the island; Uncle Kin is her brother, who is fond of partying; Chief takes her and Jesi's mother to the American shelters on Guam once Guam is secured; Grandma and Auntie Julia are sisters; Jesi likes to work in her backyard because it has a beautiful view; she has a private cove behind her house at Pago Bay.

Grandfather. Also Pops Landers, Pops, gave Johan a Bunn Special pocket watch, which he carries with him; he owned a homestead in the Catskills, where he worked the rails.

Grandfather. On Jesi's mother's side served in the navy; he built his house from ifet wood.

Jesi. Her full name is Jessica Marie Taimanglo, Jes, Sis, *Neni* (what her mother calls her, Chamorro for "baby"), age 17 at the beginning of the story; her birthday is September 30, 1944, when she'll be twenty; she has long black wavy hair tied in a ponytail; full lips; she's thin and five feet and a couple of inches; she was expected to follow in her grandmother's footsteps as a respected medicine woman; her gray eyes turn green when she's upset; her mother is taller than she is; her fingers were long and slender, and her nails were surprisingly clean and cut; she was taught English at school—graduated George Washington High School; when she was growing up other kids made fun of her eyes and skin; her mom's grandfather was in the US Navy (he died before she was born); misses her mom and grandmother who she hasn't seen since the beginning of the war; her oldest brother Tommy is killed at Pearl Harbor; she likes to swim; Mrs. T has been teaching her to sew since she was five years old. Before the war she had an American friend Suzie who helped her learn English.

Johan. Staff Sergeant Johan Landers of the United States Army in charge of a platoon; dark hair and clean teeth; was married to a woman from Texas named Lily for two years before she was killed by a drunk driver; he was not a praying kind of man; Jesi compares his muscles to Chief's and notes Johan is more muscular; he hadn't had sex in a year before encountering Jesi; he lived in the mountains in New York on his grandfather's homestead; he was married to Lily for two years and they lived in Manhattan; he doesn't smoke or drink; he was baptized and raised a Catholic but has become a heathen; his family were bankers and investors, but Johan didn't like the business; he left Manhattan in a hurry; he has two brothers in the family business, he left the brothers on good terms but hasn't heard from them; he has no sisters; was close to his grandfather and carried his grandfather's watch; he's thirty when he meets Jesi, but will have a birthday in December 1944, when he will be 31; ten and twelve years younger than his older brothers.

Johnny. What Jesi wants to name her baby; the name she calls her unborn child; the baby resembles the darker complexion of Chief; Jesi's firstborn twin.

Julia. Also called Auntie Julia; sister to Jesi's grandmother who takes care of Antonio; Jesi asks Johan to come help rebuild Auntie Julia's house; she serves as the godmother at Jesi's wedding; blesses the table at Jesi's wedding feast; she moves with Antonio to his father's house, when Grandma gives her house to Jesi and Johan as a wedding present; she's a Catholic; she goes to the hospital where Jesi gives birth.

Kat. Name of Jesi and Johan's younger twin daughter; she is lighter skinned than her brother more like her mother.

Uncle Kin. Was Jesi's grandmother's brother, and there was always a party at his house. His house was not far from the Tokcha River, along the northern edge of Talofofo village; Jesi decides to go his house when she leaves the Ylig cave where her mom and grandma were supposed to be; Uncle Kin had kept chickens and sold eggs at the Agana market; he serves as the godfather at Jesi's wedding signing her marriage license with Auntie Julia, since Johan didn't have any relatives on Guam; Auntie Rita brings eggs from Uncle Kin when Jesi is pregnant.

Lady. A Japanese woman, who had been living on Guam before the occupation, owned the Dejima store in Agana.

Landers, brothers. Johan's two older brothers who are still in the family business back in New York.

Landers, Granny. Johan's grandmother, sprinkled coconut on cake.

Landers, Johan. Also Johan, Staff Sergeant John Landers; Sergeant Landers; in the Second Battalion of the 305th Regimental Combat Team of the 77th Infantry Division of the US Army; raised Catholic; thirty years old; Was married for two years to Lily and lived in Manhattan before she was killed by a drunken driver; a muscular officer with dark hair.

Landers, Mrs. Jesi's married name; also Jessica Taimanglo Landers; Jessica Landers; Mrs. Jessica Landers.

Lily. Johan's first wife from Texas; the young couple lived in Manhattan; she was killed when she was two months pregnant by a drunken driver; Johan screams her name during a dream in Jesi's cave after he has attacked the Japanese soldiers assaulting Jesi.

Lucas, Sergeant David. Part of Johan's team in the Second Battalion landing on Guam; several inches shorter than Johan but equally fit; second in command to Landers; Landers gives him $100 to cover his shift for him when he goes to visit Jesi; Landers chides him for not saving his money.

Mames *(ma-miss).* The ancestral spirit in the story; she guides Jesi and speaks to her in whispers.

Marine Raiders. Elite group of marines who bestow the name of 305th Marines on Johan's unit.

Miller. A soldier in Johan's squad, private first class, outshone other soldiers in training in the States, but had problems with how slow the army functioned; the shortest man on the squad, 5 feet 5; would like to meet a girl on Guam; goes with Sergeant Landers to help build Auntie Julia's house; drives the jeep as the squad is leaving Orote; he calls for a medic when Johan is injured on the beach at Okinawa and works to patch up Johan; Johan thinks Miller made it out alive.

Mom. Jesi's mother; at times she is impatient with Jesi's emotional nature; she's the boss of the family, while Chief is old-fashioned.

Neni *(ne-knee)*. What Jesi's mother calls her, and sometimes her father and grandmother.

Peter. Jesi's brother, her brother closest in age to her; he still lives on Guam and is the most protective of her two brothers; the only one in the family who calls her Jes; he took on more of Chief's side of the family. Peter was darker than Jesi and almost as tall as Chief. Short hair, he lost his thumb and two fingers in a chain saw accident. He drives an old pickup truck; his prize possession is a kamyo; he tries to offer support to Jesi when she fights with her father; he used to work at the Pan Am Hotel before the war but now does odd jobs on the Orote Peninsula; Jesi asks him to be her baby's godfather; he has a pet lizard he calls after their other brother Tommy; he's very close to Tan Chai; he befriends Johan.

Pop. What Johan calls his grandfather.

Pontan *(pon-tan)*. Guam god, brother of the goddess Fo'na, in the creation story. She created the sun, moon, rainbows and the Earth from him.

Auntie Rita. Jesi's *pattera* or midwife, trained in the US navy hospital before the war; long braided hair.

Rosa. The name of Antonio's mom who the Taimonglos fear she had been murdered by the Japanese.

Saint Joseph. The patron saint of families; Jesi prays for him to protect Johan in battle; she gives Johan a Saint Joseph medal for protection; he believes it helped save his life at Okinawa.

Second Battalion. Johan's battalion in the 305th; and the Second Battalion of the Fourth Marines

Seventy-Seventh Infantry. Includes Johan's unit

706th Tank Battalion. Offered cover for Johan's unit during the battle for Barrigada, Guam.

General Shepherd. Lemuel Cornick Shepherd, Jr. (February 10, 1896–August 6, 1990), a four-star general of the United States Marine Corps; Johan tells his men they've gotten word that General Shepherd didn't need them just yet in the landing on Guam.

Smith. Specialist Smith, Smithy, soldier in Johan's platoon, courageous, pint-sized man, he's wounded in the leg fighting in the Philippines; he volunteers to help Johan build Auntie Julia's house; he's curious about the Chamorros playing baseball on Guam.

Statue of Liberty Boys. Nickname for the Seventy-Seventh Infantry from New York.

Suzie. The name of Jesi's childhood American friend who spoke English with her and filled her in about sex; Jesi had read about childbirth in Suzie's father's books.

Mrs. T. (short for *Taimanglo*), Jesi's mother, her first name is Deb; she is a couple of inches taller than Jesi and more voluptuous; described as a disciplinarian; Jesi was close to her mom; she was more affectionate and playful compared to most Chamorro mothers; the mother of four children: Teresa (died in childbirth), Tommy, Peter, and Jesi; Her son Tommy died at Pearl Harbor; she'd never talked with Jesi about sex.

Taimanglo *(tie-mang-lu).* Jesi's family name, means "without wind."

Taimanglo, Grandfather. Chief's father who was a ropemaker; he built their house out of strong ifet wood.

Taimanglo, great grandma. Was a *le'an*, able to communicate with the spirit world.

Tan Chai *(tan chai)*. Name most people use for Jesi's grandmother; a *suruhàna*, a medicine woman, in Chamorro; she's sixty-eight; Peter is very close to her; she gifts her house to Jesi and Johan as a wedding present; her house has three bedrooms with Auntie Julie and Antonio in one, leaving room for Jesi to move in when she fights with her father; she speaks in Chamorro; she is revered in the community for her skills and knowledge of medicine. she is unable to tend to her own patients after Jesi's twins are born in June 1945.

Teresa. Name of Jesi's baby sister; she died at birth.

305th Marines. The nickname given to Johan's unit by the Marine Raiders.

Tommy. Thomas, name of Jesi's oldest brother, who had joined the US Navy as a mess attendant, her mother conceived him on her first sexual encounter; he was killed at Pearl Harbor.

Tommy. The name Peter gives to the monitor lizard that crawled into his lap the day they learned that their brother Tommy had been killed at Pearl Harbor.

Tweed, George. An American radioman on Guam the Japanese were hunting. Jesi's friend Carmen's family was suspected of hiding him.

USS *Starlight*. The name of the transport ship bringing Johan to Guam.

Vicente. Antonio's dad who hid from the Japanese during the war in Umatac village near Fouha Rock; Auntie Julia and Antonio go to stay with him until Auntie Julia's house is ready.

Virgin Mary. Jesi leaves flowers at Mary's statue on the day of her wedding.

PLACES

Agana, Guam *(a-ga-nya gwom)*. Village in US territory; destroyed in the war; where Auntie Julia had a house; where Jesi and Peter are headed on the bull when they run into Johan; spelled Hagåtña *(ha-got-nya)* in Chamorro.

Agana market, Guam. Where Uncle Kin sold eggs.

Agat beachhead. Johan's battalion camps there when they land on Guam; spelled Hågat *(haw-gat)* in Chamorro.

Agat, Guam *(a-gat)*. Where Johan first lands on Guam and spends the night.

Anigua, Guam *(a-knee-gwa)*. Area along the outskirts of Agana, Jesi and Peter go there to find their mother.

Arizona, deserts of. A location of Johan's army training and where he compares the conditions on the deck of the USS *Starlight*.

Asan, Guam *(a-san)*. The Third Marine Division lands there; spelled Assan *(as-san)* in Chamorro.

Barrigada, Guam *(ba-ree-gow-da)*. Also battle for Barrigada, August 2–4, 1944; Johan is grateful he didn't lose any men in the fight with the Japanese; spelled Barigåda *(ba-ree-gaw-da)* in Chamorro.

Barrigada–Agana Road, Central Guam. Jesi and Johan find each other again.

Camp Stoneman, Pittsburg, California. Johan had completed his prewar training there before shipping out in the Pacific.

Catskills, Catskill Mountains. Johan Lander's grandfather had a homestead in the mountains and where he worked the rails in Upstate New York; Johan had tried to find peace in the mountains after his first wife died; Johan tells Jesi he'd love to show her his grandfather's land and ride horses in the Catskills.

Central Guam, Eastern Coast. Where Jesi's family lived during the war.

Dejima store in Agana. A prewar Japanese-owned store on Guam.

Eniwetok. Island in the Western Pacific in the NW Marshall Islands taken by the Americans in February 1944; where Johan trained in the jungles for battle.

Europe. WWII is still raging there, during the battle for Guam.

Fouha Rock *(fow-a)*. In Umatac Bay, where Vicente, Antonio's dad, hid during the war; location of the Guam creation story.

Gaan Point *(ga-an)*. Johan and company are supposed to meet near there in the invasion of Guam, near the village of Agat; spelled Ga'an *(ga-an)* in Chamorro.

Guam. Island and unincorporated territory of the US; where Jesi and the Taimanglo family live.

George Washington High School. Jesi and her brother Peter's school on Guam.

Hawaii. Jungles of, where Johan trained for the war. Location of Pearl Harbor where Jesi's brother Tommy was killed.

Kerama Islands, Japan. 32 miles southwest of Okinawa, or Kerama-Rettō (Japanese spelling), a small island 15 miles from Okinawa, where Johan is stationed after he leaves Guam preparing for the battle at Okinawa.

Leyte, Philippines. Where Johan landed on Thanksgiving 1944; the fighting there is worse than on Guam; he's still stationed there on Christmas, 1944, and where he's still stationed in February 1945 when he writes a letter to Jesi.

Maanot Ridge *(ma-an-ut)*. Southwest Guam, where Johan wakes up on his first morning in Guam and where his troops relieved the Second Battalion of the Fourth Marines.

Mangilao *(mang-ee-lauw)*. A village located in Central Guam, Eastern Coast, where the Taimanglos lived in a house; where the family decides to rebuild Auntie Julia's house on their property after the war.

Manhattan. Where Johan grew up and lived with his first wife Lily for two years, and where his parents still live.

Marianas. Also Mariana Islands, an island group in the Western Pacific recaptured from the Japanese in WWII; the islands are where Jesi explains to Johan that the Chamorro people live; Guam is the largest and most southern of the islands.

Matagob. Northern Leyte, Western Coast, Philippines, where Johan is stationed, Christmas 1944.

Mount Alifan *(a-lee-fan)*. Guam, where Johan is stationed in a camp near Mount Alifan.

Mount Santa Rosa. Guam, where Johan's troops are headed on the northern part of Guam; spelled Sånta Rosa *(sawn-ta ro-sa)* in Chamorro.

Mount Sasalaguan *(sa-sa-law-gwan)*. Guam, mountain in the center of southern Guam, in Merizo village (1,086 feet); sailors on the USS *Starlight* see the mountain as they near Guam; spelled Sasalåguan *(sa-sa-law-gwan)* in Chamorro.

Okinawa. Japan, where Johan is headed in the Pacific battle after he leaves Guam.

Orote Peninsula *(oh-row-tee)*. Central Guam, western coast; where the marines and soldiers met heavy fighting from the Japanese; Johan's division will move there as they prepare to leave Guam, and where Peter works; Jesi and Johan eat lunches together on the tip of the peninsula when he's on duty and spot dolphins.

Orote hospital. Military hospital on Guam where the Landers' children Johnny and Kat are born.

Pago Bay *(paw-go)*. Guam, location of the cave (Pago Bay cave) where Jesi spent the war; near where Jesi's grandmother has a private cove and spectacular view of the bay; Jesi yearns to swim across the bay during the Japanese occupation; spelled Pågu *(paw-goo)* in Chamorro.

Pan Am Hotel. Guam, grand hotel where Jesi's brother Peter worked.

Pearl Harbor. Tommy Taimanglo died there with the US Navy.

Pittsburg, CA. Location of Camp Stoneman, where Johan had been stationed before shipping out.

Plaza de Espana *(es-pa-nya)*. Guam; historic location destroyed in the war, located in central Agana, was the governor's palace during the Spanish occupation of Guam.

Saipan *(sigh-pan)*. One of the Mariana Islands already liberated by the Americans at the story's opening.

San Francisco, California. An address for Johan's mail while he is at sea.

States. Short for the United States.

Statue of Liberty. When Johan tells Jesi he lives in New York, she asks if it's near the statue.

Sumay *(sue-my)*. Guam, ancient Chamorro settlement destroyed in the war.

Taimanglo property *(tie-mang-lu)*. Jesi's family's property in the village of Mangilao.

Talofofo *(ta-low-fough-fu)*. A village in southeast Guam; where Uncle Kin's house is located; spelled Talo Ÿo Ÿo 'in Chamorro.

Tan Chai's house *(tan chai)*. Jesi's grandmother's house; where Jesi goes to live when she argues with her father; three bedrooms, where Auntie Julia and Antonio live with Tan Chai. Tan Chai gives the house to Jesi and Johan when they get married.

Tarragona. Central Leyte, Eastern Coast, Philippines, a WWII battle location where Johan writes to Jesi.

Texas. Where Lily, Johan's first wife, was from.

Tokcha Bay *(tok-cha)*. On the southeastern coast of Guam; where Johan and his platoon did reconnaissance; spelled Tokcha 'in Chamorro.

Tokcha River. Runs along the northern edge of Talofofo village; Uncle Kin's house is not far from it.

Umatac *(you-ma-tack)*. Village on the southwestern coast of Guam, Antonio's father Vincente hid there during the war; spelled Humåtak *(who-maw-tack)* in Chamorro.

Umatac Bay. Location of Fouha Rock and the Chamorro creation myth.

US Hospital Ship. Where Johan recovers from his injury at Okinawa and brings him back to Guam.

White Beach One. 400 yards inland of Gaan Point in the village of Agat, where Johan is supposed to assemble with his platoon when they land on Guam.

Ylig Bay *(ee-lig)*. Central Guam, eastern coast; also Ylig Bay Cave (south of Pago Bay); the location of Jesi's mother's and grandmother's cave; Johan follows Jesi to this cave after the attack by the Japanese soldiers.

Yigo *(jee-go).* Northeast Guam, northernmost village, where the American troops have pushed the Japanese to and where Johan and his men stop for the night; spelled Yigu *(dzi-goo)* in Chamorro.

Yona *(jo-nya).* Johan's platoon recons there after landing on Guam; spelled Yo'ña *(dzo-nya)* in Chamorro.

Zamami Shima Island. Kerama Rettō, 20 miles southwest of Okinawa, Japan; where Johan is wounded in the left leg in the fighting for control of Okinawa.

REFERENCES

BOOKS

Blaz, Ben. *Bisita Guam: Let Us Remember Nihi Ta Hasso Remembrances of the occupation years in World War II.* Guam: Micronesia Area Research Center 2008

Camacho, Olympia Q. *Legends of Guam.* Agana: Department of Education. 1986

Culbreth, Kennith. *Two Hundred Thousand Boys on a Rock Called Guam and other Asiatic Pacific World War II Stories, including a First Hand Report…Launching the Doolittle Raiders.* Alexander, North Carolina: WorldComm 2003

Cunningham, Lawrence J., and Janice J. Beaty, *A History of Guam.* Honolulu: The Bess Press 2001

Friedman, Joseph. *God Shared My Foxholes: The Authorized Memoirs of a World War II Combat Marine on Bougainville, Guam, and Iwo Jima.* New York: iUniverse, Inc. 2010

Gailey, Harry. *The Liberation of Guam 21 July – 10 August 1944.* Novato: Presidio Press 1988

Gerson, Alvin. *Guam is a Far Cry for Brooklyn.* CreateSpace Independent Publishing Platform 2013

Henry, Mark R. *The US Army in World War II The Pacific.* Oxford: Osprey Publishing Ltd. 2000

Lodge, O. R. *The Recapture of Guam.* US Marine Corps 1954

Men Who Were There. *Ours To Hold It High The History of the 77th Infantry Division in World War II.* Washington: Infantry Journal Press 1947

Morison, Samuel E. *History of United States Naval Operations in World War II. Vol. 8: New Guinea and the Marianas, March 1944 – August 1944.* Urbana and Chicago: University of Illinois Press

Newman, Samuel A. *How to Survive as a Prisoner of War.* Philadelphia: Franklin Publishing Company, Inc. 1976

Palomo, Tony. *An Island in Agony.* No Publisher Stated 1984

Rogers, Robert F. *Destiny's Landfall A History of Guam.* Honolulu: University of Hawaii Press 1995

Rottman, Gordon L. *Guam 1941 & 1944 Loss and reconquest.* Oxford: Osprey Publishing Ltd. 2004

Rottman, Gordon L. *US Marine Corps Pacific Theater of Operations 1944 – 1945.* Oxford: Osprey Publishing Ltd. 2004

Rottman, Gordon L. *US World War II Amphibious Tactics Army & Marine Corps, Pacific Theater.* Oxford: Osprey Publishing Ltd. 2004

Safford, William E. *Useful Plants of Guam.* Agana Heights: Guamology Publishing 2009

Sanchez, Pedro C. *Guahan GUAM The History of our Island.* Agana: Sanchez Publishing House 1998

Smith, Myron J., Jr. *The Mountain State Battleship USS West Virginia.* No Publisher Stated 2009

Taborosi, Danko. *Field Guide to Caves and Karst of Guam.* Honolulu: Bess Press 2004

Thompson, Laura. *Guam and Its People A Study of Culture Change and Colonial Education.* Honolulu: American Council Institute of Pacific Relations 1941

Topping, Donald M., Pedro M. Ogo, and Bernadita C. Dungca. *Chamorro-English Dictionary.* University of Hawaii Press 1973

Tweed, George R. *Robinson Crusoe USN.* Yardley: Westholme Publishing, LLC 2010

United States Army. *Guam World War II 50ᵗʰ Anniversary Commemorative Edition.* Washington: Center of Military History United States Army 1990

United States Navy. *The Bluejackets' Manual.* Annapolis: United States Naval Institute 1938

West, Charles O. *Second to None: The Story of the 305ᵗʰ Infantry in World War II.* Washington: Infantry Journal Press 1949

WEBSITE

American WWII. "Spam Again." April 08, 2013. http://www.americainwwii.com/articles/spam-again/

Catholic Wedding Help. "Rite of Marriage." September 03, 2015. http://catholicweddinghelp.com/topics/text-rite-of-marriage-mass.htm

Catskill Heritage. "Chapter XXX. Town of Shandaken. By Henry Griffeth." April 19, 2013. http://www.catskillheritage.org/heritage/griff366.htm

Daily Motion. "Video: 1940s US Occupation of Guam, Mariana Islands WWII History." April 26, 2012. http://www.dailymotion.com/video/x332jx_1940s-us-occupation-of-guam-mariana_news

Europa. "Binoculars of the U.S. Navy." February 22, 2012. http://www.europa.com/~telscope/milusn.txt

Global Security. "77ᵗʰ Infantry Division (RTU)." November 06, 2011. http://www.globalsecurity.org/military/agency/army/77id.htm

Google Books Preview. "Trout Fishing in the Catskills." September 03, 2015. https://books.google.com/books?id=iDlgBg AAQBAJ&pg=PA376&lpg=PA376&dq=fishes+in+ the+catskill+mountains+1940&source=bl&ots=Hi-4BkN5Le&sig=9F5RU1THTApxzXLtBmRv9Kkupu8 &hl=en&sa=X&ved=0CB0Q6AEwAGoVChMIvMq-0fjnyAIVBukmCh1wAgou#v=onepage&q=fishes%20in%20 the%20catskill%20mountains%201940&f=false

Google Books Preview. "World War II Letters: A Glimpse into the Heart of the Second World War Through the Words of Those Who Were Fighting It." September 01, 2014. https://books.google.com/books?id=GFOk2geCqF4C&pg=PT160 &lpg=PT160&dq=letters+to+guam+1944&source=bl&ots=1NnCY0SLZO&sig=z7uBHrkGHzljBZOwQ-kaTAXyiYQ &hl=en&sa=X&ei=nzxqVPSXLIKigwSqjIKICw&ved=0CD 4Q6AEwBDgK#v=onepage&q=letters%20to%20guam%20 1944&f=false

Guam PDN. "Ask Joyce." April 26, 2012. http://archive. guampdn.com/guampublishing/pacificedge/data/ EkkZlyEVpZngJzYIiz.htm

Guam War Survivor Story. "Lourdes Laguana Perez." February 02, 2012. http://guamwarsurvivorstory.com/index. php?option=com_content&view=article&id=75&Itemid=80

Guam War Survivor Story. "Lucia McDonald." February 02, 2012. http://guamwarsurvivorstory.com/index.php?option=com_ content&view=article&id=60&Itemid=65

Guampedia. "Folktale: Puntan and Fu'una: Gods of Creation." October 13, 2015. http://www.guampedia.com/ puntan-and-fuuna-gods-of-creation/

Guampedia. "Guam Seal and Flag." March 21, 2016. http:// www.guampedia.com/guam-seal-and-flag/

Guampedia. "Hale'ta: Amot Siha." September 03, 2015. http://www.guampedia.com/haleta-amot-siha/

Guampedia. "Mestizo (Mestisu)." September 03, 2015. http://www.guampedia.com/mestizo-mestisu/

Ibibilio. "U.S. Army in World War II The War in the Pacific Campaign in the Marianas Part Four Guam." January 29, 2010. http://www.ibiblio.org/hyperwar/USA/USA-P-Marianas/USA-P-Marianas-15.html

Kerosene Lantern. "Dietz Lanterns." April 26, 2012. http://kerosene-lantern.com/faqs.htm

Naval History and Heritage Command. "Nomenclature of Naval Vessels." December 29, 2012. http://www.history.navy.mil/research/library/online-reading-room/title-list-alphabetically/n/nomenclature-of-naval-vessels/nomenclature-of-naval-vessels-index.html

Naval History and Heritage Command. "Photos." December 14, 2012. http://www.history.navy.mil/photos/usnshtp/bb/bb67.htm

Naval War In Pacific 1941 – 1945. "Task Force 53." January 02, 2010. http://pacific.valka.cz/forces/tf53.htm

NY Daily News. "Shocking Photographs from Famed New York City Crime Photographer WeeGee." April 04, 2015. http://olive-drab.com/od_soldiers_gear_ww2pack_m1936.php

Offisland. "Guam Remembered – Part III." April 12, 2013. http://offisland.com/feature/bobquinn2.html

Olive-Drab. "Bag, Canvas, Field, M1936 (Musette Bag)." September 01, 2014. http://olive-drab.com/od_soldiers_gear_ww2pack_m1936.php

One Jones Family. "First Letter Home." June 29, 2012. http://www.aboutjonesfamily.com/PAGES/WAR2.HTM

Patriot. "Personal Log of Arthur Alvater aboard U.S.S. Relief (AH-1) Cover Feb. 13, 1945 through Sept. 10, 1945." September 01, 2014. http://adams.patriot.net/~eastlnd2/rj/alt/al/Alog.htm

Patton HQ. "The Famous Patton Speech." March 01, 2015. http://www.pattonhq.com/speech.html

Railroadiana. "Railroad Lanterns." April 26, 2012. http://www.railroadiana.org/lanterns/pgLanterns.php

Smithsonian Institute Postal Museum. "Postal Censorship and Military Intelligence during World War II." May 31, 2012. http://www.postalmuseum.si.edu/symposium2008/Pfau-Postal_Censorship.pdf

The Pacific War Online Encyclopedia. "Rations." June 07, 2012. http://pwencycl.kgbudge.com/R/a/Rations.htm

Together for Life. "Hispanic Wedding Tradition: Wedding Coins (Arras)." September 03, 2015. http://togetherforlifeonline.com/wedding/traditions/wedding-coins-arras/

U.S. Army Fort Jackson. "50th Anniversary History, 1917-1967, Fort Jackson, South Carolina." January 2, 2010. http://www.jackson.army.mil/sites/garrison/pages/542

US Army Quartermaster Foundation. "Army Operational Rations – Historical Background." June 07, 2012. http://www.qmfound.com/army_rations_historical_background.htm

USDA Mann Library Cornell University. "Census of Agriculture 1940." April 26, 2012. http://usda.mannlib.cornell.edu/usda/AgCensusImages/1940/04/16/1471/Table-01.pdf

USS Ormsby. "Guam War Diary." January 02, 2010. http://ussormsby.com/pdf_files/1944_07_Guam_War_Diary.pdf

Wartime Press. "Infantry Divisions 043 77th Infantry Division." April 26, 2012. http://www.wartimepress.com/archives.asp?

TID=043%2077th%20Infantry%20Division&MID=Infantry
%20Divisions&q=91&FID=89

West Virginia Division of Culture and History. "USS West
Virginia Remember Pearl Harbor." December 30, 2012. http://
www.wvculture.org/history/usswv/remember.html

Wikipedia. "Deck (ship)." July 29, 2012. https://en.wikipedia.
org/wiki/Deck_(ship)

Wikipedia. "Joseph E. Muller." June 29, 2012. https://
en.wikipedia.org/wiki/Joseph_E._Muller

Wikipedia. "Pine Hill, New York." June 29, 2012. http://
en.wikipedia.org/wiki/Pine_Hill,_New_York

Wikipedia. "Shandaken, New York." June 29, 2012. http://
en.wikipedia.org/wiki/Shandaken,_New_York

Wikipedia. "USS George Clymer (APA-27)." January 03, 2010.
https://en.wikipedia.org/wiki/USS_George_Clymer_(APA-27)

Wikipedia. "World War II U.S. Military Sex Education."
January 24, 2016. https://en.wikipedia.org/wiki/World_War_
II_U.S._Military_Sex_Education

WW2 In Color. "US Army Rations – World War II." November
01, 2011. http://www.ww2incolor.com/forum/showthread.
php/3551-US-Army-Rations-World-War-II

WW2 US Medical Research Center. "WW2 Hospital Ships."
September 01, 2014. https://www.med-dept.com/articles/
ww2-hospital-ships/

BLOG

Absolute Write. "Swearing During WWII." March 01, 2015.
http://absolutewrite.com/forums/archive/index.php/t-442
78.html

Paleric Blog. "I Siette Na Sakramenton Guinaiya." September 03, 2015. http://paleric.blogspot.com/2014/04/i-siette-na-sakramenton-guinaiya.html

HOOK A WRITER UP

"Hook it up" was a favorite phrase in one of my husband's platoons when he was in 414th Signal Company, Mannheim, Germany. I smile every time I think of it. The soldiers sounded off "hook it up" during formation in honor of one of the many wonderful platoon sergeants leading our company. In the summer of 1997, as a recently married wife, a girl in a foreign country, and a new college graduate, I was blessed to have been welcomed in to the 414th family. They were a supportive, loving group of men and women that made my experience as a military spouse one of the best times in my life.

Did you write that review yet? Yes? Thank you! Soon? Thank you too! Oh, and if you want to tell all your friends and family about *Conquered,* I would appreciate that as well.

Connect with me on Facebook/Instagram as pquinene, and YouTube/Google+ as Paula Quinene. If you don't have any social media accounts, feel free to write to me at pquinene@paulaq.com.

Send me an e-mail so I can add you to my mailing list and give you a heads up when my next Guam book is released.

Always,

Paulaq

About the Author

Paula Quinene was born and raised on Guam. She graduated from the University of Oregon in 1997 with a bachelor's of science degree in Exercise & Movement Science hoping to return to the island as an anatomy teacher. A resident of North Carolina since 2000, Paula's homesickness – or "mahalangness" – has motivated her to write *A Taste of Guam*, *Remember Guam*, both cookbooks, and her first novel, *Conquered*. Paula is enjoying life with her husband Ed, and her children, Carson and Evalie. Paula's home on the web is www.paulaq.com.

Lightning Source UK Ltd.
Milton Keynes UK
UKHW021533170820
368380UK00012B/2555

9 781495 811067